Over Too Soon

Over Too Soon

Avril Sabine

Cracked Acorn Productions
Australia

Over Too Soon

Published by

Cracked Acorn Productions

PO Box 1365

Gympie, Queensland 4570

 Australia

978-1-925131-89-5 (Kindle)

978-1-925617-45-0 (EPUB)

 978-1-925131-90-1 (Print)

Genre: Young Adult Contemporary/Paranormal

Copyright 2017 © Avril Sabine

Cover design by Caitlyn Petersen

Seventeen-year-old Kayla finds life a breeze. She has plans for her future and friends to hang out with. Life is exactly the way she wants it to be. Until she realises that not every person she can see is actually alive. Or friendly. Her world is crumbling, her twin brother is suicidal, a ghost moves in and her own death seems a distinct possibility.

*

This story was written by an Australian author using Australian spelling.

Chapter One

Kayla leaned back against the wall of the hospital corridor and stared at the door in front of her. It was only a few more steps, but she couldn't bring herself to take them. She knew she had to go back in the room. There was no point in standing here all night. She needed to be on the other side of the door with her brother. There was no one else by his side. And wasn't she partly to blame? How many times in the past couple of months had she told him life was tough, get over it? She took a hesitant step forward. He'd tried to go one better. He'd tried to get over it permanently.

They'd been born fifteen minutes apart, another five minutes and she would have had a separate date of birth. They'd shared a womb for eight months, a cot for a year and a bedroom for five years. With all that enforced time together, you'd think they'd have more in common than a last name, the same birth date and identical dark brown hair. She hadn't one single thing in common with Jeff. Actually, not many people had anything in common with him.

Kayla forced herself to open the door and step into the hospital room. Her courage deserted her and she stood there, frozen. She listened to the click of the door close behind her as she stared at the floor. One of her shoelaces had come undone and trailed under her sneaker. For a moment she was tempted to stop and retie it, but instead she forced herself to move forward, her gaze on the industrial carpet. The edge of the bed came into view and her gaze slowly travelled up along the bed frame, across a beige blanket, halting when she saw a young man leaning over her brother. The palm of one hand rested on Jeff's pale forehead.

"Hey! What are you doing in here?"

The young man straightened. "You can see me?"

"Of course I can see you." Kayla took a step back. He might be good to look at, but he sounded like he'd escaped from the psychiatric ward. "You shouldn't be in here." She took another step back, unable to look away from him. If he started to run towards her wielding an axe or something she wanted plenty of warning.

"Wait. Don't go." He moved forward.

She turned and raced for the door. His hand captured hers before she could grasp the door handle. She faced him as she tried to pull away. "Let me go before I scream."

"Please. I've been here for days."

He stepped closer and Kayla was forced to tilt her head back to meet his dark eyes. She shook her head, trying to pull away from him.

"No one sees me. Only you. Don't go. Talk to me. Just talk to me. Please."

Kayla ignored the pleading tone. "Let. Me. Go."

His grip loosened, but he continued to hold her hand. "I just want to talk."

The door swung open and forced them to break apart so they could jump out of the way. Kayla pressed her hand against her chest as she glanced first at the nurse and then the boy.

The nurse held the door with one hand, the other resting on her hip. "Your parents rang. They want to remind you not to stay too late as you have school tomorrow."

Kayla sent a nervous glance towards the boy. "Ahh, I was wondering…" Kayla faltered. What did she say? *Can you have someone cart this lunatic back to the asylum?*

"She can't see or hear me." He stepped in front of the nurse to wave, grinning as he faced her.

"Yes?" The nurse continued to look at Kayla, giving the boy not the smallest amount of attention.

Kayla stared then shook her head, sighing deeply. "Never mind." She slowly walked to the chair near the bed and sank onto it. She dropped her head into her hands. It had obviously been too long a day. It wasn't the boy who was the lunatic. It was her. Just great. She wondered if she should ask the nurse to cart her off to the psychiatric ward.

"Are you okay?"

Kayla raised her head to see the nurse in the doorway, looking at her through the waving boy, half hidden by him.

Kayla laughed abruptly, a sharp sound that made her think of a lunatic sharpening an axe as he muttered to himself. "Yeah, about as much as you can expect." She kept the words to herself that she wanted to blurt out. Just great for someone who's completely lost her mind. Instead, she watched as the nurse nodded and left the room. Kayla looked back at the boy who remained in her brother's hospital room. Maybe she should have asked the nurse to bring a bed in for her too.

Although how she'd thought up someone who

looked as good as him, she didn't know. He had olive skin, short brown hair a shade darker than her own and eyes equally as dark. He looked like he'd be taller than her brother who often reminded her of a scarecrow with how tall and thin he was. There was nothing scarecrow-like about the boy she stared at. He filled his white cotton shirt nicely.

He stepped forward and held out his hand. "I'm Brett, by the way."

Kayla stared at his hand.

"Most people shake hands and offer their name."

Kayla closed her eyes. This was dreadful. No. This was worse than dreadful. Maybe she was hallucinating from all the drugs her brother had taken to end his life. Didn't twins often experience the same things? That they'd never done so before didn't mean it couldn't happen.

"You know, just because I'm dead doesn't mean I enjoy being ignored. I didn't like it when I was alive, not about to start liking it now."

Kayla's head jerked up at his words. Her mouth opened twice before she managed to speak. "Dead? As in a ghost?"

Brett dropped his hand. "Dead. As in no longer living."

"There are no such things as ghosts." She frowned

and reached out to touch him on the arm. "You're real. I can touch you." She wrapped her fingers around his warm arm. "Hold you. You can't be a ghost."

Brett shrugged. "I don't understand it either. No one else can see me. Everyone walks through me. To you, I'm real. In the past nine days I've talked to one other person. Someone like me. Another ghost. Do you know how lonely it is when you have no one to talk to? When no one can see you?"

Kayla's eyes narrowed. "What were you doing to my brother?"

"What do you think I was doing?" Brett asked warily.

"He can't die. Do you understand? He's not to die."

"He wants to. His soul is barely holding on."

"No!" Kayla rushed to her brother's side and grabbed hold of his hand. "Do you hear me, Jeff? You're not to die. I couldn't stand to live without you. Remember when we were really little and we thought 'cause we were born on the same day we'd die on the same day? Well don't go, in case we were right. I have heaps of stuff I want to do." She turned to Brett. "Can't you reach him? Tell him to come back. Please?"

"I don't know how."

"What were you trying to do before?"

Brett shook his head. "It doesn't matter."

"I think it does. You were trying to kill him. Weren't you? Why?"

"What's your name?"

"Huh?"

"Your name. I already told you mine."

She hesitated. "Kayla."

"Kayla, I've been dead nine days. I talked to some old guy who's been dead a total of six times. That's it. The measly bit of info he gave me is all I know about being a ghost. I have no chains to rattle, I don't feel the need to throw things about the room, or at least I didn't until I met you. And, I shouldn't be dead."

"Obviously you should be since you're here."

"I'm not meant to be dead. Unlike your brother I didn't try to kill myself. I wasn't drink driving when we went out the night I died. I had someone, who didn't plan to drink, organised to drive. I did everything right. Ate properly, played sport, got into uni, made no trouble for anyone. I did everything right. Then bang! All over. Do you know what that's like?"

Kayla shook her head. Of course she didn't. She was alive. And he knew that. She glared at him.

"None of that has anything to do with my brother. You leave him be."

"He doesn't want to be here. It wasn't a cry for help. You weren't meant to come home. Why did you come home?"

"How do you know?"

Brett smiled. "I heard it in his thoughts. So, why did you come home?"

"I forgot my phone."

"It wouldn't take much to show him how to let go so I can step in." Brett brushed the hair back from Jeff's forehead. "A little on the pale side and he looks like he's never played sport, but I can deal with that."

Kayla leapt forward and shoved Brett away from her brother and against the wall. "No." She held his gaze. "Don't touch him."

"I have six months to find a new body before I permanently become a ghost. He doesn't want his. I do."

"You can't have it."

"What do you expect me to do? Let go? After all that's happened? Die? Never live again?"

Kayla frantically held onto Brett so he couldn't return to Jeff's side. "I don't know. All I know is that you can't have my brother. Please. Leave him be." A tear escaped and she blinked, trying to hold onto her emotions.

Brett swore and sank to the floor, his back resting against the wall. Kayla went with him, unwilling to set him free. Brett swore again then reached out to wipe the tear from her cheek. He leaned back, his head against the wall and his gaze on the ceiling. "I'll leave your brother alone. But if he figures out for himself how to let go I'm not going to encourage him to stick around and I will take his body."

"Thank you," Kayla whispered.

"The first body in days I've felt I could take and you have to ruin it."

"He's my brother. My twin."

Brett glanced between the two of them, surprise on his face. "You have to be kidding. I had you pegged as being half siblings or something."

"I know. We don't look much alike." She sat beside Brett, her shoulder touching his, and let go of him. "I didn't know things had got so bad for him. I would have done something. I don't have a clue what I could have done, but I'm sure there must have been something. I can't believe I didn't realise how he felt."

Brett took her hand. "No one can know what's on another's mind."

"Yes but-" Kayla broke off as the door swung open.

The nurse stood there again, looking extremely annoyed. "You might want to give your parents a call and let them know what your plans are. I am not a messenger."

"I'm sorry," Kayla said.

"I understand you don't want to leave your brother's side. But while your friend is here he can take a turn sitting with him. Since there doesn't seem to be anyone else willing to share the duty with you."

"They-" Kayla started to defend her parents and then the rest of the nurse's words registered. "My friend?"

The nurse pointed to Brett. "Boyfriend maybe?"

Kayla started to pull away from him, but his hand tightened on hers. "I... that is-"

"Don't worry. I'll make sure she calls her parents," Brett said.

"Thanks." The nurse turned and left the room.

Brett grinned. "Did you hear her? She saw me. And spoke to me."

Kayla frowned. "But she couldn't before."

Brett let go of her hand and reached out to the wall. He pressed against the wall and his hand slid through it like it wasn't there. He pulled back, grabbed her hand and tried to do the same trick. This time his hand met a solid surface. He pulled Kayla to him, hugging her tightly. "You make me exist."

Chapter Two

Kayla drew away from Brett, shaking her head. She ignored the grin she had the urge to return. "Whatever you're thinking... no. Absolutely no. Definitely no. No way in hell. No-"

"Okay, I get the idea."

"Good. Because I don't like you very much. You tried to kill my brother."

"I didn't try and kill him. He was the one who did that."

"I need to ring my parents and you're coming with me. I'm not leaving you alone with Jeff."

Brett grinned. "Don't you trust me, Kayla?"

"Not at all. Are you coming willingly or do I have to drag you with me?"

"On one condition."

"Which is?"

"You buy some food. Any food. I don't care if it's

from a vending machine. Then you hold my hand when we come back here so I can see if I can eat it."

Kayla hesitated. It wasn't like she planned to go home tonight. And if it kept him away from her brother it was a small price to pay. She was surprised at how calm she was. She guessed it was shock. Maybe when everything fully sank in she'd be screaming like a lunatic. She frowned. Maybe this was all a nightmare. It had all the right ingredients for one. If only it didn't feel so real.

"Well?" Brett interrupted her thoughts. "Is it a deal?"

Kayla nodded. "But you're to stay in sight every moment I'm out of this room."

"Deal." Brett held out his hand.

Kayla shook his hand and turned towards the door. "Let's leave you invisible for now. I don't want to have to keep remembering to hold your hand all the time we're outside this room."

"Fair enough." Brett fell into step beside her.

Resting her hand on the door, she turned to face him. "And don't expect me to talk to you when I leave this room. I'd look like a lunatic."

Brett chuckled. "That's a bit boring of you."

Kayla ignored Brett and pushed the door open. The corridor was empty. She supposed that was to be expected at this time of night. She hurried to the public phone since there were signs all over the place requesting mobile phones be turned off. Once she picked up the phone, she dug in the pockets of her jeans for some coins, dropped them in the slot and dialled her home number before she changed her mind.

"Hello?"

"Mum."

"Where are you? You should have been home over an hour ago. You know you're not meant to be out after ten when you have school the next day. You'll never manage to get up in the morning and off to school on time."

"Mum!"

"No need to raise your voice to me, Kayla."

"I'm not coming home tonight. Someone has to stay with Jeff."

"The doctor said Jeffery wouldn't be alert before morning. There's absolutely no need at all for you to spend the night with him. Stop carrying on and come home."

"Who will be here with him in the morning?"

"I'll call in and see him for a few minutes on my way to work. Your father has an early appointment so he won't have time until tomorrow night. Which is why we have private medical insurance. At the press of a button Jeffery can have a nurse at his side. I want to see you home within half an hour. I don't have all night to sit up and wait for you."

Kayla shook her head in disgust. "I'll be home in time to get ready for school in the morning. And you've never waited up for me before so I don't expect tonight to be any different. Oh, and don't keep ringing the nurses, they're getting annoyed and I've told them there's no need to pass on any more messages since they have more important things to do." She hung up before her mum had a chance to say another word. Her gaze collided with Brett's and she turned away to find a vending machine.

They silently walked the corridors and Brett pointed to the packet of chips he wanted when Kayla shoved a crumpled note into the machine. She grabbed the packet and headed back to the room. Anger kept her silent. She worried that if she opened her mouth she'd scream. Or ring her mum back and abuse her. Sometimes she found it impossible to understand why her parents had bothered to have children. Kayla shifted a chair closer to Jeff's bed and reached out for his hand as she dropped onto it. The words she would have spoken caught in her throat. Spilling emotions in front of a stranger wasn't her thing. Actually, spilling emotions to anyone had never been her thing. But she guessed that was to be expected with the way they'd been raised. Emotions were messy and unnecessary.

Brett took her hand. "You do realise it's been over a week since I've tasted food. I hope you don't expect me to wait the rest of the night before I can eat."

Kayla glanced at her watch. "Not that you'd have much of a wait. Sunday's nearly over. It's not long till midnight."

"Help me open the packet. I can't do it one handed without making a mess."

Kayla let go of Jeff's hand long enough to pull on one side of the packet. She reluctantly smiled when Brett closed his eyes the moment he'd put a chip in his mouth. "They aren't that good."

Brett stared silently at her for a moment. "You tell me that when you've gone days without food. I might not feel hunger, but I'm left with a hollow feeling. Like something's missing."

Kayla remained silent. What could she say? Instead she watched as Brett slowly ate the packet of chips. When he finished, he sat on the floor beside her, his arm resting against her leg.

When Kayla began to struggle to keep her eyes

open, she tapped Brett on the shoulder. She waited until he faced her. "What happened?"

"When?"

"How did you die?" He stared at her long enough she began to think he wasn't going to answer. Not that she could blame him. She guessed it wasn't something he wanted to think about.

He turned his head to stare straight ahead. "My eighteenth birthday actually landed on a Friday. We had all these plans…

Brett grabbed his wallet and smiled at the sound of the horn out the front. He stepped out of his room and nearly ran into Brian who held his hand out. Brett grinned. "What, not going to give me a break since it's my birthday?"

"And risk you drinking the rent money? Be real. I wasn't born yesterday." Brian continued to hold out his hand.

Brett pulled his wallet from a back pocket of his black jeans and handed over the correct money. When Brian tucked the money in his shirt pocket, Brett grinned. "Not going to hand some of it back with a happy birthday?"

Brian laughed. "My great grandfather was Scottish. What do you think the chances of that are?" He clapped Brett on the shoulder. "But I'll say happy birthday. Only because it doesn't cost me a cent."

"I bet they'll bury you with the first dollar you ever earned."

Brian nodded solemnly. "Yep. It's a family tradition."

The car horn sounded again. "Gotta run. Don't wait up for me. I won't be home before daybreak."

"As if I'd bother," Brian called out after him. "I'll probably wake up in the morning about the same time you're walking in the door."

Brett hurried across the front lawn to the car parked on the side of the road. He grinned when heads and hands were poked out of the windows, to cheer, the moment they saw him. A can of mixed spirits was shoved in his hand as he opened the rear door.

The boy beside him opened a similar can. "How's it feel to be of legal drinking age? Finally."

"Great. Means I no longer have to hassle you to buy my drinks for me." Brett dropped the cold can beside him while he buckled up.

The laughter was punctuated with happy birthdays and Brett glanced around at his friends as he opened the can. Nick drove tonight, Jake sat in the front passenger seat and Trevor was next to him. The only one missing was his girlfriend, Chelsea. She was at her cousin's engagement party and hadn't been able to get out of attending. He had a feeling she hadn't tried hard as she desperately wanted to be a bridesmaid.

Jake turned in the seat to face Brett. "You ready for a big night?"

"Where are we off to first?" Brett asked.

"We couldn't decide where to take you so we've worked out a schedule. Three parties, two pubs and four nightclubs. Hope you've had your Weetbix." Trevor grinned.

"No probs. I could hit twice that many places." Brett had a mouthful of his drink and grinned. "The question is, can you lot keep up?"

There was good-natured arguing on the heels of his question and before long they pulled up in a crowded street. Brett looked out the car window. He guessed this was one of the parties.

Nick took out his phone. "Time check peoples. Mine says eight forty-two." Phones were taken out and they made sure they all had the same time.

"Isn't this a bit extreme?" Brett checked the time.

"Set alarms for nine-thirty." Nick ignored Brett's question. "If we get separated, we meet back at the car at that time."

Brett shook his head, with a grin, as he set his alarm to vibrate. Otherwise there was no way he'd know his alarm was going off once the noise of a party surrounded him. "Mission accomplished."

Nick pointed at Brett in warning, a grin barely held back. "I'd be nice to me if I was you. I managed to talk them out of some of the more interesting pranks they wanted to play on you for your birthday. I could let them go ahead."

Brett swung his door open. "We going to party or sit in the car and talk all night?"

Trevor threw his door open and yelled over his shoulder as he raced towards the party. "Last one inside buys a round at the first nightclub."

Brett slammed the door behind him and raced after Trevor, rapidly catching up with him. They burst through the open front door, grinning and arguing over who was first. Within minutes of arriving, Brett felt like he'd said thanks a million times to birthday wishes and had been offered so many drinks he'd begun to wonder if the night would end in alcohol poisoning. Trevor and Jake offered to help drink the cans so he didn't risk it.

By the time they'd been to the two pubs, the other party and one of the nightclubs and were on their way to the next one, Brett felt hungry. He pointed to the twenty-four hour service station.

"Think we can pull up? I want to grab something to eat. They should have something in the hotbox. Even if it's crumbed oil."

Nick pulled up at one of the bowsers. "Might as well put some fuel in while we're here." He took out his wallet and handed over thirty dollars. "Pay for it while you're in there, will ya?"

"And grab me something to eat. Not oil. An ice cream. One with a chocolate coating." Trevor handed him a ten dollar note.

Brett looked to Jake. "Anything for you?"

Jake shook his head, an exaggerated look of disappointment on his face. "We're meant to be drinking, not stopping for food. You lot won't last till daybreak at this rate."

Brett grinned. "Just refuelling. I bet I outlast you."

"Ten bucks says you pass out before me." Jake held out his hand.

Brett shook it. "Done." He got out of the car, headed inside and grabbed an ice cream from the freezer to the left of the door. He crossed the room and eyed what the hotbox had to offer. A frown formed when he glanced over to where the attendant served someone at the other counter. It looked like a whispered argument was in progress. He sighed. He didn't want to be stuck in here all night waiting to be served. He grabbed a packet of chips instead and headed for the attendant.

The man with a hooded shirt whirled when Brett dropped the chips and swore. Brett's gaze was drawn to a gun pointed at him. There was a loud sound and he saw the attendant cover his mouth with his hands. A scream cut through the silence.

The ice cream slipped from Brett's fingers and pain exploded through him. The man with the gun ran towards him. Another loud sound and then the world became hazy until it ceased to exist. His last image was of the gunman running past, his mouth open and moving, his eyes filled with terror. Brett's last thought was that the gunman was only a kid. One younger than him.

Chapter Three

"And that was it. All over too soon."

"I'm sorry." Kayla leaned forward to rest her hand on Brett's shoulder. "Do you know if they caught him?"

Brett shook his head. "I'm stuck in this hospital. The old fellow I told you about, he said I died here. Minutes after I arrived. I don't know what's going on in the rest of the world. Right now, this hospital is the only place I can be."

Kayla didn't know what to say. So she stayed silent. Brett remained quiet too. Time slowly passed. Her eyes grew heavy and she yawned. She didn't realise she'd drifted off to sleep until she tried to roll over into a more comfortable position. She ran into the arms of the chair and was startled awake. Her first thought was for her brother. Then she glanced around for Brett. He paced the floor by the door.

Brett stopped abruptly. "Checking I was still here?"

"I..." What could she say? She'd worried he might have turfed her brother out while she'd slept? That would have gone across real well. She sighed, rose to her feet and winced as muscles protested. She smothered a yawn with her hand. "I can understand how you need a new body, but he's my brother. Can you understand that?"

Brett shook his head. "Not really. I don't... didn't have a family. No siblings, father was never in the picture and my mother died when I was eleven."

"Where did you live?"

"Foster homes."

"Oh."

Brett smiled. "Don't stress it. They were good families. Just not my family. I never had a closeness to them like what you have for your brother."

Once again Kayla was lost for words. She was relieved when a noise from her brother drew her attention. She took the couple of steps that brought her to his bed and reached out to brush his hair back from his forehead. "Jeff?"

His eyes slowly opened. He tried to speak but shook his head instead. Kayla picked the cup up off the metal cabinet by the bed and held the straw to his lips. She waited for him to have a drink, noting the shadows under his eyes, the paleness of his skin and the tremble in his hand as he reached for her.

"Sorry."

She grasped his hand tightly. "What did you think you were doing? Didn't you think about how we'd feel?"

"We?"

"Mum. Dad. Me."

Jeff snorted. "That's crap and you know it. All they're probably worried about is how this might cut into their time."

"What about me?"

Jeff sighed. "You're the only person who'd miss me. What does that say about my life?"

"Jeff–"

"Who's that?"

"Who?" Kayla turned, but could only see Brett.

"The guy behind you."

Brett stepped over to the bed. "You can see me?"

"My head might be completely screwed up, but there's nothing wrong with my eyesight," Jeff said.

"Life keeps getting odder," Kayla muttered.

Brett turned to Kayla. "Am I the only one or can you see all ghosts?"

"How would I know? You look alive to me." Kayla reached out her hand and pressed it against his chest.

She could feel the warmth of his skin through his shirt. "And feel alive." She let her hand fall to her side.

Jeff looked from one to the other as they spoke. "Ahh. I've figured it out. I'm hallucinating, aren't I? You're at home in bed." He pointed to Kayla, then at Brett. "And I don't know who you're meant to be. Probably the son my father wishes he had. Do you play football? Cricket? Have a million friends?"

Kayla squeezed her brother's hand. "Of course I'm here. I'll probably be grounded for hanging up on Mum, but I wasn't letting her send me home. You'll be left on your own for most of the day since there's no way I'll be able to get out of going to school. Sorry."

A nurse came into the room and caused Brett to step back from the bed. Kayla grinned as the nurse nearly walked through him and he had to step back further. The nurse smiled at Jeff and took the hand Kayla held. With her gaze on her watch, she checked his pulse. She was a different nurse to the one who'd been forced to play messenger.

Her smiled brightened. "So how's my patient feel?"

"A lot better than I'd hoped," Jeff said dryly.

"Now, now, no need to think along those lines. I have someone who'll come and talk to you later." She patted his hand before she lowered it back to the bed.

"You can tell whoever it is I'm not interested," Jeff said.

"Actually," Kayla said when the nurse looked like she was about to leave. "Jeff mentioned seeing someone over in the corner of the room. He was arguing about it with me. Do you see anyone?"

The nurse looked through Brett, shaking her head.

"Oh come on, Kayla. You were talking to him too." Jeff tried to sit up.

The nurse pressed him back against his pillows. "Don't get yourself all worked up. There's no one over there. Only you, your sister and me are in the room. Can you still see him? Maybe it was earlier? It might have been a dream. You know you popped quite an interesting cocktail of tablets. You're lucky your sister found you."

"I'd tell her you can't see me. They might think you have some psychiatric disorder." Brett grinned. "Well, one more severe than they probably already think you have."

Jeff stared at the corner where Brett stood before he turned back to the nurse. "You're probably right. I can't see anything now. Maybe I was disorientated when I first woke up." The moment the nurse left the room, he sat up to glare at Kayla. "What the hell's going on here? Why couldn't she see him?" Jeff gestured towards Brett.

"Because he's dead."

"Then what's he doing hanging about my room?"

"Ahh…" Kayla looked away.

Brett returned to the bed. "Because I need a body. Unlike you, I want to live."

"Twice," Jeff yelled. "Twice you kept me alive. I didn't ask you to."

"Don't you dare do this again. Do you hear me? You have to live. You're my brother. It's always been you and me. Who sat with me when I had nightmares when we were little? Who always had a birthday present for me, even if it was only a worm? Don't do this to me."

"I was three-years-old. I liked worms."

"Did you hear what I said?"

"You can't tell me how to live my life." Jeff continued to glare at her.

"You can live it however you want. As long as you do live it. We used to share our problems. Figure them out together. Why didn't you come to me?"

"When was the last time you came to me with a problem?"

Kayla frowned. "I don't know. But that's because I

don't have any. I haven't stopped going to you with them."

"Exactly. We started high school and you coasted along. Plenty of friends, welcome on any team, good at everything. Me? I'd have to be the joke of the entire school."

"Jeff-"

Jeff shook his head. "Don't spin fairytales for me. We aren't three anymore. Name one person other than you who speaks to me."

Kayla was lost for words. She didn't think he'd appreciate her listing people he knew online. She sighed and reached for his hand instead. "If you can't stay for you, then stay for me. Please."

"Kayla I-"

"Give me one year. Please. One year where I don't have to worry about what you're up to." When Jeff shook his head and opened his mouth to speak, Kayla pressed her fingers to his lips. "Then till the end of this year. Come on, Jeff. How am I meant to get through the rest of year twelve if I spend every moment worrying about what you're up to? You know how much effort it takes for me to keep my grades up. The rest of this year and then we'll renegotiate."

"This deal expires first of January."

Kayla nodded.

"A pity that's more than six months away," Brett said.

Kayla turned on him angrily. "You'll have to find yourself another body. This one's already taken."

Jeff laughed derisively. "I'd like to oblige, but my sister can be fairly insistent."

Brett nodded. "I know."

"Either that or I'm weak," Jeff said.

Brett shook his head. "We'll go with the first option."

"She got to you too, huh?"

Kayla ignored them and checked her watch. "I have to head home and get ready for school."

"What am I meant to do?" Brett demanded.

Kayla shrugged. "I wouldn't have a clue. What do you normally do?"

"Pace the corridors and rooms looking for a body. I refuse to take on an old one. Or a baby. I'm not stealing a new life."

Kayla sighed. She had enough problems to deal with. She wasn't taking on anyone else's. "Then I guess you go back to doing that." She dropped a kiss on her brother's forehead. "But I have to go."

"I want to try something before you do," Brett said.

Kayla looked at him suspiciously. "What?"

Brett grinned. "Come over here to the wall."

Kayla crossed the room slowly. She pulled away when Brett reached out and grabbed a fistful of her hair. "What are you doing?"

"Quiet for a minute." Reaching out to touch the wall, he pressed his hand against it. The moment he let her hair go, his hand sank into the wall. He turned to face her. "Can I have some strands of hair?"

"I haven't got any scissors."

"Pull a few out." He held out his hand.

Kayla sighed before she randomly pulled strands of hair from her head and laid them across his palm. When he continued to hold his hand open, she frowned. "How many do you want? I'm not about to go bald for you."

Brett chuckled. "A few more. I want to plait them together."

"And how do you expect to keep it from coming undone?"

"Don't worry. I've done it before. I used to have long hair. When I cut it, my girlfriend wanted me to make her a bracelet with some of it."

Kayla pulled out a few more strands. "That's all. If those aren't enough, too bad."

Brett closed his hand and stared into her eyes. "Thank you," he said softly.

Kayla met his gaze. Her mouth went dry and she

could only nod. Looking away, she returned to Jeff's side. "I'll see you after school." She left the room before he had a chance to answer and ran most of the way to her parked car.

She sat in the driver's seat and rested her head against the steering wheel. What was that about? She sat back and closed her eyes. Brett had tried to kill her brother. Well, maybe not exactly tried to kill him, but he had tried to encourage him to die. She should hate him, not be drooling over him. She forced herself to open her eyes and clear her mind. Starting the car, she reversed out. She had enough problems without falling for a ghost. He had six months to find a body or be stuck as a ghost.

Kayla shook her head. What was she thinking? He was dead. Live ones came with enough problems. Hooking up with a ghost wouldn't be the best plan. She was mad to even think about him like that. Right now she had to focus on getting through a day at school. Everything else had to wait.

Chapter Four

Kayla's feet slowed the closer she came to her brother's hospital room. She stopped completely when she saw Brett walk towards her. Someone stepped out of his way and her gaze was drawn to the thin plait of hair around his wrist. When her gaze returned to his face, he grinned.

"Thank you." Brett's arms went round her and his lips lightly brushed her cheek. "You can't imagine how good it is to be visible again."

Kayla was momentarily speechless. She wanted to throw her arms around him and show him how she preferred to be kissed. Certainly not the quick, friendly one he'd given her. Instead, she held herself still as he stepped back from her.

Brett's grin faded. "You okay?"

Kayla nodded as she tried to think of something

to say. "Jeff–" she stopped, took a breath and started again. "Is he okay?"

Brett's face became closed. "You don't have to check to see if I've turfed him out. As you can see, I'm still here."

Kayla shook her head. She met his gaze, which was filled with anger, and for a moment she would have also said hurt. Her next words surprised her, but she realised they were true. "I trust you to leave his life alone. I was wondering how he was doing. You know. If he still felt the same as this morning."

Brett looked startled. "Thanks." He slipped his hand in hers and walked with her towards the room. "He keeps alternating between anger and indifference."

"He's not going to want to live past the end of this year, is he?" Kayla's words broke as she tried to hold back tears.

"Not unless there are some drastic changes between then and now."

Kayla stopped several metres from the room. "What am I going to do?"

Brett shrugged. "I wouldn't have a clue. I've never thought death better than life."

"I didn't know it was that bad for him. He's always quiet. He loves playing computer games and he spends heaps of time online. I thought that's what he preferred."

Brett shrugged again. "Maybe he does. But maybe he also wants something else in his life too."

"Like what?"

Brett stared at her for a moment. "For people to see him and not treat him like he doesn't exist. Or when they do see him, not treat him like he's crap."

"How do I give him that?"

"I wouldn't have a clue."

"I need help. I don't know how to make him want to live. Can you-"

Brett took a step back from her, a hand held up as if to keep her away. "Don't even think about it. I have my own problems."

"I'll help you with yours if you help me with mine."

Brett swore and rubbed his forehead. He sighed. "Fine."

Kayla grinned, resisting the impulse to thank him like he'd thanked her earlier. She knew if she threw her arms around him for a kiss it wouldn't be as innocent as his had been. "So what do we do first?"

"Give me a break. I've only just agreed to help out."

"Sorry. But we don't have a lot of time."

"He has more time than I have. A month more. I could ask you the same. I have less than six months."

"Sorry." Kayla was lost for words. She gestured towards Jeff's room. "I guess I better see how he is."

Brett nodded. "His emotions seem all over the place. Don't be surprised if you're having a friendly conversation one second and he's angry with you the next."

Kayla stepped into the room, surprised to see her brother sat on the chair by the bed, his head bent low as he put on his shoes. He was dressed in the clothes he'd been rushed to hospital in. "What do you think you're doing?"

Jeff glanced up before he returned to putting his shoe on. "Going home."

"Did the doctor say you could?"

Jeff rose to his feet without answering and strode to the door. He stopped when Kayla grabbed his shoulder. "I'm going home. Are you going to give me a lift or do I catch a taxi?"

"Mum-"

"Don't start. You want to know how concerned Mum is? She rang this morning. Said she was hoping to find the time to call in and see me on the way home from work. And Dad? Haven't heard from him at all."

"Jeff, I-"

He pulled away from her. "I don't want to hear it."

Kayla watched as he left the room. She didn't know

what to do. Surely the hospital wouldn't let him go home. She nearly jumped when Brett's arm encircled her shoulders. Her gaze met his. "What do I do?"

"Give him a lift?"

"You're a great help."

"What can you do? If they let him sign himself out, you can't exactly force him to stay. And he was pretty convincing earlier today when the shrink came to talk to him. Spoke about making a promise to you that he wouldn't kill himself this year and he's never broken a promise to you. They don't believe his life is in any immediate danger."

Kayla sighed before she reluctantly pulled away from Brett and went to look for her brother. She found him arguing with a nurse. For a few seconds she thought it meant he wouldn't be able to leave. She watched as Jeff headed for the lift, the nurse shaking her head. She hurried after him.

"I hope you're not planning to hassle me about leaving." Jeff crossed his arms over his chest.

"Would it change your mind?"

When the doors slid open, Jeff entered the lift. "Not at all."

Kayla followed her brother, a quick glance in Brett's direction as he followed her. She turned back to Jeff. "I wish you weren't so stubborn."

"I guess we had to have something in common since we're related."

Brett's laughter ended when Kayla turned to glare at him. "Do you think I can stay with you pair? It's not like I can turn up at my home. Knowing Brian, he's probably already rented my room out."

"Why can't you stay here?" Kayla asked.

"Would you like to stick around here?"

Kayla hesitated as she tried to think of a reason why he couldn't stay with them. He might be willing to help, but he'd also bring a heap of problems with him. "I thought you couldn't leave the hospital."

Brett glanced at the bracelet of hair. "I walked outside earlier."

"I don't know how I'll be able to explain you." Kayla stepped out of the lift when the doors opened.

"I'll tell them he's a friend from school." Jeff walked beside her.

"You haven't had anyone stay before," Kayla said.

"So you think that means I shouldn't ever have anyone stay over?" Jeff demanded.

"I didn't say that. I'm worried they'll think it's strange."

Jeff snorted. "As long as what I do doesn't affect them they couldn't give a shit."

Kayla reached for her brother, but he stepped

further away from her. She dropped her arm to her side. "That's not true. They do care. They just get busy with work."

"Yeah, right." Jeff faced Brett. "I can offer you a mattress on the floor. Hope that's okay."

"I don't sleep. I don't need to eat either, but I prefer to." Brett turned to Kayla. "Where are you parked?"

She felt outnumbered. But what choice did she have? Of course she'd give Jeff a lift home. She couldn't make him catch a taxi. And Brett, well she needed someone's help to find a way to make Jeff want to live. She didn't have anyone else who'd be willing to help. Somehow she'd cope with whatever problems having a ghost in the house would cause. She sighed. To think a couple of days ago she'd thought she didn't have a care in the world. She hadn't realised her world was crumbling around her. "Come on then."

The drive home was silent and Jeff headed for his ensuite to take a shower the moment they arrived, leaving Brett scrolling through search pages on his computer.

As soon as she heard the water running, Kayla turned to Brett. "What are we going to do?"

"About?"

"My brother."

"Hmm."

"Are you paying attention to me?"

"Hmm."

Kayla strode across the room and grabbed the back of the office swivel chair and turned Brett to face her. "You promised to help."

"So did you. What have you come up with to help me find a new body?"

Kayla growled and spun away from him to pace the room. "I don't know. I thought it'd be easier to help Jeff first."

"Are you going to help me at all? Or was it a way to get me to agree to help you?"

Before Kayla could answer, the doorbell rang. She hesitated. "This conversation isn't finished." She strode through the house to the front door and swung it open. "Red. What are you doing here?" She stared at the girl with dyed, cherry red hair, pale green eyes and porcelain white skin. They'd been best friends from the moment they'd met in grade eight.

"I thought I'd come over and see how you are. You were a bit distracted at school today."

Kayla stepped back so Red could come inside. "Yeah." Red had been waiting outside for her when she'd found her brother.

"How is he? I rang the hospital and they told me he'd been discharged."

Kayla shrugged. "Discharged himself is more accurate."

Red grabbed Kayla's arm, speaking softly. "Oh my god. I've died and gone to heaven. Who is he?"

Kayla turned to see Brett walked towards them. She waited until he was closer before she spoke. "Brett, this is Red, a friend from school."

"Friend. Whatever happened to best friend?" Red grinned at Kayla before she stepped closer to Brett. "Where did Kayla find you?"

"You might say Jeff introduced us."

Red's mouth dropped open. "You're Jeff's friend? Jeff has a friend?"

"Red!" Kayla glared at her friend.

Red shrugged. "Bet you were as amazed as me to find out he has a friend. A real one. How did you meet him?"

"Long story," Brett said.

Red grinned. "Ahh, I bet it was online. Were you disappointed when you met him in real life?"

"Hello, Mildred."

Red's eyes narrowed as she looked towards Jeff. "Hello, Jeffery." She stressed his name.

Jeff looked around at everyone. "Why are we standing near the front door?"

"Red popped in to see how you are," Kayla said.

Red shook her head. "No, I came over to see how Kayla is. I couldn't care how the inconsiderate bastard you call a brother is." She turned on Jeff. "Do you know how freaked your sister was when she found you? How could you do that to her?"

Kayla put a hand on Red's shoulder. "Leave him."

"Why should I? He's so selfish."

"I guess that's a trait you'd easily recognise," Jeff said.

"Why you–" Red began.

Kayla stepped between them. "Enough. Both of you."

"He started it," Red muttered.

"You were the one who called me an inconsiderate bastard." Jeff glared at her.

"You called me Mildred."

"So? That's your name."

Kayla threw her hands up. "Fine. Verbally slay each other. See if I care." She moved away from them to stand near Brett. "Did you find anything online?"

"Too much. Mostly ghost stories though."

"Cool. Ghosts are interesting. My aunt thinks she can see ghosts and talk to them," Red said.

Brett turned to Red. "Where does she live?"

"Just north of the city. A bit over an hour away. She's odd though. Thinks she can do magic too." Red rolled her eyes.

"Can I see her?" Brett asked.

"I don't know. She's a bit of a nutcase. Why do you want to see her?" Red eyed Brett. "You don't look like the kind of weirdo that normally wants to meet her."

Kayla spoke before Brett could tell Red the truth. "I doubt she'd be able to tell you anything more than what you can find online. Red doesn't believe she can see ghosts or do magic."

Brett stared at Red for a moment. "You don't?"

Red shook her head. "Nah. Like I said, she's a bit of a nutcase."

"Why is she?" Brett asked.

Red laughed. "Well, hello? I thought that'd be obvious. She believes in ghosts and thinks she can do magic."

Chapter Five

Kayla reached out to Brett when she saw him start to remove the bracelet. "No." She was too slow. She closed her eyes as he let the bracelet fall from his fingers. There was dead silence. Kayla reluctantly opened her eyes. Red stood, finger pointed at Brett, who she couldn't see, her mouth open. Brett stood with hands on his hips and Jeff started to laugh as he watched Red.

Red turned on Jeff. "This is your doing, isn't it? How'd you do it? I hate you. You've always got to hassle me."

Kayla picked up the bracelet and held it out. "Brett. Show yourself again."

Red looked at Kayla, a shocked look on her face. "You're in on this too? How could you? I thought we were best friends."

"Brett. Enough. You're making a mess of

everything." Kayla continued to hold the bracelet out.

Brett took it from her and slid it back on his wrist. He stared at Red. "Ghosts do exist."

Red stretched her hand out to Brett, drawing back before she came into contact with him. She tried again. This time her fingers grazed his cheek before she pulled back. "You… it can't be… but you were… how…" she shook her head. "This has to be some sort of trick."

"Don't I wish," Kayla muttered.

Red turned to Kayla. "How does he do that? Disappear."

Kayla looked from Red to Brett. She knew her friend wanted her to say it was all a joke. She could see the pleading in her eyes. She also saw Brett waited for her to explain the situation. She couldn't. With a shake of her head, she hurried through the lounge and kitchen and down the corridor to her room, locking the door. Sitting on the edge of her bed, she stared at the door, not wanting to face a single thing that was on the other side of it. This was a nightmare. Maybe she'd been caught up in one since the moment she'd found her brother had tried to kill himself. Any minute she'd wake up and find out the last two days hadn't happened. She jumped at the knock on her door.

"Come on, Kayla. You can't run off and leave me wondering what's going on," Red called through the door.

Kayla listened to the whispered conversation on the other side of the door. It wasn't loud enough for her to figure out who spoke. She dropped back onto the bed, feet still on the floor as she stared at the ceiling. When Brett came to stand over her she closed her eyes. "A locked door means keep out." She felt the bed dip beside her as he sat close enough for his leg to press against her. Sitting up, she faced him.

"Ghosts don't follow locked door rules."

Kayla looked away from him. "What do you want?"

"You promised to help me."

"You heard Red. Her aunt only thinks she can do that stuff." Kayla moved over on the bed. The warmth of his body against hers was distracting.

Brett took hold of her hand. "I want to see her. I don't care how small a chance it is that she can help. It's more than I have now."

"I'm sorry. It's…" What could she say? She'd doubted her own sanity for a moment? She no longer knew what to think or say. That her nice safe world had disintegrated and she didn't know what to expect?

"What?" Brett prompted when she was silent too long.

"I don't know." She glanced towards the door. "Where's Red?"

"With Jeff."

Kayla leapt to her feet. "What? They can't be left alone. They'll kill each other."

Brett held onto her hand, tugging her back to him when she tried to move away. He rose to his feet. "I want to see Red's aunt."

"Fine. Now let me go so I can make sure Red hasn't driven Jeff to try and kill himself again."

"When?"

"I don't know. As soon as Red can arrange it."

Brett let her hand go. "Thanks."

Kayla unlocked the door and hurried along the corridor to find Red and Jeff. They were in his room. She hovered in the doorway, staring at them in surprise. They were actually talking, without insults.

Red sat at Jeff's computer and he had one hand on the back of the chair and the other on the desk as he leaned in to see what she pointed to on the screen. Kayla took a step back and ran into Brett. When he opened his mouth to speak, she placed her hand over it with a shake of her head. Glancing back in the room, she was relieved to see they hadn't noticed her. She pushed Brett away from the door and grabbed his hand, pulling him with her as she retreated to her room. Pausing at her door she picked up the circlet of hair and held it out.

Brett took the bracelet and slipped it on his wrist. Stepping into the room with her, he closed the door behind them. "What was that all about?"

"They were talking. And Red even laughed."

"And?"

"They don't talk. They've hated each other since the moment they met."

Brett shrugged his shoulders. "Red said something about seeing if she could find info online. She reckons we probably don't have a clue what we're looking for."

Kayla smiled. "That sounds like Red."

"What? An insult with every second breath?"

Her smile widened into a grin. "Yeah."

"You have an interesting friend. Has she always been so... abrasive?"

Kayla nodded. "Yeah. When I met her, the first day of year eight, she had fire engine red hair..."

Kayla stepped between the older boy and her brother.

He was about a head taller than her and definitely stronger if his broad chest and thick arms were any indication. On either side of him stood a boy, one tall and thin, the other slightly shorter but with a similar build. She didn't know what she was doing between them and her brother. Instinct, she guessed. But it wasn't the best way to start grade eight.

"Get out of the way, kid. This isn't any of your business," the ringleader said.

Kayla took a deep breath. "He's my brother."

The ringleader and his mates laughed. He nudged the one on his left. "Hear that? He can't even stick up for himself. Has to have his little sister do it for him."

"We're the same age," Kayla muttered.

"You're still shorter than him," the ringleader said. "Now get out of the way."

"Three against two. How fair is that?"

They all turned to see a girl with hands on her hips and short, fire engine red hair that made her porcelain skin seem paler. She was shorter than each of the boys, but stood like she towered over them, her green eyes narrowed as she slowly surveyed them.

The ringleader laughed. "Don't tell me. When you grow up you want to be the girl on the matchbox."

"How original. Not! Like I haven't heard that before. If you had more than one brain cell to share between the three of you I'd be surprised." She turned to Kayla with a grin. "I'm Red."

"Kayla."

"Now look who's being original," the ringleader sneered.

Red shrugged. "You don't like my name, take it up with my parents. They're the ones who named me."

"Yeah, right. What do you take me for?"

Red laughed. "Do you really want me to answer that question?"

"Why you-" the ringleader took a threatening step forward.

A senior, who walked towards them, called out, "Red! You got a problem there?"

Red grinned as he stopped beside her and dropped an arm around her shoulders. "These oxygen thieves are hassling my friend Kayla."

The ringleader took several steps backwards, both hands held up and his head violently shaking back and forth. "It was a misunderstanding." He turned and hurried away, his two mates close on his heels.

The senior ruffled Red's hair and grinned. "Stay clear of him. He tends to pick on you little kids."

Red pushed his hand away. "Little kids." Her tone was full of disgust and her eyes narrowed again

With a chuckle, the senior ruffled her hair one last

time and sidestepped when she tried to punch him in the arm. "See ya later, Red."

Red turned to Kayla, shaking her head. "Cousins. I mightn't have a single sibling, but I have over a dozen cousins." She made a face. "And nearly all of them are at this school."

"Thanks." Kayla waved towards the direction the ringleader had disappeared in. She glanced at Jeff who ducked his head and hurried off in the opposite direction.

"Who was the kid hiding behind you?"

"My brother."

"Then why didn't he step in and help you?"

Kayla didn't think Red would be impressed that she'd been the one to step in to save him. She kept that bit of information to herself and searched for a way to change the topic. She glanced at her watch. "Guess I'd better head towards my classroom. If I can find it."

"Who's your homeroom teacher?"

"Ms Magana."

"Really?" Red linked her arm through Kayla's. "Me too. I'll take you there. My cousins have already shown me where all my classrooms are. They're handy to have sometimes."

Kayla listened as Red chatted non-stop all the way

to their classroom, her sentences regularly punctuated by laughter.

Chapter Six

Kayla smiled, her eyes unfocused as she thought back over the years. "She came home with me that afternoon and we've been best friends ever since."

"What's her natural hair colour?" Brett asked.

"Sandy blond. But other than photos of her as a little kid, I've only ever seen her hair a shade of red." She reached out to link her fingers through Brett's. "You okay? You looked… I don't know. Funny… no… strange for a second."

"Yeah." Brett pulled away, rising to his feet. He strode to the window and stared outside, his back to her.

Kayla made her way to his side. She rested her hand against his back. "Brett?"

He turned to face her and her hand ended up on his arm. "I'll never be able to get my old life back. Even when I manage to find a new body I'll have no past. No stories of what I've done, who I've known. Nothing. All my things, they're probably at the tip. I'll be dead to my friends."

"Brett…" she wrapped her arms around him and rested her head on his shoulder. "I'm sorry. I wish I could–"

"Forget it. You can't change it."

Kayla tilted her head to stare up at him. "I'll help you find a new body as soon as possible."

Brett smiled wryly. "And then I lose the last bit of my old life. I'll no longer look like myself. I'll be someone else completely. What if I become them? Take on their memories until mine no longer exist?"

Kayla didn't know what to think. She could only stare at him, surprised by the tears that tried to form. "The man who died, he must have remembered his old lives to be able to say he'd died six times."

"Or he remembered his deaths." Brett framed her face with one hand and his head came closer.

Kayla pressed her fingers against his lips. "Not because I'm convenient."

Brett stared at her for a moment then nodded once. He spoke when her fingers fell away. "Sorry."

It was Kayla's turn to smile wryly. "As appealing as I find you, I'm not desperate enough I'll tolerate being used."

"Appealing, huh?"

Kayla laughed softly. "As if you don't know how good you look."

"It's been a while since anyone's mentioned it."

"Ten days maybe?"

Before Brett could say anything the bedroom door swung open and Red strode into the room. They sprang apart. It had taken her a couple of seconds to spot them, but she'd still caught them in mid motion.

Red faced them, hands on her hips. "Your brother is impossible. And what's with you? He's dead. You only dumped the live one a fortnight ago."

Kayla sighed. "Stop fighting with my brother. And it's not what you think."

"Hello? Not blind here. And I wasn't fighting with him. He was fighting with me."

"Your aunt. Would it be possible to visit her?" Brett interrupted.

"She's certifiable," Red warned.

Brett grinned. "Why do I get the feeling that runs in the family?"

"Watch it or I won't take you." Red turned to Kayla. "You okay with that?"

Kayla nodded. "As soon as you can arrange it."

"Okay. I'll let you know once I talk to her. But

you'll owe me big time." Red pointed at Kayla in warning.

"It's not for me. Brett's the one who needs to see her."

Red grinned. "No point collecting a debt from the dead, they can't be held legally responsible. Anyway, I'm going. I don't want to be around here when your mum gets home. Her icy stare could freeze a volcano mid eruption."

Kayla covered her open mouth with her hand. "No one's rung her to say Jeff's not at the hospital anymore. She's going to be livid if she drops in to visit him."

"I'm so outta here." Red stepped out of the bedroom and, with a quick wave over her shoulder, bolted for the front door.

Kayla hurried to her bed so she could sit before her legs gave out on her. She glanced at her watch. Too late. They'd have already reached the hospital by now if they were going to visit Jeff. She groaned. "I hope she doesn't have time to go to the hospital and comes straight home."

"What are the chances of that?" Brett asked.

"Pretty good." Jeff appeared in the doorway. "I forgot all about ringing them."

Kayla pointed at her brother, who didn't look at all

concerned about the fact. "You're dealing with them. Not me."

Jeff shrugged. "If you hadn't called an ambulance, this wouldn't be a problem."

"Yes it would. They'd have had to take time out for your funeral." Kayla groaned, momentarily closing her eyes. "Forget I said that."

Jeff laughed. "Not likely."

"Where does that door lead to?" Brett pointed to the closed door in her room.

Kayla glanced at the door. "Ensuite."

"Doesn't Jeff have an ensuite too?" Brett frowned.

Kayla nodded. "So do our parents and then there's a bathroom near their home office."

Brett shook his head slowly. "Do you think you have enough bathrooms?"

"It's basically a six bedroom house. Except one of the bedrooms has been turned into an office and one into a home gym," Kayla said.

"Seems a bit excessive for four people." Brett opened the ensuite door and peeked inside.

Jeff chuckled. "It doesn't feel big enough some days. Especially when Mum's out for blood. I'm going to see what I can find for dinner. Hungry anyone?"

"Not at all. But I'll eat." Brett closed the door.

"Kayla? Hungry?" When Kayla shrugged, Jeff asked, "Anything in particular you want?"

Kayla shrugged again. "Anything. I don't care. I don't feel very hungry." And the thought of what her parents would say was making food seem less appealing.

"How about steak? A thick rump with mashed potato, gravy and veggies?" Brett asked.

"Are you peeling the veggies?" Jeff said over his shoulder as he started for the door.

Brett stepped into the hallway. "I guess so."

Kayla watched as they headed for the kitchen and lay back on her bed with a groan, her arms spread out. How could life change so quickly? Her brother planned to die in seven months, a ghost lived with them and her parents were due home any minute. Normally the last wouldn't be a problem. Jeff forgetting to ring them and mention he was discharging himself from hospital on top of her hanging up the phone on her mum last night, didn't make it an event to look forward to. She hoped her mum didn't go to the hospital first.

The front door slammed shut, making her sit up quickly. That hadn't sounded good. She sat on the bed a moment longer, trying to convince herself Jeff could handle the confrontation. She sighed heavily, rising to her feet. "What a joke." She reached the kitchen seconds before her parents did.

Terry had the same slightly tanned skin as Kayla, light brown eyes like Jeff and a solid build. In one hand he carried several manila folders crammed with paper and a set of car keys. In the other he held his tablet and scrolled through his emails. Robyn was tall and willowy, her dark brown hair tied at the nape of her neck, as neat as when she'd first pulled it back that morning. She wore black slacks with a matching jacket and an autumn coloured blouse. Her hazel eyes were filled with the ice Red had fled from.

"What are you doing at home?" Robyn's tone was as frosty as her eyes when she spotted Jeff.

Terry glanced around the kitchen before his gaze rested on his wife. "You have everything under control here? I have another meeting I need to change for."

Robyn waved him away without taking her gaze from Jeff. "Well, Jeffery? What is the meaning of this? Do you realise how much extra time it took for us to call into the hospital? Your father will be lucky if he isn't late for his meeting."

Kayla saw her brother physically wilt under Robyn's gaze. She took another step closer and if there'd been the space would have stood between her mum and brother. "We didn't think there'd be any point in letting you know."

Robyn rounded on her. "No point?" The level of her voice didn't change, only the quantity of frost in it. "And why did you think there was no point informing us Jeffery wasn't in the hospital?"

"We didn't expect you'd bother."

"Not bother? Of course we bothered. You make it sound like we don't care. Is that what you think?"

Kayla shook her head. "Not at all. I thought it'd be like this morning when you had more important things to do." Out of the corner of her eye, she noticed Jeff had returned to helping Brett cook dinner. She guessed she shouldn't be surprised Jeff was as willing as ever to let her handle the dramas in his life.

"Are you trying to insinuate something, Kayla? If so I'd appreciate if you came straight out and said it. I don't have time for these games."

"Are you home for dinner?" Kayla glanced to where Jeff used a fork to turn the meat in the frypan.

"I beg your pardon?"

"Dinner." Kayla gestured towards Brett. "That's Brett. He's staying the night. He's a mate of Jeff's. Dinner's nearly ready. Do you want a plate?"

Robyn stared at Brett for several seconds before she turned back to Kayla. "I will eat later."

Kayla watched as her mother stalked from the kitchen. She didn't turn to face her brother until she was certain the battle was over. The dread that had ruined all sense of hunger earlier was now gone. "Is dinner nearly ready? I'm starved."

"What the hell happened?" Brett mashed the potatoes, a glance in her direction.

Kayla grinned. "Topic change and a reminder we have company. She doesn't know who you are or who your parents might be. They're big on networking. Once she finds time to interrogate Jeff or me she'll decide you're unimportant and you'll lose your guest immunity."

Brett shook his head. "Odd." He glanced at the cupboards. "Where are the plates?"

Kayla took three plates out and put them on the kitchen bench. "They've always been the same. Everything relates to how they can further their careers." She shrugged. "A lot of the time it's a pain, but occasionally it's helpful."

"It means they don't bother us unless we get in the way of their careers." Jeff stabbed the steaks with a fork and put one on each plate. He glanced at the two left in the pan and added them to one of the plates. A cup of cornflour was tipped in next and water added to the pan. He used the fork to stir the liquid. "Kayla, put those extra steaks, that are on my plate, in a container and into the fridge."

Kayla rummaged in one of the lower cupboards. "It's been a while since we've had a cooked meal. I'm surprised the potatoes weren't growing."

"Nah, I bet Mrs Guillory buys fresh fruit and veggies every week and takes the old ones home to her family." Jeff turned the element down as he continued to stir.

"Mrs Guillory?" Brett spooned mashed potato onto each plate and then served the steamer of vegetables.

"She comes every Wednesday to clean the house and buy the groceries." Kayla put the extra steak in the fridge and leaned back against the shiny surface to look at Brett. "You'll have to make sure you're not about, or at least not visible, when she's here."

Jeff poured the gravy into a jug, turned off the element, grabbed his plate and picked up the jug of gravy. "Bring cutlery with you, Kayla." He headed for the table.

Brett picked up the other two plates. "Water would be good too." When Kayla stared at him with narrowed eyes, he smiled. "Please?" At her nod he followed Jeff.

Kayla joined them at the table with a jug of water, three glasses and a fistful of cutlery. She handed the cutlery around and paused to watch Brett savour his food. She smiled. It vanished as she thought of why he was so fascinated by the meal. But maybe it wasn't because he'd gone without eating for days. "Have you always been so into food?"

Brett paused, his fork halfway to his mouth. "No."

"Sorry," Kayla said softly.

"It's not like we can avoid the topic. It's a pretty big part of my…" He shook his head. "I can't very well say life, can I?" Brett popped the food in his mouth. Silence settled over the table.

Kayla kept her gaze on her plate, not so hungry anymore. They weren't the best company to share a meal with. One wanted to die, one wanted to live. Put like that it sounded half positive. Until you were reminded the only one who wanted to live was the one who no longer had a grip on life. Kayla glanced towards Brett. His plate was half empty. She stared at her plate, only a few mouthfuls gone, and swirled the gravy through her mashed potato. There had to be some way to sort out this mess.

Chapter Seven

Saturday morning Kayla paced restlessly in the lounge room while she waited for Jeff and Brett to join her and Red. She stopped her pacing to glare at her friend. "Do you have to do that?"

Red continued to slowly flick through the music channels. "Yep. Sit down, why don't you? You've worn a track in the carpet already."

"Choose a channel and stick with it." Kayla dropped into an armchair.

"There's three good songs on. I can't decide which one to listen to." Red changed the channel again.

Kayla got to her feet as Jeff and Brett entered the lounge room. Her mouth hung open as her gaze landed on her brother. "Wow. Those clothes suit you a lot better than the ones you normally wear."

"They're not as comfortable," Jeff muttered.

Red abandoned the remote to circle Jeff. She

reached out to mess up his hair. "Looks like you've had a haircut. Not bad, Jeffery."

"Am I meant to be pleased by your praise, Mildred?"

Red made a face at him. "You're the one going to all the bother."

"No I'm not." Jeff gestured towards Brett. "He's the one who dragged me shopping and to a hairdresser. I don't know what was wrong with the barber I've been going to."

"Then you obviously haven't looked in a mirror in the past decade," Red said.

"Shut up, Mildred."

"Oh, the pair of you shut up," Kayla snapped. "Let's get out of here." She picked up her car keys and handbag she'd dropped on the coffee table earlier.

"I still think we're wasting our time." Red followed Kayla to the front door. "We'd have been better off seeing the psychic I found online."

"Ease the path for restless spirits doesn't sound like what we need." Kayla waited until everyone stood on the front porch before she locked the door. She strode towards the car parked on the side of the road and pushed the central locking button.

"At least she sounded like she knew something about ghosts. Aunt Andrea thinks she can see them because she's the seventh daughter of a seventh daughter. She doesn't believe anyone when they say it doesn't count when there are two brothers ahead of her in the family so she's actually the ninth child." Red slid into the front passenger seat.

"Nine kids." Brett stared at her.

Red grinned. "Yep. Grandma and Grandad didn't own a TV until after Aunt Andrea was born. At least that's what Dad reckons."

Jeff got in the car. "He can't talk. He's one of six kids."

Brett shook his head, getting in the back of the car with Jeff. "I've never met anyone with such a large family before. What about you? How many siblings do you have, Red?"

"Absolutely none. Thank god." Red glanced at Jeff. "I might have ended up with a brother like Jeffery. I seriously don't know why Kayla bothered to call the ambulance."

"Red." Kayla started her car with a warning glance at her friend.

"What? You want me to start lying?"

"I want you to shut up and stop hassling my brother." Kayla checked over her shoulder before she pulled out onto the road.

"Where's the fun in that?" Red muttered, but she

managed to restrain herself from tormenting Jeff in the hour and a bit it took to reach Andrea's house.

They sat out the front of the house, silence filling the car. Brett was the first to speak. He handed the circlet of hair to Kayla. "Look after this for me. I want to find out if Andrea can see ghosts."

"I hate it when you do that." Red turned to glare at the spot where she'd last seen Brett. "You are still there, aren't you? What am I thinking? I can't hear you answer so there's no point in asking you questions."

"He's still there." Kayla pushed the bracelet in her pocket. "I guess we should get this over and done with."

"Good idea. Sooner we get in there and talk to her the sooner we can get out of here. Then I say we ring the psychic I found online." Red opened the car door. They followed her to the front door of the house and stood back as she knocked. She glanced around. "Where's he standing?"

Jeff pointed to a spot near Kayla. "There. But stop talking about him. You'll give him away."

Before Red could reply, the door swung open and a woman in her late twenties grinned. Her blond hair hung loose down her back and she wore a flowing black dress. "Mildred. So good to see you." She threw her arms around her niece. "It's been far too long. Come inside. And your friends too, of course."

They followed her inside. Kayla looked around the lounge room they entered. In the middle of the room was a low table with a large bowl of polished stones sitting on it. Against one wall was a bookcase with books and crystals filling the shelves, a pile of cushions sat in one corner and an armchair in another. Gauzy curtains framed the windows and faceted crystals hung from the curtain rods, spinning rainbows of light around the room. In another corner sat a small table where a lazy trail of smoke rose from an incense stick.

"Grab a cushion, find a place to sit and make yourselves comfortable." Andrea waved towards the pile.

Red continued to stand. "Aunt Andrea–"

"No, no. Sit first. Get comfortable."

Red sighed and grabbed a pillow. She dropped it on the floor near the low table. "Aunt Andrea–"

"Can I get you something to eat? Drink?"

"No." Red's tone was sharp and her lips were pressed tightly together.

Kayla sat on a pillow she'd taken over to the low table. "Ah… Andrea?" She wasn't certain if she should call Red's aunt by her first name, but it seemed preferable to letting Red lose her temper. "We actually came to ask a favour of you."

Andrea perched on the edge of the table and, without looking, took one of the polished stones from the bowl. She rubbed her fingers over it. "A favour?"

Kayla nodded. She noticed Jeff had chosen the armchair to sit in and wished she'd thought of it. Brett leaned against the wall near the front door. "Ah… that is… well, Red said you can… ah-"

"I told them you can see ghosts," Red interrupted. She sent Kayla a look. "How hard was that? They're just words."

"You want me to see any particular ghost?" Andrea dropped the stone back in the bowl and took a different one out.

Kayla's gaze remained on the pale pink stone. "Yeah, we were wondering if you could see any right now."

Andrea glanced around the room. "Of course I can. There's one behind you."

Kayla looked over her shoulder. She frowned. She wouldn't exactly say Brett was behind her. He was more to the side than directly behind. She turned back to Andrea. "What does… ah… the ghost look like?"

"It's a bit hazy. More of a glow. I can sort of make

out the shape. A male I believe. An older male. Maybe a grandfather or great grandfather watching out for you. Has he tried to make contact with you?" Andrea changed the stone she held for yet another one.

Brett pushed away from the wall. "She's full of it. Red was right."

Jeff laughed. "Don't tell her. She'll be unbearable."

"What did he say?" Red demanded. "Was he talking about me?"

"You can hear the ghost too?" Andrea looked from Red to Jeff.

"Make him appear. I told you she wouldn't be able to see him." Red looked around the room. "Where is he now?"

Brett rested his hand on Kayla's shoulder. "I'm here."

Andrea made a noise that was half yelp and half squeal as she leapt to her feet. The stone she held fell to the floor and came to a rest against the pillow Red sat on. "He… there's… what the… how did…" She pointed at Brett. "Where did he come from?"

Red grinned. "He's been here the whole time. Didn't you see him? Not exactly a grandfather, is he?"

Andrea took a cautious step towards Brett. Her hand stopped centimetres from him. When Brett disappeared again, she jumped back with another strange sound, her hand covering her mouth.

Red laughed when Brett reappeared. "Glad to know I'm not the only one who's bothered by that trick."

Kayla took the bracelet from her pocket and handed it to Brett. "Stop playing." She turned to Andrea. "We need help. He doesn't want to be dead. There's a way he can live by taking over someone else's body if he turfs them out. We hoped you knew of a better method."

"Oh my." Andrea tried to sit on the edge of the table, but missed and landed on the floor. "Oh my."

"Guess you don't." Red rose to her feet. "We might as well go."

Andrea stumbled to her feet, becoming tangled in the skirt of her dress. "No, no. I might be able to help you. Not me personally. I know someone who might be able to help. My mentor. She's in her sixties but you'd swear she looks forty. If anyone knows what else you can do, it'd be her."

"Another nutcase," Red muttered, rolling her eyes.

Brett stepped closer to Andrea who took a nervous step backwards. "Can you ask her?"

"Give me a few minutes while I call her. I'll be right back." She took another couple of steps backwards.

"Ahh… you lot… ahh… make yourselves comfortable." She fled from the room.

Chapter Eight

Red dropped back onto the cushion she'd been sitting on. "That went real well, didn't it? I did tell you it was a waste of time."

Brett sat beside Kayla, not bothering with a cushion. "Maybe not."

"Her mentor will be just as warped. The only difference is she's more than twice her age." Red picked up the stone Andrea had dropped earlier and tossed it in the bowl.

"I hate to agree with Red on anything, because most of the time she's full of it, but I think she's right." Jeff made a face like he was in pain.

Red smiled sarcastically and gestured towards him with her middle finger. "You'll want to be careful with all those compliments. They'll go to my head. I might fall madly in love with you and follow you around like an obsessive stalker."

"I couldn't be that unlucky," Jeff said.

Red grabbed a stone from the bowl and pegged it at Jeff. "When I came to my senses I'd have to kill myself. I wouldn't be able to live with the thought of having been in love with you."

"Red!" Kayla glared at her friend.

"What?" Red had an exaggerated look of innocence on her face.

"Stop hassling my brother."

"Stop sticking up for him all the time. He won't grow a backbone if you do." Red picked up another stone.

"Throw one more at me and I'll dump the whole bowl of them over you," Jeff warned.

"See, he can stick up for himself when you don't jump in." Red let the stone fall into the bowl. "Or was it the killing myself comment you were going on about? I'm not about to censor my comments because he's stupid enough to try and do himself in."

Kayla sighed. There were times when she could easily dump a bowl of stones over her friend's head too so she could understand her brother's threat. She just wished they didn't have to constantly bicker. It made her feel like her loyalties were torn in two different directions. She nearly shouted in relief to see Andrea appear in the doorway.

"What did she say?" Red demanded.

Andrea shook her head. "She wasn't home. I rang a couple of mutual friends, but they don't know where she is either. I'll keep ringing her until I get hold of her." Her gaze was drawn to Brett. "Do you mind if I ask you a couple of questions about when you died?"

"I won't be able to answer them. Jeff's already grilled me. One minute someone shot me, the next I woke up in the hospital," Brett said.

"What about a tunnel of light?" Andrea came further into the room.

Brett shrugged. "If there was I didn't see it."

Andrea sighed. "I finally have a ghost I can question and he can't tell me anything." Her gaze turned to the ceiling as she spoke.

"See, told you she doesn't see ghosts," Red said.

Andrea turned to her niece. "Of course I see them. I am unable to question them. They only impart the information they wish me to have."

Red rolled her eyes. "We might as well head. No point wasting more time here."

Brett pushed himself up off the floor before he turned to help Kayla. He faced Andrea. "You'll let us know the moment you've talked to your mentor?"

Andrea nodded. "Of course. And if you recall anything that happened to you between being shot and waking in the hospital, could you let me know? I'd be interested to know what happened to you during that space of time."

Brett shrugged. "Probably. But I don't think anything happened."

Minutes later they were in the car and Kayla turned the key in the ignition. "Are we going straight home? Or was there somewhere else we had to go first?"

"I don't suppose we could drive past where I used to live?" Brett asked.

"Where is it?" Kayla watched Brett as he hesitated to tell her.

Brett gave her an address and smiled wryly. "It's over an hour from your place on the other side of the city. If it's too far-"

Kayla interrupted him. "It doesn't bother me." She turned in her seat to look at Red and Jeff in the back. "What about you two?"

"Can you drop me home first?" Jeff asked.

"Me too. Or even at your place. I should probably take my bike home in case I need it," Red said.

"We don't have to go," Brett said.

"I don't mind." Kayla smiled. "I'm curious to see where you lived."

Red laughed. "Why doesn't that surprise me?"

Kayla pulled out onto the street and drove towards

home. When she arrived, she left the engine running while Jeff and Red got out. With a wave, Kayla headed for Brett's home. It was late afternoon when they arrived. She pulled up out the front and turned the engine off. They sat in silence, looking out Brett's window at the old timber house shaded by three jacaranda trees with wide spread branches.

Kayla saw a shadow cross in front of one of the windows. "I think someone's at home."

"Probably Brian."

"How do you know?"

"That's his room."

"Oh." Silence filled the car again. Kayla didn't know what to say to break it.

Brett sat quietly in the passenger seat, his gaze drawn to the house. Finally he turned to Kayla. "I want to find out if my stuff is here." He slipped the bracelet off and handed it to her.

Kayla slid the bracelet on her wrist, but immediately removed it because she was afraid it would slip off and she'd lose it. She pushed it into her pocket. "Don't take too long. I don't want to sit out the front of someone's house for ages. It'd be my luck someone'd call the police and say I was a crim checking the place out so I could break in."

Brett nodded before he slid through the car door.

Kayla shook her head as she watched him disappear through a wall of the house. She glanced at the time on her dash and turned her music on while she waited, tapping her fingers against the steering wheel. Another glance towards the house showed Brett must still be inside. Kayla sighed. So much for him not taking long. She frowned as another song began. What if he'd run into trouble? She continued to tap her fingers on the steering wheel, no longer keeping time with the music, frequently glancing towards the house. Hitting the steering wheel, she turned off the ignition.

"Enough sitting around," she muttered as she got out of the car. She didn't have a clue what she'd say to Brian, but she couldn't sit in the car all afternoon. She knocked firmly on the front door and tapped her foot as she waited for it to be opened.

"Yeah?"

A man, who looked to be a few years older than Brett, opened the door. Kayla hadn't expected him to be so young and it took her a few seconds to gather her thoughts.

Brian continued to stare at her, a frown forming and a question in his blue eyes. He ran his hand through his short brown hair and smiled crookedly.

"Are you going to speak or has my good looks rendered you speechless?"

Kayla couldn't resist smiling. "Not quite. I'm not sure how to start this conversation. Could I come in?" She moved her foot so it'd stop the door from being closed if he said no.

Brian hesitated. "I haven't met you before, have I?"

Kayla shook her head. "And I guess I should check if you're Brian."

"Yeah. That's me. Brian Macrae. And you are?"

A crash inside saved Kayla from answering. Brian swore and spun away from the door as he automatically gave it a shove, hard enough to close it. Kayla winced as the door hit her foot and bounced back. She shut the door behind her as she ran quietly after Brian. He paused in a room with an unmade queen-sized bed and a painting lying face down on the floor. Brian moved to pick up the painting while Kayla's gaze was drawn to Brett. He wrestled with a man who had reddish-brown hair, blue eyes, a barrel chest and arms that looked like they'd snap firewood without any help from an axe. The man had a slightly faded look about him, like a photograph left sitting in the sun for years.

Kayla ran towards them, touching each of them as she tried to push them apart. "Enough." Her hands remained against their chests as she looked from one to the other.

The painting slipped from Brian's fingers. He swore, shook his head and swore again. "Someone want to tell me what's going on here? Is this some sort of hidden camera show?" His gaze stayed on Brett. "It's pretty damn sick if it is."

Kayla groaned as she realised what she'd done. She stepped back from the two males who'd stopped fighting. Facing Brian, she spotted the portrait that was now face up. "Who's that?" She pointed at the painting.

"Haven't ye eyes, lass? That's me of course. Douglas Macrae."

Kayla spun back towards Douglas. "But... I mean... I know it's a portrait of you. I didn't... I wasn't..." Kayla closed her eyes for a second and took a steadying breath. "What I meant to ask, Douglas, is who are you?"

"You're talking to him?" Brian took a step forward, a hand in front of him like a blind man trying not to run into something.

Douglas pointed to Brian. "That there's me great grandson. I don't know what's so great about him though. I'd been working for years by the time I was his age. No' still stuck in school. By twenty-three I owned my own house."

"It's a different era. These days you normally earn more money by continuing your education," Kayla said.

"What's he saying? Is he talking about me? And where is he? Why can't I see him anymore?" Brian glanced around the room, still walking cautiously forward.

Brett held out his hand to Kayla. "Bracelet. This isn't getting us anywhere. I want to ask Brian about my gear."

"Do you think that's a good idea?" Kayla pulled the bracelet out of her pocket, but didn't hand it over.

"Of course it's not a good idea, but I think you pretty much ruined keeping this quiet when you ran in here and tried to drag us apart," Brett said.

"What was I meant to do? Let you get pounded into the ground by Paul Bunyan?" Kayla demanded.

Brett took the bracelet from her and slipped it on his wrist. "I didn't need any help. I was doing okay on my own."

Brian sat heavily on the bed when Brett appeared again.

Douglas grinned. "Paul Bunyan. I like that, lass."

Kayla shook her head. "This is getting too confusing."

Chapter Nine

Kayla reached out and took hold of Douglas' hand. "I don't suppose there's anything you want to tell your great grandson."

Douglas looked down at her hand, dwarfed by his. "He can hear me?"

Kayla nodded. "And see you."

"Guess that's why the lad looks like a dead fish washed up on the shore." Douglas shook his head slowly. "Can't say I'm all that impressed with the lot of them. I can't count the amount of times I've wanted to give 'em a clout across the ears to knock some sense into them. You're a sore disappointment to me lad."

Brian finally closed his mouth. "Can't say I'm impressed by you either. You nearly died a pauper. Only had the house you lived in and a few pounds.

Everyone said you never spent a penny and yet there weren't any to be found."

"Pauper! I had thousands of pounds by the time I died. What did that hen-witted boy of mine do with it all?" Douglas pulled away from Kayla and strode towards the painting, trying to pick it up.

"Where'd he go?" Brian rose unsteadily to his feet, glancing around the room. "And where are you going?" He grabbed Brett by the arm when he tried to step out of the room.

"What'd you do with my stuff?" Brett pulled away from Brian.

"It's in boxes in the shed." Brian grabbed Brett again when he tried to leave the room. "But you can't take it. You're dead. I mean… you can't be real. This has to be some sort of hoax. It's not your stuff."

"Get over here lass and help me pick up my portrait. Can knock the dammed thing off the wall, but can never lift it." Douglas beckoned her over.

Kayla looked between Douglas and Brett. "Okay. Enough. All of you. Brett, wait. We'll sort you out in a minute. Douglas, if you stop insulting your descendants I'll pick up the portrait. Actually, let's try something else instead." She pulled a single strand of hair from her head and handed it to Douglas.

"What do I want this for?" Douglas peered at the strand he held between two fingers.

Brian open and closed his mouth several times before he managed to speak. "I can see him again."

"Good. That means he should be able to pick up his own painting." Kayla turned to Brett. "Instead of demanding your gear, why don't you convince Brian you're real?" Kayla rubbed the left side of her forehead then pressed her fingers against her temple. "This day has been a disaster."

Douglas looked up from where he squatted in front of his face down portrait. "Get me something to pry the nails up so I can remove the back of me portrait, lad."

Brian stared at him, standing in the doorway so Brett couldn't leave the room. He shook his head and then pressed his palm against his forehead.

Kayla grinned. "You're not sick and this isn't a hallucination. As much as I wish it was sometimes." She looked pointedly at Brett.

Douglas rose to his feet. "Do I have to do everything myself? Ye must have cotton between yer ears, lad."

"It's Brian. Stop calling me lad. You make me sound like a little kid."

"Ye are a little kid. Must be since yer still in school. Wonder ye still aren't living with ye ma."

Kayla glanced at the back of the portrait. "Brian, can you please get a bread and butter knife? Or a small flat screwdriver. I don't have all night. I have to get home before it's much later."

Brian glanced around the room warily. "None of you move." He hurried away.

When Brett started to leave the room, Kayla jumped over the painting and grabbed him by the arm. "Have some patience."

"It's my stuff." He met her gaze, determined.

Kayla sighed and let Brett's arm go. "Give me a few minutes to sort Douglas out first. You were the one fighting with him."

"He started it. I was trying to look in my old room when he threw himself at me." Brett glared at the older man.

"He was trespassing." Douglas' glared back more fiercely. "Ye don't live here anymore and this place isn't big enough for two ghosts."

"I don't care who started it. If you hadn't been fighting we wouldn't be in this mess." Kayla's hands went to her hips as she looked from one to the other.

"Good thing we were fighting then," Douglas said.

Kayla stared at him for a moment. "How on earth can you reach that conclusion?"

Douglas looked past her. "About time, Brian." He stressed the name. "What'd ye have to do? Make it?"

Brian slapped the knife onto Douglas' outstretched hand. "I think I liked it better when I couldn't see or hear you."

"No need to rattle ye cage." Douglas bent down to pry the nails up on the back of the painting. He carefully lifted the back away and grinned, looking towards Brian. "What do ye say about that, lad?"

"It's Brian," he muttered as he came forward to peer at the paper randomly lying on the back of the portrait. His jaw dropped. "Are they what I think they are?"

"Money, lad. Money. Now try and tell me I died a pauper."

Brian reached out to touch the notes, a finger gingerly brushing across the corner of one. "They're in perfect condition. There must be a couple of thousand pounds here."

"Of course there is. A lifetime of working. Ye didn't think I had nothing to show for it, did ye?"

Brian shook his head, his gaze focused on the notes. "I don't suppose you have a fifty pound note with a

Y prefix and small numbers. Or better yet, one of the ones issued between 1914 and 1917."

Douglas held up a fifty-pound note. "How about this one?"

Brian reverently took it. "Close. Bold numbers. This has to be worth over seventy thousand. Are there any more like this one?"

"Seventy thousand, huh?" It was Douglas' turn to look surprised.

Brett pulled Kayla close to him and bent his head to her ear. "Think we can search the shed now he's occupied?"

Brian put the money back. "We shouldn't be touching it. We don't want to damage any of them. I need to call Dad. And go online and find out some prices." He rose to his feet. "I need to…" he stared at Douglas. "You can't be here. Dad'd freak."

"Wait," Kayla whispered to Brett.

"If Camden had more between his ears than sawdust he would have had the money when I died. Sorriest excuse for a son. And the way he raised Colin guaranteed your father would be no better."

"If Grandad had spent the money when you died they wouldn't have been worth anywhere near as much as they're currently worth." Brian took his mobile phone from his pocket. "Don't say a word." He stared at Douglas for a moment.

"Before you ring your dad, can we talk about Brett's gear?"

Brian turned towards Kayla, startled. "I forgot all about you two."

"Thanks," Brett said dryly.

Kayla waved towards the painting. "Can we have Brett's gear? Think of it as a way to say thanks for putting you in touch with your great grandfather and his money."

Brian grinned. "My favourite topic." He took a set of keys from his pocket and threw them towards Brett.

Brett caught them effortlessly. "Thanks. I won't be long."

"Think you could grab a cap from one of the hooks on the back door to wear? I don't want to have to explain to the neighbours what's going on," Brian said.

Brett laughed. "Sure." He turned to Kayla. "Your car keys?"

Kayla reluctantly handed them over. "I'll be out in a minute."

Brett nodded then left the room. Kayla turned back

to Brian. She smiled apologetically. "Sorry about all the dramas."

Brian continued to grin. "I'm not about to complain. I might have a heart attack when the shock wears off though."

Kayla chuckled. "So, you'll be right then? I didn't mean for you to find out like this. And I guess I don't have to ask you to keep quiet about Brett."

Brian sobered. "I'd be an idiot to mention him to anyone. Is he staying with you?" At Kayla's nod, Brian cleared his throat. "Do you think I could get your number? It'd be nice to talk to him when I manage to get over the shock." He put her number in his phone as she said it. "And do you think I can get a couple more strands of your hair? In case we lose that one."

Kayla ran her fingers through her hair. When she found no loose ones, she pulled a couple of strands out and handed them over. "I swear I'm going to be bald at this rate."

"Thanks." Brian looked at the dark brown strands. "I guess I should find somewhere safe to keep these."

"What about somewhere safe for me money?" Douglas waved towards the notes lying on the back of the painting. "No' so sure about yer priorities, lad."

Brett appeared in the doorway. "I thought you said you wouldn't be long."

Kayla shrugged.

Brett turned to Brian. "Thanks." He tossed the keys to him.

Brian caught the keys and nodded. "I… it was…" He smiled wryly. "Not exactly how I expected my weekend to turn out."

Brett laughed. "I'll catch you around. Hopefully."

"Yeah. I hope so too."

Brett dropped an arm around Kayla's shoulders and ushered her out of the room, barely giving her time for a quick wave and smile for Brian and Douglas. Reaching the car, she glanced at the boxes piled on her back seat as she opened her door. Not much to show for a lifetime. Even a short life. But she guessed if you didn't count the furniture in her room she wouldn't be able to fill many more boxes.

Once they were back on the road, Kayla glanced at Brett. "Are you happy to have your gear?"

Brett was quiet for several minutes. "It hasn't changed my six month deadline. I don't want to spend forever like Douglas. Half a century of not being seen. Of having nothing to do other than watch and listen to life going on around him. I want to be part of life, not an observer."

"We're working on it. Remember? Andrea is asking her mentor."

"We should look at other options too. I don't want to be stuck between life and death for centuries."

Kayla nodded. What could she say? Not much at all. She remained quiet and was relieved when Brett turned her stereo up and closed his eyes to listen to the song.

When Kayla pulled up in front of her home, she was surprised to see Red near the front door yelling at Jeff. She'd expected her to be long gone. Hours ago.

"You're full of it." Red rammed Jeff's shoulder with the heel of her palm.

Jeff rubbed his shoulder, his smile not slipping in the slightest. "You're only mad because I'm right."

"Not even. It was because–" Red cut her words off abruptly when she spotted Kayla and Brett. She turned her back on Jeff, speaking to Kayla instead. "I'll give you a call as soon as I hear from my aunt." She stalked to her bike.

Still trying to figure out what was going on, Kayla nodded and waved to her friend. She turned to Jeff when Red was halfway down the street. "What happened?"

Jeff shook his head. "Why don't you ask your

friend?" He turned away from her, about to head back inside.

"Jeff, do you have space in your room for a handful of boxes?" Brett gestured towards the car.

Jeff shrugged. "I guess so."

"Give me a hand?"

Jeff grumbled as he walked beside Brett to the car. "What are you trying to do? Turn me into a body builder? If I wanted to lift weights I'd use the home gym. It's bad enough you drag me swimming every morning. When do I get to sleep in?"

"Swimming?" Kayla stared at Jeff.

Jeff glared at her once he picked up one of the boxes. "It's all your fault you know. If you think getting me in shape is going to make me want to live longer you have to be kidding. I hate strenuous activity. I should have been born a sloth."

Brett carried two of the boxes. "You don't hate it. You hate people seeing you be uncoordinated. Some people need to practice more than others."

"Yeah, right." Jeff stepped inside and headed for his room.

Kayla stared after them, trying to grasp the concept of her brother dragging himself out of bed early in the morning to go swimming. He loved to sleep in as much as she did. She shook her head and then reached into the car for one of the boxes. Nothing had been normal since her brother had tried to kill himself and she had no idea when it was likely to be normal again. Or if it ever would be.

Chapter Ten

Kayla hid a yawn behind her hand. It was annoying having a ghost, who didn't need to sleep, wandering around the house of a night looking for something to do. She'd suggested he might want to do her homework if he was bored. He hadn't been interested. Not that she could blame him.

She bit back an exclamation when she saw Brett step through the wall and into her classroom. She wanted to tell him to go home. What was he doing? He sat on the edge of the desk beside her and stared down at the equations she struggled to complete.

"The second one is wrong." Brett pointed towards it.

Kayla opened her mouth to tell him to leave her alone. She turned it into a yawn and tilted her head further forward. She was tempted to reach out and touch him. Just for a second. That would liven the class up.

"Do you need a hand with it?" Brett grinned when she glared at him.

"What's your problem?" The girl sitting beside Kayla hissed.

She supposed the girl had thought she was glaring at her. "Sorry. Trying to think how to do the second question. It doesn't look right to me." Kayla tilted her page so the other girl could see what she meant.

The teacher rose from his desk and cleared his throat. When Kayla looked towards him, he spoke. "If you're having trouble, raise your hand and I'll help you. Otherwise I expect heads down and pens in motion."

Kayla angled her head down. She clenched her teeth together and forced her hand to stay on her pen and not reach out to Brett. She ignored his chuckle and read the next question. She had to read it four times before it made the slightest bit of sense.

She nearly bolted from the room when the bell rang. Heading for the library, she found a quiet corner towards the back. She was relieved to see Brett followed her. "What are you doing here?" She kept her voice low. The last thing she needed was to be found talking to empty air.

"It's Wednesday."

"Usually lasts a full twenty-four hours too," Kayla said dryly.

"Very funny. Mrs Guillory is cleaning."

Kayla swore. "You can't follow me around all afternoon. Why don't you go and hassle Douglas."

"You have to be kidding. You want me to visit Douglas."

Kayla closed her eyes momentarily and sighed. "Okay. Bad idea. But you can't follow me around. There has to be something you can do." When Brett reached out to clasp her hand, she looked around to make sure no one saw.

"There's no one here but us. When will Andrea know something? The days are disappearing. It's been four days. How hard can it be to track down one old lady?"

"I don't know. Look, I know how–"

"You don't know. Quit trying to patronise me."

"Well stop taking your problems out on me. I'm doing the best I can."

"Shouldn't you be in class?" A sharp voice cut into their argument.

Kayla mentally swore when she turned to find the librarian glaring at her. "Yeah. We're heading there now." She kept hold of Brett's hand. There wasn't much else she could do. She frantically thought of where she could drag him to so she could let him disappear. Somewhere close so she wasn't caught holding hands with a boy who wasn't wearing a school uniform. "If you weren't already dead-" she sent him a threatening look as they stepped out of the library.

Brett grinned. "At least I've made the day more interesting. You looked so bored earlier you were about to fall asleep."

"That's because you keep waking me up every night. How am I meant to sleep when you don't let me?" Kayla turned at the sound of a sudden indrawn breath behind her. She kept her face expressionless when she spotted one of the worst gossips in the school.

Samantha grinned delightedly as she stepped closer. "Hi, I'm Samantha. Are you Kayla's boyfriend?"

Kayla answered before Brett could speak. "No, he's not."

Samantha glanced down at their hands clasped together. "Really? And yet he stays at your place each night."

"We're friends," Kayla protested.

Brett laughed softly. His smile widened when Kayla's gaze met his. "Friends. Hmm. I guess that term will do." He reached out and pulled a single strand of hair away from her head and slowly wrapped it around his index finger. He tugged it out when his hand was close to her head.

Kayla let his hand go as a wave of relief washed over her. It was short lived when he leaned close and lightly brushed his lips across hers.

"I'll see you at home this arve." With a grin, Brett strode away from her.

"Friends." Samantha nodded her head. "Right."

Kayla could see it would be a waste of time to argue. Instead she shrugged. "I've gotta run. I'm late for my next class."

Kayla found it difficult to concentrate for the rest of her classes. Even Red and Jeff commented about it when they saw her. Red during English and Jeff when they were headed for her car after school. Kayla stopped mid stride when she saw who leaned against the car.

"Great," Kayla muttered. Her eyes narrowed as she tried to figure out if Brett was visible to the rest of the world. It was hard to tell at a distance.

"You can't stand here all day." Red glanced at Kayla while she waited for her phone to turn on. "I swear it's pure torture they expect us to turn our phones off in class. Why don't they ever check if yours is turned off?"

"Because you've been regularly caught answering your phone in class." Kayla continued to stand where she was, her gaze on Brett.

"If you're not planning on going home, can I have the keys?" Jeff held his hand out.

Kayla pushed his hand away. "Not on your life."

Jeff laughed.

"How come you can make comments like that when I'm not allowed to," Red demanded.

Kayla shook her head and started towards her car. She nearly stopped again when she spotted Samantha near another girl, her head close to her ear as she passed along some news that made the other girl's mouth round in surprise. They both looked towards Kayla's car and she was left with no doubt what the gossip was about. And no doubt that everyone could see Brett. Kayla glanced down when Red grabbed her by the wrist. She tried to shake her friend off.

"They're not worth it. Ignore them."

"Have you heard what they're saying?" Kayla stared straight ahead.

"Yeah. I was going to tell you later." Red glanced at Jeff.

Kayla shrugged. "It doesn't matter."

Red glanced at Jeff again. "You sure?"

"If you want to whisper and share secrets behind my back, how about you say so?" Jeff strode ahead of them.

"Jeff–"

Red linked her arm through Kayla's. "Forget about him. Do you want to hear what they're saying or not?"

"I guess."

"Brett has moved in with you and you're having sex with him, but it's only casual." Red grabbed Kayla's arm with her other hand. "Forget about them. You'll make it worse if you say anything to her."

"I hadn't planned to say a single word," Kayla said through clenched teeth.

"That's worse." Red checked her phone when it beeped. "It takes so long for messages to come through when you first turn your phone on."

Kayla unlocked her car and glanced at Samantha as she slid into the driver's seat. She ignored Brett when he greeted her.

Brett got in the front passenger seat. "Are you still mad at me for turning up here today?"

Kayla continued to ignore him as she buckled her seat belt and her brother got in the back with Red.

"That was Aunt Andrea. She wants me to call her back."

"Did she find her mentor?" Brett turned in his seat to face Red.

Red shrugged as she dialled her aunt's number and held the phone to her ear. "How do I know? She said to ring. Nothing else." She made a shushing motion with her hand. "Hey, Aunt Andrea. You wanted me to call… yeah, it's Red… sounds great… okay, give me a couple of minutes." Red disconnected. "Talk about centre stage. Haven't any of you got anything better to do than stare at me?"

"Don't push it, Red. What did she say?" Brett demanded.

"No need to act like an axe wielding psycho. I was joking," Red said.

Kayla shook her head. "I swear you'd tease a caged tiger and then wonder why he came after you the moment his door was opened."

Red grinned. "Thanks for the advice. I'll be sure to padlock it first."

"Red!" The three of them yelled at the same time.

"Okay. No need to yell. Mentor found. If you want to meet at Aunt Andrea's house tonight we have to let her know in the next half an hour. Otherwise, they have somewhere else to go."

"Ring her back and tell her we'll be there," Brett said.

"We have to be home by ten," Kayla said.

"If we're running late we'll tell our parents something was wrong with the car," Jeff said.

Kayla shook her head. "They'll expect to see a mechanic's invoice."

"No problem. I know a mobile mechanic who'll charge you for some minor repair and swear he actually fixed it," Jeff said.

"For someone who doesn't have friends you know some really useful people." Red redialled Andrea's number.

"Red. Quit hassling-"

Red made a shushing motion at Kayla. "Yeah, it's me again… yeah…. Okay, I'll tell him… see you." She disconnected. "Aunt Andrea said you have to bring something from when you were alive. Baby teeth, nail clippings, lock of hair, blood stained item. Something like that."

"I have hair in one of the boxes in Jeff's room, from when I had it cut," Brett said.

"Guess we're headed home first." Kayla started the car.

It was a silent trip. Kayla couldn't help wondering what Andrea's mentor would be like. All the

Hollywood images of witches flittered through her mind. She hoped the mentor wasn't anything like the evil ones. Maybe someone like Sabrina would be okay. She pulled up in front of her home and locked the car once they were all out.

"Can I borrow something to wear?" Red asked.

Kayla nodded. She needed to change too. She turned to Brett and Jeff. "Will half an hour be long enough for you two?" When they nodded, she retreated to her bedroom with Red.

In less than half an hour Red and Kayla headed for the lounge room where they usually met up. Only Jeff was there. Kayla glanced back the way they'd come. No one followed. "Where's Brett."

Jeff shrugged. "He was looking at stuff in his boxes. Said he'd be a minute."

Kayla frowned. "Did he find the hair?"

Jeff nodded.

Kayla stared in the direction her and Jeff's bedrooms were in. "I'll see what's holding him up." She found him on the floor, leaning against Jeff's bed, a photo album in his hands. She sat beside him.

Brett turned another page before he looked up at her. "I went and saw him today."

"Who?"

Brett snapped the album shut. "He stole all that

from me." He gestured towards the boxes before he rested his hand on the photo album.

"The kid who shot you?"

Brett nodded. "I asked Brian to drive me over to where they're keeping him. He was playing basketball. I couldn't believe it. He might be locked up, but it wasn't bothering him. Well, it wasn't until I rocked up there."

Chapter Eleven

Kayla rested a hand on the photo album Brett held. "Can I?"

He hesitated then let her take it. "I took a couple of strands of your hair from your brush. I didn't want to risk losing the bracelet." He glanced down to where it encircled his wrist.

Kayla opened to the first page and smiled at the young couple in the wedding photos. She saw similarities between Brett and the man. "Didn't your father skip out on you and your mum?"

"Yeah. Two months after the wedding. By then he'd got her pregnant and spent all her money. She didn't have a fortune, but enough to make him want to marry her. She'd inherited it when her parents died a few months before." He gestured towards the wedding photo.

"Oh." She turned the page to see photos of Brett as

a baby. She grinned at one of him with food mashed through his hair. She looked up to see he watched her. Her grin faded. "What did you do to the kid?"

"I waited until he was alone. Then I picked up the piece of your hair I'd been carefully blowing in the direction I wanted it to go."

Kayla turned another page and saw photos of Brett a little older. A skinny kid with missing front teeth, one skinned knee and a bruise on his jaw. "What happened here?"

Brett glanced at the picture. "Got in a fight." He frowned.

"Who won?"

Brett raised an eyebrow, looking at her like she was crazy. "Me of course."

She grinned. "Okay. Sorry. You were telling me about your day." She turned another page and watched as his skinny body started to fill out and become taller.

"I don't think he's going to sleep tonight."

"What did you do to him?"

Brett shrugged. "Not much. Told him he better sleep with one eye open because if I decided to end his life he wouldn't end up as a ghost, he'd be going to hell."

"Oh. I bet he didn't take that too well." She turned

another page. She couldn't look down. Her gaze was held by Brett's.

"I think if he hadn't just used the bathroom he'd have wet himself." Brett grinned.

Kayla couldn't resist returning his grin. "Feel better after that?"

Brett's grin vanished. "No. Not even punching the little bastard helped." He sighed.

Kayla looked down at the album and her breath caught in her throat. She didn't even notice the girl on his arm. It was a studio photo and Brett looked absolutely gorgeous. Her fingers traced the edge of the photo that took up most of one page.

"My formal."

"Oh."

"Do you think we should join the other pair before they come looking for us?"

Kayla looked up at Brett. She nodded, closed the album, handed it back to him and let him help her to her feet. They walked quietly to the lounge room in time to see Red shove Jeff backwards.

He caught himself and turned towards Kayla. "Call your friend off." His hands were fists at his sides.

Kayla sighed. "Red–"

"He started it." Red stalked to the front door.

With another sigh, Kayla followed her.

The trip was silent and they remained quiet when they pulled up in front of Andrea's house. No one moved. Between Brett and Kayla sat a plastic bag with a hank of hair in it.

"I would have brought food if I'd known we were going to stay out the front forever," Red muttered.

Brett picked up the plastic bag and placed it in Kayla's lap, then slipped the bracelet off to hand it over to her. As soon as he was invisible to Red, Brett spoke to Kayla. "We'd better move before I'm tempted to murder your friend."

Jeff laughed. "I know exactly how you feel."

"I hate it when he does that. What's he saying?" Red glared at the front passenger seat.

"He wanted to know if we'd help dispose of your body after he murders you." Jeff was out the door in time to miss the punch Red aimed at him.

Red slid across the back seat and followed him. "He did not. You're so full of it." The door slammed shut.

"What if she makes the problem worse?" Kayla asked as soon as they were alone.

"Worse than being a ghost? I want to live."

Kayla met his gaze, unable to say anything. She looked away. "Let's get this over with." She locked the car as soon as Brett had slid through the door and then mentally called herself an idiot. A locked door wouldn't have stopped him from being able to get out of the car. She slowly walked towards Jeff and Red, who knocked on the door when she saw Kayla coming towards her.

The front door swung open. Andrea glanced around. "Is he here?"

"Guess you still can't see ghosts, huh, Aunt Andrea?"

"He's here." Kayla spoke before Andrea could. She didn't want any arguments that might make them refuse to help Brett.

Andrea stepped back and waved them inside. "Come in. Make yourselves comfortable."

Their gazes were drawn to the woman who sat in the chair Jeff had used last time. She had short, silver hair, her face was barely lined and her smooth skin could have belonged to someone a couple of decades younger than sixty. Her dark eyes carefully looked them over. She pointed first to Jeff and then to Kayla and beckoned them forward.

"If either of you are interested in exploring your abilities further, you're welcome to give me a call," the woman said.

"What abilities?" Kayla asked.

"Being able to see the deceased."

"I guess you can't see them either," Red said.

The woman looked her over. "It's not one of my abilities." She turned back to Jeff. "How long have you been able to see the dead?"

Jeff shrugged. "I don't know. The first time I knew I could see them was when I met Brett. I actually thought it might have been from the drugs. Guess that's why they suggest you say no to them. Messes with your head."

The woman looked at him for nearly a minute. "Maybe you should remember that next time you think you might want to kill yourself."

Jeff's gaze dropped to the floor and he took a step back.

With a sympathetic glance at Jeff, Brett stepped forward and rested his hand on Kayla's shoulder. "Can you help me?"

The woman looked him over. "You must be Brett." When he nodded, she said, "I'm Irene."

"But can you help him?" Red moved closer to them.

"That will be up to him. He might not want my help. There are certain conditions that must be fulfilled." Irene's gaze remained on Brett.

"Like what?" Brett asked warily.

"Did you bring something with you?" Irene held out her hand when Brett nodded. Kayla handed over the plastic bag and watched as Irene opened it and pulled out the hank of hair. She nodded as she let the dark brown strands run through her fingers. "Perfect."

"Does that mean we can do something about a new body for me?" Brett asked.

"If you keep your body for two months it's yours for life. Let it die and there's no second chance."

Brett took the bracelet Kayla handed him and slipped it on his wrist. "That doesn't sound too hard."

"And isn't that what got you in this predicament in the first place? How difficult was it to die the first time?" Irene dropped the hair back in the bag.

"I'd like to try," Brett said softly.

Irene nodded. "I'm sure you would. Give me your hand." She held hers out and waited for him to place his hand in hers. She turned his hand, looking at it from several angles. She finally let it go. "Come back Saturday. I'll expect you at eight in the morning." She took a business card from a pocket. "Call me if you have any questions."

"Thanks." Brett handed it over to Kayla to look after.

"You'd better go if you expect to be home by ten. There's a bit more traffic than usual on the road tonight." Irene smiled at their dazed expressions.

Once they were in the car, Red demanded, "How'd she know we had to be home by ten? That's your curfew, not mine."

Jeff shrugged. "Does it matter? I think she was trying to show off with that comment, anyway."

Kayla started the car. "What's it matter? We know there are odd things in life. Seems like every direction I look in, there's a ghost."

Red looked interested. "Really? You've seen more? You never said."

Kayla shrugged. "I guess I don't think anything about it. I realised I've always seen them. A faded old man who sits on the same park bench every afternoon, a woman who wanders along a certain street looking at each window she passes like she's desperate to find something and a cat that sits in the same tree at the end of our street and has done ever since I can remember. I've seen them for years but didn't register they were ghosts or that they were always in the same place every time. Not until I started looking around and wondering."

"Hey, I've seen that cat," Jeff exclaimed. "I didn't know it was a ghost."

"The ones that have been around for a while have a slightly faded look. Like if you'd bought two shirts and one you always hung inside to dry and the other you put out in the sun. It's hard to tell when you don't have the original to compare them to, but I'm starting to figure it out," Kayla said.

"And the new ones?" Red asked.

Kayla smiled wryly. "I'm not so good at figuring them out. Sometimes I can, but I'm never certain."

"What are we going to do with Brett when he's real again?" Red asked.

"I am sitting here, you know," Brett said.

"You're talking about him like he's a stray dog," Jeff said.

"Stray part sounds pretty accurate. He's meant to be dead. You can't bring him back to life and expect there to be no problems. He doesn't exist. There'll be no birth certificate or anything. Well, I guess there will, but there'll also be a death certificate," Red said.

"I know someone who can take care of that problem for a price," Jeff said.

Red rolled her eyes. "I should have known. Don't you know any normal people?"

Jeff smiled slightly as he looked Red over. He shook his head. "Nope. Not a single one."

"Why you–" Red began.

Kayla interrupted before another argument could start. "How are we going to pay your friend? I'm guessing he won't be cheap."

"There's ten k in your bank."

"What? How long has that been there? How did it get there?" Kayla glanced at Jeff in the rear view mirror and saw him slowly shake his head. "No. You didn't."

"I couldn't take it with me."

Kayla shied away from that thought. "Where'd you get it from?"

"Our parents."

"Yeah, right."

"Credit card. I kept taking more off it each month and they never said anything. No matter how much I spent or how many cash advances I got. I've been doing it for years. I told you they don't pay attention to what we do."

"Yes they do. What about our ten o'clock curfew on a school night?"

"I've broken it plenty of times without a problem. I send them a text with some lame excuse. Even you didn't get in trouble for staying at the hospital with me."

Kayla fell silent as she dwelled on Jeff's comments. She thought back over each time she'd been in trouble and grounded by her parents. She winced as she began to see the pattern. Her parents did care. She had to believe that. They just weren't good at showing it. She glanced at Brett when he rested his hand on her arm momentarily.

"Do you think you can put up with a ghost around your house a bit longer?"

Kayla smiled. "I suppose you're looking forward to Saturday."

"I hope Irene knows what she's doing."

Kayla reached over and squeezed Brett's hand. "So do I."

Chapter Twelve

Kayla strode towards the car park, relieved school was finished for two days. She hoped whatever Irene planned to do to Brett would mean he'd need to sleep again. His restless pacing each night was driving her mad.

"Hey! Kayla."

She turned to see Karl, a boy from her homeroom, wave as he hurried towards her. She stopped and waited for him. He wasn't as tall as Brett, or anywhere near as good looking, but with his blond hair, blue eyes, athletic build and easygoing nature, he didn't have a lack of girls wanting to hook up with him.

Karl reached her side. "I haven't seen you around much in the past couple of weeks. Are you doing anything this weekend?"

"You're busy," Brett said from behind her.

Kayla started to turn and speak to him, but when

there was no reaction from Karl, she guessed Brett was invisible. "I have some plans." Like catching up on sleep.

"Do you think you can spare a few hours Saturday night to see a movie with me?" Karl grinned. "I'll let you pick, as long as it isn't too mushy."

Kayla laughed. "Well…" she dragged the word out.

Brett stepped in front of her. "Tell him you have other plans. I should be alive Saturday night. I want you to celebrate it with me."

Kayla hesitated, moving sideways so she could see Karl. "It's tempting."

"Come on. Surely you can get out of whatever else is on. You don't sound like you're interested in it anyway."

"Kayla," Brett began, breaking off when Red joined them.

"What's happening?"

"I'm trying to talk Kayla into seeing a movie with me Saturday night. Think you can help me?" Karl appealed to Red.

"Of course she'll go," Red said.

"No." Brett reached for Kayla.

She took a step back and smiled at Karl, annoyed by Brett's demanding tone. "Okay. I'll meet you in the city centre. I'll check online and text you with the movie and what time." She had his number from when they'd worked on a school project together. "But I have to run right now." She took another step away from Brett's glare.

"You'll text tonight?" Karl stepped forward.

Kayla nodded. "Yeah, sure. I'll do that." She waved and hurried towards the car, Red on one side and Brett on the other.

"I know exactly how Jeff feels about Red. She should stay out of things," Brett muttered.

"Can you believe it? I know he's been talking to you a bit in homeroom, but I didn't think he'd want to go somewhere with you. Doesn't he make your brain stop functioning when you look at him?" Red asked.

Kayla sighed. Saturday morning couldn't come quick enough.

"Stop functioning. I didn't know her brain ever started functioning." Brett glared at Red.

Red rambled on about Karl as they continued towards the car. She eventually slowed her steady stream of compliments. "What's wrong? Didn't you want to see a movie with Karl?"

"I guess." Kayla glanced towards Brett.

"He's here, next to you, isn't he? That's so rude.

Tell him to go away and stop spying on everyone. Did you hear me, Brett?" They reached Kayla's car.

Jeff, who leaned against the car, straightened. "He's not deaf. Just invisible."

"I wish I was deaf sometimes." Brett glanced towards Red as he spoke.

Jeff laughed. "I don't blame you. What's she done this time?"

"It's not fair talking about me when I can't hear half the conversation." Red's eyes narrowed when she looked at Jeff.

"Everyone get in the car. Before we draw attention." Kayla unlocked the doors and got in. She started the engine the moment they were seated and reversed out of the car park.

Other than some bickering in the back seat, between Jeff and Red, the drive home was quiet. As soon as everyone was out of the car, Kayla locked it and headed inside.

"Kayla. What's wrong?" Red called after her.

Kayla heard Jeff speak to Red, but it wasn't loud enough for her to hear the words. Red's uncomplimentary reply to him was loud enough the neighbours probably heard it. As soon as she entered her room, Kayla locked her bedroom door behind her and left her schoolbag on the floor before dropping onto her bed. She closed her eyes as she tried to sort out her thoughts.

The last couple of days she'd spent reminding herself not to get too attached to Brett because it looked like he'd have his life back soon. He'd have no reason to hang around once Jeff sorted identification for him. It made sense to accept Karl's invite. Of course it made sense. So she couldn't understand why agreeing to see a movie with Karl made her feel disloyal to Brett.

Kayla's eyes opened when she felt the bed sink near her waist. "I'll be glad when you can't walk into my room whenever you feel like it."

"Then you shouldn't take off to sulk instead of sticking around to talk."

"I'm not sulking." Kayla sat up, feeling at a disadvantage looking up at Brett.

"What would you call it?"

"Regrouping."

"Why didn't you want to celebrate with me tomorrow night?"

"You didn't ask me."

"Yes I did. And you went ahead and agreed to go out with Karl."

Kayla shook her head. "You told me. You didn't ask. And you left it until someone else wanted to do something with me before you thought to say anything."

Brett reached out and took hold of her hand. "Sorry. I want you to celebrate with me tomorrow night. Please?"

Kayla noticed the bracelet of hair was on his wrist. She guessed he'd left it in her room. She drew her hand from his, shaking her head. "No. I've already told Karl I'd go to a movie with him."

"Then go early and come out with me afterwards."

Kayla hesitated, then shook her head. "That sounds wrong."

Brett grinned. "Afraid it'll give Samantha something else to gossip about."

Kayla groaned, thinking of exactly how Samantha would twist that situation. "Yes. It's bad enough with the rumours she's spreading. She doesn't need any more ammunition." Her mouth dropped open as a thought occurred to her. Why had Karl invited her to see a movie? Did he believe some of the rumours? She stood up, heading for her door. "I can't go. Is Red here?"

"What?" Brett followed behind her.

"I have to find Red." She threw Jeff's bedroom door open and stared open mouthed at Red and Jeff who broke apart. "I... what... how..." Kayla closed her eyes, swallowed, took a deep breath and opened her eyes again. "What's going on?"

Brett laughed softly at her side. "If you don't know, Samantha's not even close in the rumours she's spreading."

"Shut up, Brett," Kayla muttered. She stepped forward and grabbed Red by the hand. "I need to talk to you." She started to drag Red from the room then stopped to face Brett. She held a finger out in warning. "And you will stay out of my room while I talk to her."

"What's going on?" Red demanded as soon as Kayla locked her bedroom door.

"I should be asking that. What did you think you were doing?"

Red shook her head. "A dare gone wrong?"

"Huh?"

"Never mind. What's your emergency?"

"Why did Karl ask me out?"

Red rolled her eyes. "Because he likes you. Obviously."

"What if it's because of the rumours Samantha's been spreading?"

"Oh." Red looked horrified. "The rumour that you're casual about sex?"

Kayla nodded.

"Hmm." Red stared at her a moment, frowning. Her expression brightened. "I've got it." She hurried from the room.

"Got what?" Kayla followed her to Jeff's bedroom.

Red stood in the doorway and pointed at Brett. "We're going to the movies tomorrow night."

"Why him?" Jeff demanded.

Red turned to Jeff. "Because he'd be more useful in a fight."

"What fight?" Brett was at Kayla's side in seconds. "What's going on?"

"Nothing." Kayla glared at Red.

Red shrugged. "It's the best plan. It's not like we can read minds." She turned to Brett. "Unless you can."

Brett shook his head. "Only those close to death."

"How close?" Kayla blurted out the question then instantly decided she didn't want to know. She covered Brett's mouth with her hand when he started to answer. "I changed my mind. Don't tell me."

Brett nodded, removing her hand from his mouth. "What fight are you worried about?"

"We're not." Kayla couldn't meet Brett's gaze.

Red had no problem divulging the answer. "We're worried about the rumours Samantha's been spreading. And what Karl might be thinking because of them."

Brett's hand tightened on Kayla's that he still held. "We'll be there."

"What about me?" Jeff demanded.

"You'd need a girl to take with you. And a mannequin doesn't count," Red said.

Jeff glared at Red for a moment and then grinned. "Sure. I'll bring a girl. She won't be a mannequin either."

"Why do I suddenly think a mannequin is the better choice?" Red asked.

Kayla rubbed the left side of her forehead before pressing her fingers against her temple. "Why do things seem to end up out of control when you're involved, Red?" What had made her think her friend would know the answer?

"Not in the slightest out of control. It's a triple date." Red grinned.

Kayla slowly shook her head. "I'm going back to my room. I want to have a look online at what movies are on."

"How about an action?" Brett asked.

"Or horror," Jeff suggested.

Kayla ignored them both as she returned to her room. She also had to get through the not so pleasant

task of telling Karl their plans had become a group
activity.

Chapter Thirteen

The drive to Andrea's house had been done in complete silence. Even Jeff and Red hadn't tormented each other. Brett wore the bracelet this time as they knocked on the front door of the house. Andrea opened the door immediately.

"Come inside. All of you. I'm sure you're anxious to see what will happen." Andrea waved them in with a sweeping motion of her arm.

Irene was in the armchair again and they slowly crossed the room to stand in front of her. She held a plastic bag out to Brett.

"I didn't need all the hair for the tincture. But I need one more ingredient. Which one are you drawn to the most? The boy or the girl?" Irene waited for Brett to answer.

Brett frowned as he took the plastic bag. "What?"

Irene smiled. "What am I thinking? You're a

heterosexual male. Of course it'd be the girl." She beckoned to Kayla and took hold of her hand.

"Ow!" Kayla tried to pull back, but Irene had a surprisingly strong grip. "Why did you do that?" Kayla stared as a drop of blood formed on her finger.

"Hold still for a moment." Irene opened a small blue bottle, the lid an eyedropper. She held Kayla's finger over the opening and let a single drop of blood fall in. Letting go of Kayla's hand she closed the bottle, shook it, then held it out to Brett. "Four drops once a day for three days. At the same time each day."

Brett stared at the bottle. "I have to drink this?"

Irene smiled. "Think of it as medicine. It's not meant to taste good."

"It has blood in it." Kayla stared at the bottle. "My blood."

Irene nodded. "To strengthen the tincture. You can see the deceased." She shrugged. "You don't have to use it. I've given it to you. It's up to you if you choose to use it. But it must be destroyed after four days. It'll be no good then. Destroyed with fire, even the inside of the bottle must be cleansed with fire."

"This will give me back my life?" Brett's gaze was fixed on the bottle.

Irene nodded. "You'll be as alive as the rest of us."

Brett's finger's closed over the bottle. "I'll use it."

"Then I suggest finding somewhere quiet and alone. I've been told the process is a little painful. But what birth is easy? You might want to use Andrea's bathroom if you plan to have it now."

Brett turned towards Andrea.

"Third door down the hallway." Andrea pointed towards the doorway that led to the rest of the house.

"Thanks."

Kayla watched as Brett left the room. She wanted to run after him and tell him to take some time to think about it. But she didn't. She continued to stand as quiet as Jeff and Red. Remembering Irene's comment of taking the tincture at the same time each day, she took out her phone and set the alarm to go off daily.

"I can't wait around in here. I'm going outside." Red headed for the front door.

"I'll go with you." Jeff hurried after her.

Kayla watched them, until the front door closed. She wanted to run and never return to this house. She sucked her finger and the metallic taste of blood filled her mouth, causing her to wince. Holding another finger against it to stop any more blood drops forming, she glanced at the doorway Brett had left the room by and then looked over at the other occupants of the room. Andrea sat on the coffee table, fiddling with the rocks in the bowl. Irene read a book that had been on the floor near the armchair. Kayla didn't know what to do. Another glance towards the doorway made up her mind and she followed the directions Andrea had given Brett.

She tapped on the bathroom door. "Can I come in?"

"It's unlocked."

Kayla swung the door open. Her gaze was drawn to Brett who sat in a corner, his back against the wall, his arms wrapped around his legs that were drawn up to his chest and his jaw was clenched tight. She hurried into the room, letting the door swing shut behind her, kneeling beside him. "Are you okay?"

"Other than the fact that my heart might explode from my body, my veins are on fire and it feels like I've been shot again… I'm absolutely great."

"That doesn't sound like a little painful. Maybe she got the tincture wrong."

Brett closed his eyes and shuddered. "I hope not." His words were a whispered gasp.

"What can I do?"

"Help me out of this shirt. I need to see where I was shot."

Kayla helped Brett unbutton his shirt and slip it off his shoulders. She gasped when she saw the two marks on his torso. Pin pricks of blood seeped from them. "Do you think that's meant to happen? Maybe I should get Irene."

Brett clutched her arm when she started to move away from him. "Stay. Please." When Kayla hesitated, Brett smiled weakly. "It's not as bad now. I think I'm over the worst of it."

Kayla sat beside him, leaning against the wall, and draped her arm around his shoulders. Closing her eyes, she rested her head against his arm. She nearly drifted off to sleep as she waited for Brett.

"Are you awake?"

Kayla struggled to open her eyes. "Yeah, but I desperately need some sleep."

"Me too."

She stared at him, certain she couldn't have heard right. "You need sleep?"

Brett grinned. "It's a good feeling."

"You're planning on going to sleep?"

"As soon as we get back to your house."

"Then let's go. I plan to sleep until it's time to get ready to go out tonight." Kayla stumbled to her feet. Her gaze was drawn to the marks on Brett's torso, two smudges of dark colour where he'd been shot. She hesitantly reached out to touch them when he stood up. "It's like they've been bruised for days."

"It feels like it."

She looked at her fingers. They were clean. "At least they've stopped bleeding." She shuddered. "Actually, let's not mention the word blood again. I can't believe it was part of the ingredients. I don't want to think what else went in the tincture."

"Eye of newt? Wing of bat?"

Kayla laughed. "Yeah, something along those lines."

"A small price to pay to be able to return to life."

Kayla sobered. "I guess it is." She slid her hand in his. "Let's go home."

* * *

Kayla yawned and stretched, her eyes tightly closed. She rolled over in her bed, savouring the feel of being well rested. Her eyes slowly opened and instead of looking at the time on her alarm clock, she saw Brett.

He grinned. "I was beginning to wonder if I should wake you. Unless you've changed your mind about going to the movies with Karl."

Kayla sat up, checking Brett over, trying to see if there were any changes in him. "How do you feel? Any different?"

"Yeah, but it's hard to describe. Sort of like being

here, not like the world is out of reach, no matter how hard I try and grab hold of it."

Kayla threw the bedding back and stood up. Her gaze travelled over his body before returning to his face. "You look exactly the same." When Brett smiled slightly, she demanded, "What's so funny?"

He shook his head, the smile becoming a grin. "Nothing."

"Fine!" Kayla turned her back on him and crossed the room to her wardrobe, opening the door. She felt him step close, but pretended to be absorbed by the clothes she ran her hands along. The occasional noise of coat hangers sliding on the rod was the only sound. She could feel the heat of his body as he continued to stand behind her. She forced herself not to turn. After pulling a pair of black pants from a coat hanger, she looked through her tops.

Brett reached over her shoulder and took out a long sleeved shirt that dipped low in the front and had more lace than fabric. "What about this? That's the problem with so many clothes, it takes ages to choose."

"Too cold." She stepped away from him.

"Wear a jacket. Although you won't need it at the cinema. It'll be warm there."

"Who do you think you are? My fashion consultant?"

Brett grinned. "Nope. Getting impatient waiting for you to make a decision."

"What were you grinning about before?"

"If I said, you'd probably be offended."

"I already am, so you might as well tell me."

Brett took the pants from her hands, throwing them on the bed along with the shirt he held. "Have I thanked you for helping me get my life back?"

"Are you certain you have it back?"

Brett nodded. "Red could see me without the help of your hair."

Kayla ran her fingers across the bracelet he wore. "Then why are you wearing it if you don't need it anymore?"

Brett shrugged. "I guess I kinda got used to it." His gaze steadily held hers.

"Well now you've said thanks, either tell me what you found so funny or get out of my room so I can have a shower and get ready."

"Who said I've thanked you?"

Kayla frowned. Hadn't he? "Hurry up then."

There was a hint of a smile before his lips met hers. It was nothing like the last time he'd kissed her in thanks. Kayla's eyes automatically closed and her hands linked behind his neck. When he finally pulled back slightly, her eyes opened and she stared up at him, speechless.

His lips curved into a smile. "I'll let you get ready. Don't keep me waiting too long."

It wasn't until Brett reached her bedroom door that Kayla was able to speak. "I'm going to the movies with Karl, not you."

Brett paused, one hand on the door, and looked back at her. "Are you?" He closed the door before Kayla could reply.

She stared at the door, not certain what had happened. Brett had kissed her, that much she obviously understood. She wanted to know why. Staring at a closed door wasn't going to give her the answers she needed. Grabbing the clothes off her bed, and underwear from her duchess, she headed for her ensuite.

Within half an hour she was knocking on Jeff's bedroom door. It was opened by a girl with purple hair and so much body jewellery Kayla thought she might sink if she ever went swimming. Her eyes narrowed as something about the girl made her think ghost. A mannequin looked like it might have been the better option.

"Hey. You looking for Jeff or Brett?" The girl

continued to hold onto the door, the other hand on her hip.

"Ahh… both?"

The girl swung the door open and turned to bellow, "Hurry it up boys. Someone's looking for you."

Spotting her brother, Kayla stepped forward. "I need to talk to you for a minute." She grabbed him by the upper arm and dragged him back to her room. "What do you think you're doing?" For a moment she thought he might play dumb.

Jeff shrugged. "No one said anything about ghosts. Only mannequins."

"You can't go around making ghosts real. Have you thought about what'll happen if too many of them know about using our hair so they can participate in life again?"

"Of course I have. That's why I laid a couple of strands on some tape and put it on her back. I'm not about to tell her how I'm making her real for the night. You're the one who told someone about it once Brett figured it out."

Kayla took a deep breath instead of arguing like she wanted to. "Fine. Make sure she doesn't figure it out. The last thing we need is every ghost in the world turning up on our doorstep wanting to make us bald."

Jeff laughed. "I don't think that look would suit you, sis."

"Don't leave her side. She better not work it out."

"You were the one who dragged me away from her."

Kayla opened her mouth to speak, but closed it when the doorbell rang. "That's probably Red."

Chapter Fourteen

Kayla headed for her door then paused, turning back to Jeff. "You better not ruin tonight for me." Stepping through her doorway, she strode towards the front door and swung it open."

"Wow, you're certainly sending a message tonight." Red stared at Kayla's top.

"Don't you start." She turned away, Red's comment reminding her she needed a jacket.

"What's your problem?" Red stopped halfway through the lounge room. "Who the hell is she?"

"I wouldn't have a clue. I wasn't introduced." Kayla stared at Jeff's friend who clung to him like he was the only life raft, after a ship went down in a stormy sea.

Red crossed the room and stopped in front of Jeff. Her hands went to her hips, her gaze on the girl. "I'm Red. Who are you?"

"What's it to you?" the girl demanded.

Jeff grinned. "Looks like I'm not the only one who finds your personality far from bearable. This is Pallas. Pallas, that's Kayla, my sister, and Mildred is her friend."

"Watch it, Jeffery," Red muttered.

Brett entered the room. "Is everyone ready to go?"

"I have to grab my jacket." Kayla was nearly out of the room when Brett spoke.

"I like the top you're wearing." He grinned when Kayla turned to look at him.

She stared at him for a moment then decided it wasn't worth commenting. She hurried to her room, grabbed her jacket and handbag then returned to the lounge room where everyone waited. She took her keys from her bag and they were soon on their way to the cinema.

Pallas sat between Red and Jeff. She shifted closer to Jeff with a contemptuous look at Red. "Don't you have a car, Jeff?"

Red laughed sharply. "Nope. He totalled his a few days after he got his licence. His parents said he'd have to buy the next car himself."

"Why didn't you use the money, you put in my bank, for a car?" Kayla asked.

"I wouldn't have been able to explain it," Jeff said.

"How do you know Pallas?" Red demanded.

"I've known her for a bit over a year. I often run into her in the city centre."

Kayla was tempted to ask how she'd died, but stopped when Jeff met her gaze in the mirror. He slightly shook his head. She sighed. It looked like it was going to be a long night.

Brett reached out and rested his hand on her thigh. "Are you having second thoughts?"

She shook her head. She could honestly answer no. She was way past second thoughts.

"Thought he was meant to be with her." Pallas pointed first to Brett and then to Red.

Kayla pushed Brett's hand away. "He is."

Brett grinned. "For tonight."

Pallas shook her head. "And people said I was weird. You lot are way weirder than I've ever been."

Kayla pressed her lips together to prevent any reply she might make. Why had she agreed to a triple date? She was still asking herself that question when she arrived at the cinema and greeted Karl, joining him as he lined up to buy tickets.

By the time they were seated and the movie was starting, Kayla was ready to go home. There'd been too many awkward silences. At least now she could use watching the movie as an excuse not to speak. She soon found it didn't help. Sitting between Karl and

Brett was distracting. A million thoughts ran through her mind and the movie couldn't compete with them.

She had no idea how much time had passed when Karl held a container of popcorn towards her. Taking a handful, she slowly ate them, reaching for more when they were finished. She glanced at Karl when their hands bumped and she wondered if it had been deliberate on his behalf. If the glint in his eyes was anything to go by, it probably had been. On her other side, Brett shifted and bumped her as he did. She faced straight ahead and tried to focus on the movie. She hoped Karl wasn't the type who liked to discuss a movie in depth afterwards. Time slowed to a crawl and she had no idea what she'd been watching.

She managed to hold back a sigh as she tried to unobtrusively check the time on her watch. When she realised there was almost an hour left, she nearly groaned. She grabbed another handful of popcorn. This time Karl didn't reach for some at the same time. She began to think she'd panicked over the date for no reason. She wished she'd said nothing to Red. Maybe then she might have been able to enjoy herself.

Between Brett regularly bumping her, Red leaning back in her seat to look past Brett, her and Karl to where Pallas and Jeff sat and Pallas' nearly steady stream of remarks about the movie, Kayla wanted to go home. She blinked, barely managing to hold back a scream as Douglas stepped through Karl to stop in front of her. She opened her mouth to demand what he was doing there when she remembered Karl sat beside her. She heard a soft chuckle from Brett and a hushed conversation between Pallas and Jeff.

"I need to talk to ye, lass."

Kayla ignored Douglas and suppressed the urge to lean closer to Karl so she could see the movie. She'd never wanted to be able to see ghosts. Actually, she hadn't thought about it until recently, but she couldn't imagine she ever would have wanted to see them no matter what her age.

"Are ye listening to me, lass? We need to talk. I can mess the place up a little if I need to so I can get yer attention."

Brett nudged her. When Kayla turned to look at him, he raised an eyebrow. Kayla almost wished Brett could go invisible so he could tell Douglas to go away. But if last time was anything to go by, she guessed they would have ended up fighting. She almost regretted giving him a strand of her hair, which had cut his ties to his painting and allowed him to go where he wanted.

"Come on, lass. Give me a few minutes and then I'll let ye get back to watching yer picture."

Kayla hesitated. She already had enough problems to deal with. A persistent ghost wasn't her idea of a great night. She finally came to a decision and leaned closer to Karl. "I'll be back in a few minutes." Rising to her feet, she walked sideways, her legs brushing against the seats in front of her. When Red started to rise and follow her, she shook her head.

Within minutes Kayla reached the ladies and started to push the door open.

"I can't go in there, lass."

Kayla ignored him and stepped inside, letting the door slowly swing shut behind her. She checked the cubicles were empty then faced the door in time to see Douglas step cautiously through it.

"I can't stay in here, lass. It's no' right."

Kayla folded her arms across her chest. "You have five minutes. Better make the most of them."

"The lad is letting some dolly lead him around by the nose. She keeps trying to get him to spend money on her. I tried to talk to him, but he took the hair off me. Said he doesn't have to bother with me anymore."

"Look Douglas, Brian's a big boy and more than

capable of looking after himself. He doesn't need you lecturing him on who he can and can't see."

"But-"

"You can't take over his life."

"I'm no' about to stand by and let him make a cake of himself."

"Douglas, stay out of his life." Kayla fell silent when the bathroom door swung open and two girls walked in. She hurried to the mirror and fussed over her hair and makeup. Anything to make her look busy until the two girls left. As soon as they did, she turned to Douglas. "Fine. I'll talk to him. But you need to remember you can't run his life."

"I'm no' about to watch some little gold digger walk away with all me money."

"You can't interfere. Not if you want me to deal with this."

Douglas glared at her a moment longer before he nodded sharply. "When?"

"Tomorrow. And don't go turning up at my place thinking you can wake me early. I won't be interested in helping if you do. I'll get there when I'm ready. I can't give you a time."

"Make sure ye do turn up." Douglas disappeared through the wall.

Kayla sagged against the vanity, her back to the

mirror. She should return to the movie, but she couldn't bring herself to move. She checked her watch. A little over half an hour. How long could she hide in the bathroom without Karl sending someone to find out if she was okay? She pushed away from the vanity and stepped out of the bathroom, freezing when she saw Brett standing there. "What are you doing here?"

"Are you okay?"

"Of course I am."

Brett moved closer. "What did he want?"

"It has nothing to do with you."

"What's your problem?"

"I didn't think you'd be nearly sitting in my lap. Couldn't you have sat a row or two back?"

"I don't trust him."

"Why?"

Brett shrugged. "I just don't."

Kayla stared at him for a moment. "You'll have your life back soon."

"And?"

She hesitated, uncertain how to word what she was thinking. "A year from now we'll probably never hear from you again. You'll be too busy living your own life."

Brett smiled slightly and stepped close enough

there was only centimetres between them. He reached out and brushed a lock of hair back from her cheek. "No I won't."

Kayla broke eye contact with him. "I have to get back to my seat." She started to move away and then frowned as Brett fell into step beside her. "Don't even think about walking in with me. What sort of message are you trying to give Karl?"

Brett grinned and took a step back. When he didn't answer, Kayla's eyes narrowed and she stalked back to her friends. Slipping into the seat beside Karl, she ignored the empty place on the other side of her. Jeff leaned forward and tried to catch her attention. She deliberately looked away from him. It wasn't like she could explain the problem to him with Karl beside her. He'd have to wait until later. She also ignored Brett when he sat down a few minutes later. Out of the corner of her eye she could see he smiled, his arm encroaching on her space.

Chapter Fifteen

Kayla nearly bolted from her seat the moment the movie was over and the lights slowly brightened. She managed to slow her pace so she wasn't miles ahead of everyone. They stepped outside into the cool night air and Kayla pulled on her jacket, shivering at the change in temperature. Something caught her attention. It was little more than a shadow in her peripheral vision. When she turned her head, it was gone. Yet she was left with the uneasy sensation that someone had been following them. She pushed the thought from her mind, telling herself it was probably another annoying ghost.

"Did you want to go somewhere and get a coffee? You don't have to head home yet, do you?" Karl asked Kayla.

Red yawned. "I was up really early this morning. I didn't think we'd go anywhere after the movie."

"What about you, Kayla?" Karl persisted.

Kayla held up her car keys. "I'm the driver."

"Don't any of the others have a licence? I can drop you home later," Karl said.

"I guess-" Kayla began.

Brett dropped his arm around Red's shoulders. "Come on, Red, the night's still young. A coffee will help keep you awake anyway." He grinned when Red nodded and Karl frowned.

"As long as we're home by eleven," Red said. "You don't want to be sprung with more than one passenger in your car, who's not related to you, and lose your license."

"Yeah, we need our chauffeur." Jeff grinned.

"Great. All sorted." Brett turned to Karl. "Do you want to follow us?" Before Karl could answer he headed towards the car, his arm remaining around Red. Jeff and Pallas trailed after him.

"Are you happy with that plan?" Karl asked Kayla.

"It sounds good."

"Are you doing anything tomorrow?"

Kayla nodded.

"Then maybe next weekend you and I could go somewhere. Without the crowd." Karl glanced towards the four who waited at her car for her.

Kayla smiled. "That sounds good, but I'm not sure what I'm doing during the school holidays."

"I'm not going anywhere these holidays. Give me a call when you know what you're doing."

"Okay." Kayla gestured towards her car. "I'd better unlock it before they start complaining."

"I'll see you shortly."

When she was in her car, Kayla waited until she saw Karl start his vehicle before she headed towards a cafe. They stayed nearly an hour and she was relieved it wasn't as awkward as watching the movie had felt. Surprisingly it was Jeff and Pallas that kept the conversation going with their cutting remarks about the movie.

"Next time, how about we pick an action," Pallas said when they all rose from the table.

Kayla groaned. "Not you too."

Pallas grinned as they headed for the door. "Do I look like I'm into chick flicks?"

Kayla laughed as her gaze was drawn to the body jewellery. "I try not to judge a book by its cover."

"Some covers give a pretty good indication," Red muttered.

When they'd nearly reached the two cars parked next to each other, Karl took Kayla's hand and stopped walking. She turned to face him, still smiling.

"I had a great night." Karl grinned. "Even if it wasn't an action movie."

Kayla grinned back. Before she had a chance to reply, Karl leaned close and kissed her. She didn't have time to get over her surprise at his move, before the kiss ended. She stared at him, not knowing what to say.

"I'll call you." After a fleeting grin, Karl strode to his car.

Kayla turned towards her car and froze at the look Brett gave her. His arms were crossed over his chest and his body tense. She slowly walked towards him. Karl hit his horn and she forced herself to smile and wave as he drove off. Her gaze returned to Brett, who hadn't moved.

"You going to unlock the car?" Red called out, oblivious to the undercurrents.

Kayla pushed the central locking button, her gaze still on Brett. He stood in front of her door, not moving even when the other three got in the car.

"Are you going to get out of the way?"

Brett stood there silently a moment longer. Then he stepped close and wrapped his arms around her. His lips met hers and she clung to him. Her eyes closed and one of her hands slid around his waist.

When he pulled back slightly to stare down at her she continued to cling to him.

"You don't like him, Kayla."

"How can you say that?"

"Because you don't look like this when he kisses you."

Kayla drew away from Brett and looked at a point past his left shoulder. "You're in my way."

Brett laughed softly. "And I plan to keep getting in your way." He strode around to the passenger side and got in the car.

Kayla took a deep breath before she slid into her seat. She glanced at the rear view mirror and was relieved to see the three of them were in the middle of a heated discussion. She started the car, keeping her gaze away from the front passenger seat and her thoughts blank. She'd never felt so confused, in her entire life, as she did right this minute.

* * *

The insistent sound of the alarm on her phone dragged Kayla from sleep. It took her a couple of seconds to remember why she'd set it. She staggered out of bed and stumbled to Jeff's room, her eyes half closed. She fumbled with the doorknob, swinging the door open. There was a buried lump in her brother's bed and on the floor was a mattress with Brett, one arm flung wide so it rested on the carpet. She paused in the doorway, her gaze travelling down Brett's body.

The sheet pooled at his waist, his chest bare. The house was always kept at the same temperature, summer or winter, so there was no need for heavy blankets. His other hand was tucked behind his head and she caught a glimpse of the bracelet amongst his dark hair, the thin strand a slightly lighter shade of brown.

Kayla crept quietly over to the mattress and knelt beside it. She leaned forward about to whisper in his ear, so she didn't wake Jeff, when his eyes opened. There was a moment of confusion and then he smiled.

"Morning," Brett said softly.

"Medicine time."

Brett closed his eyes again, sighed heavily then opened them. Kayla sat back on her heels as he sat up, throwing the sheet aside. Her gaze fleetingly dropped to his boxer shorts before it returned to his face. His smile was back. She turned away as she rose to her feet, Brett beside her in a second.

He glanced at Jeff before he looked at Kayla again. He lowered his head to her ear. "Can I use your bathroom so I don't wake Jeff? I guess he can sleep in since we've missed our early morning swim." Kayla pulled away from him and nodded. She hurried back to her room and stood in the doorway of her bathroom. She looked around. Everything seemed fine. No dirty clothes on the floor, or anything else lying around that she'd prefer him not to see. She turned as she heard her bedroom door close and saw the small bottle in Brett's hand.

"Do you want me to stay with you while you have it?"

Brett hesitated and then nodded. He stepped into the bathroom when Kayla moved out of the way. She watched as he put the bottle on the vanity and squeezed the dropper lid before he opened it. He let four drops fall into his mouth and swallowed. Grimacing, he turned on the tap to cup his hand under it for a drink. He closed the bottle and went to sit on the floor, his back against the wall. Kayla joined him on the cold tiles, her arm pressed against his. She felt him tense a moment before he doubled over, his breath hissing through his teeth.

She wrapped her arms around him, surprised when he straightened enough to clasp her to him, his arms tightening as he gasped. She felt something on his chest grow damp and wondered if it was blood like yesterday. She didn't bother to pull back and check, only held onto him.

Minutes dragged by as Brett continued to cling to her. Eventually his grip loosened and she ran her fingers through his hair. "One more day. Then you'll have your life back."

"If I live through the next two months."

"Of course you will. Just no stepping in front of bullets again."

Brett drew back from her and looked at his torso. Kayla stared at the smeared blood where he'd been shot. The skin was slightly puckered this time, like old scars. Brett lightly ran his fingers over the bloodstains on Kayla's nightie. She shivered and her mouth went dry as she met his gaze.

"Brett…"

He closed his eyes, leaning back against the wall. His hand fell away from her. "I'm sorry about last night."

"What?"

He opened his eyes and turned his head to face her. "About Karl. I'm sorry. It's your choice. I shouldn't…" he glanced away again before he faced her. "My life is uncertain. I shouldn't…"

Kayla started to smile. She pressed her lips against his. Karl's kiss hadn't made her feel anything like

Brett's kisses did. There was no comparison. She deepened the kiss, relieved when he kissed her back.

When they broke apart, Kayla smiled. "Karl? Who's Karl?"

Brett grinned and pulled her close again. "I should probably get this blood cleaned off me."

"Later. I'm too comfortable to move."

"Sitting on the cold tiles?"

"Barely notice them." She smiled when his arms tightened around her, trying not to think about needing to visit Brian later. Douglas better not think he could hassle her whenever they had a disagreement.

Chapter Sixteen

Kayla glared at Brett who sat in the passenger seat of her car. "I might need more than ten minutes."

"I'm not sitting out here all morning."

"The morning's nearly gone. Besides, you were the one who insisted on coming along. I told you I wanted to talk to them alone."

"Brian is my friend."

"So? Douglas asked me to do this."

Brett's eyes narrowed. "I don't trust Douglas."

"Only because he attacked you."

"Ten minutes and then I'm coming in."

"I said I might be half an hour. And you still wanted to come."

"Fine. Twenty minutes."

Kayla reached over and grabbed the cap off the back seat. She shoved it at him. "Wear this when you come in. You're not meant to be alive. Remember?"

She handed the car keys to him, got out of the car and slammed the door shut behind her. She strode to the front door and knocked sharply on it. She was startled when a tall woman with long blond hair opened it.

"Yes?"

"Is Brian home?"

"Who are you?" The woman continued to block the doorway.

Kayla saw Douglas stride up behind her, a scowl on his face. "I need to see Brian. Is he home?" She kept her gaze on Douglas as she asked.

"He's out the back. Hanging washing on the line. She doesn't let anyone in to see him," Douglas said.

"Why don't you try ringing next time you want to see him? Let him know you're coming." The woman shut the door in her face.

"Rude bitch," Kayla muttered as Douglas stepped through the door to stand beside her.

"I wouldn't have put it so nice." Douglas pointed to the side of the house. "There's a gate that way. Hurry if ye want to catch him without his jailer."

Kayla hurried around the side of the house and through the gate, stopping when she saw Brian hanging out washing. She grinned as he threw another garment over the line and shoved a single peg in it. "Morning."

Brian looked over and grinned when he saw who spoke. He walked across the lawn to greet her. "How are you?"

"I'd be a lot happier if your grandad didn't come looking for me last night while I was at the movies."

Brian glanced around. "Is he here? That-"

"I'm beginning to think he might be right to be worried about you," Kayla interrupted.

"Of course I am, lass."

"Your new girlfriend slammed the door in my face after insinuating you weren't home. Have you been having a lack of visitors lately?"

"Are you sure?" Brian glanced at the house.

"Of course I'm sure. Anyway, Douglas asked me to have a talk to you. He said you've hidden all my hair so you don't have to listen to him."

"It's bad enough having Dad lecture me on investing and being sensible with the money, but he has no idea about the value of money today."

"Money is money, no matter what year it is," Douglas growled. "He spent a fortune on that girl."

Kayla grinned. "He said you spent a fortune on your girlfriend."

Brian sighed heavily. "Three dollars. For a drink. He whined about it all night. I got fed up listening to him. Look, I know she's hanging out with me because I have money. Eventually she'll figure out I'm not going to waste it on her and disappear. But until then, I'm going to enjoy having her around. Coming home to a lecture every night isn't enjoyable."

"Told ye there was nothing great about him. It's a stupid reason to keep someone around. He can do better than her," Douglas said.

Kayla sighed. "Do you think you can give us some space, Douglas? You were the one who wanted me to talk to him. The least you can do is let me." She held up her hand when he opened his mouth. "Without the interruptions." She waited patiently while Douglas glared at her, snorted, then stalked away. She turned back to Brian.

"He's gone now?"

Kayla nodded. "I think he's bored. He's been stuck following his portrait for around fifty years. And even though he doesn't have to follow it anymore, there isn't much else he can do. Maybe you should teach him about the value of money today."

"I don't know."

"He does love making money. I bet if you bought him some books on the sharemarket and trading and set him up an online trading account he'd probably make more money. He's going to be around a long time. You should find a way to keep him busy."

Brian frowned. "What if he loses it?"

"How much did you make from selling those notes?"

Brian shrugged and looked away. "Enough. We decided not to sell all of them. We don't want to flood the market and lower the value."

"So give him ten grand. I bet you'd barely notice it. And do you honestly think he'd start trading before he was ready to? Remember, we're talking about the guy who hid his money in his portrait because he obviously didn't trust banks."

Brian laughed. "You're right. He wouldn't think about trading until he knew every single thing about it. Thanks. I'll pick up a few books later to get him started. And probably a dictionary since there's so many words he keeps asking me the meaning of."

"And let him have some strands of my hair. I don't want him turning up and hassling me about them." She turned her head to see what had caught Brian's attention. She frowned as Brett walked towards her. "I think your watch must be fast."

Brett grinned. "I wanted to see if I could get past the gatekeeper." He turned to Brian. "Is there a reason why you don't want to see anyone?"

"She wouldn't let you in either?"

Brett shook his head. "And I was my most charming, which usually works." His grin widened.

Kayla elbowed him at his comment and sent him a daggered look when he laughed, draping an arm around her shoulders to pull her close. She looked over to Brian. "I have to agree with Douglas and say you could do way better than her."

Brian sighed. "Probably. But…"

"She looks better out of clothes then in them?" Brett suggested.

"Something like that," Brian muttered.

"That's pathetic." Kayla shook her head. "Ditch her before she takes over your life. I think she's trying to."

"She won't be staying here again, that's for sure. Friends are welcome to drop in at any time. Not when she thinks they should."

"Well… we'll leave you to it," Kayla said. "Do you need any more hair before we take off?"

Brian shook his head. "Do you mind if I have a word alone with Brett before you go?"

Kayla turned to Brett. "I'll meet you in the car." She held out her hand for the keys. She smiled at Brian. "I'll see you later."

Brian returned her smile. "Yeah, and thanks for your idea."

Kayla strode back to the car and slid into the

driver's seat. She turned the ignition on and used the remote for the stereo to find one of her favourite songs. Turning up the volume, she leaned back, closing her eyes as she waited for Brett. She could have done with another couple of hours of sleep.

Chapter Seventeen

Monday afternoon, Kayla strode towards the parking lot with Red beside her. She stared at the ground, going over the scene with Karl, wondering if there'd been something she could have said different.

"Quit brooding. You're annoying me," Red muttered.

"Yeah well, I keep thinking I made an absolute mess of it."

Red laughed. "You did. I think he's going to hate you for life."

"I didn't exactly want to come out and tell him I'd picked someone else over him in the space of a couple of days. But he kept hassling me."

"You have to at least give him top marks for persistence." Red glanced around. "You know that Pallas girl." Red waited for Kayla to nod before she continued. "What do you know about her? How long has Jeff known her? Where does she live? Has he been anywhere with her before?"

Kayla held up her hand, grinning. "Slow down. Do I hear jealousy there?"

"Of course not. As if. I just like to know everything that's going on."

"Really?"

"Oh forget about it."

Kayla relented. Red always had to know everything. She supposed this wasn't anything different. "I don't know much about her. I've never seen her before Saturday. And I haven't seen her around since. But that doesn't mean she hasn't been around. I wasn't home much on Sunday."

"Why? What'd you do? That's what I hate about year twelve. There's not enough time to talk during classes, lunch is far too short and exam week is pathetic. Too much studying, kids stressing and no one making any sense."

"We went to the beach. Me and Brett. It was great. And Sunday night I slept like the-" Kayla broke off.

"Dead?" Red raised her eyebrows.

"Yeah."

"He's had all his medicine, hasn't he?"

Kayla nodded. "And got rid of the left over bit and cleaned the bottle."

"Then what's the problem? You're home free now."

"Yeah, I guess." But she still worried about him. "I can't help thinking about the two month thing. Why would Irene make a point of mentioning it if it wasn't important? Anyway, don't say anything in front of Brett. I just–" she shrugged.

"I don't think it's going to be a prob–" Red fell silent as they both saw Brett and Jeff leaning against Kayla's car.

"What are you doing here?" Kayla asked as she stopped in front of Brett.

"Completely and utterly bored. I caught a bus over. I'm not used to so much free time."

Kayla unlocked the car. "What did you fill your time with before?"

"Uni, sports, friends, work." Brett shrugged. "There always seemed to be something happening."

Kayla started the car and headed for Red's home first. "How do you feel? Other than bored?"

"Like I'm me." Brett grinned. "It's good to be able to walk down a street and know if people don't get out of the way, they'll walk into you, not through you."

"Uh, hello? What about you getting out of their way?" Red asked.

Brett laughed. "Where's the fun in that?"

"You didn't-" Kayla glanced towards him and caught the slight shake of his head.

"That's so rude and inconsiderate. It sounds like the world was better off with you dead," Red snapped.

"Gotta make sure they realise I'm alive," Brett said.

"How old are you? Two?" Red glared at him. She turned on Jeff when he laughed. "What?"

"He's stringing you along. Hey. No need to hit." Jeff blocked the second punch Red tried to give him.

"Then stop being childish." Red kept her glare focused on Jeff.

"Do you want to do something this arve?" Brett reached over to rest his hand on Kayla's thigh.

"Ah… I've got studying to do."

"Yeah, some of us take life a little more seriously than others." Red glanced towards Brett and then focused her attention on Jeff.

"Finally." Jeff looked out the window. "We can ditch Mildred in a few seconds."

"You're not getting out of it that easy. If you don't make decent arguments, during our debate, mine will seem lame." Red poked him in the chest with her finger.

"What's going on?" Kayla glanced in the rear view mirror.

"We were paired in modern history. I'm pro and he's con. We have to pick one of the topics we've studied this semester and argue the pros and cons of it the middle of this week. We found out today who our partners are and our exam is Wednesday," Red said.

Kayla sighed. She hated exam week. Many students only turned up for their exams. She went for most of the day and spent every spare second in the library. She knew she had no chance of a good grade if she didn't put in extra time studying. The one good part about exam week was that they didn't have to wear their uniforms.

Kayla pulled up in front of Red's house and turned to face her brother. "Why aren't you putting any effort into studying?"

"Because I won't need it next year." Jeff met her gaze.

"No. I want you to pass your exams. Please, Jeff."

"If we don't pass our debate for modern history I swear I'll make every second of the rest of this year pure hell for you," Red warned Jeff. "Get out of the car and get your arse inside. We have a lot of prep to do."

"You already make my life hell." Jeff shrugged. "So it won't be any different."

Red stared at him for a moment. "I need to pass this subject. You're not screwing up my plan to become a lawyer."

Brett laughed. "Why doesn't that surprise me? What a perfect career choice."

Jeff started to laugh too. "I know, isn't it just?"

Red flung the car door open, pressed the release button on both her and Jeff's seat belt and grabbed him by the arm. "You will put your best effort into this debate." She dragged him across the seat.

When Jeff pulled easily away from Red, Kayla sighed. She turned further in her seat and reached out to place a hand on his arm. "Please, Jeff? I know you can breeze through your exams if you want to. Please."

Jeff stared at her for long silent moments. "There isn't any point, Kayla."

"Humour me. Let me think there is a point."

Jeff rested his hand over hers, for a second, before he removed it. "Okay." He turned to Red and pushed her towards the door. "Hurry up then. I have better things to do with my time than spend them studying with you."

"Like what?" Red got out of the car.

Jeff grinned. "Wash my hair." He shut the car door and followed Red as she stalked towards her house.

Kayla momentarily closed her eyes when they went inside. She looked over to Brett when he took her hand. "We haven't made any difference, have we?"

Brett shrugged. "I don't know. Would he say that and not mean it?"

"I don't think so. He isn't like that. Not to me."

"We'll keep trying. Hey, did I tell you he was talking to a few of the regulars at the pool this morning? And he's swimming really good now. When I first started taking him I kept thinking he'd drown."

Kayla smiled sadly. "I know. He looks uncoordinated no matter what sport he's doing."

"Not when he's swimming. He just needed practice."

Kayla pulled out onto the road and headed for home. "I'm glad. Maybe that'll help. I mean, it's only been two weeks and he's already improved. That'd have to make him feel better about himself, wouldn't it?"

"Let's hope." Brett opened the car door when Kayla pulled up in front of her home. "Are you sure you have to study?"

"Yes."

"Do you think I can borrow the car?"

Kayla hesitated.

"I can drive. I've been driving longer than you. And I haven't had any accidents like Jeff."

She'd been more worried about him not having a license. "Where do you want to go?"

Brett shrugged. "I don't know. I'm sick of pacing the rooms of your house. There's only so much TV I can watch and so long I can work out in the home gym. I need to get out for a while. Besides, do you really want me hovering around you while you're trying to study?"

Kayla laughed. "When you put it that way…" She dropped the keys in his hand. "Don't be out all night. My parents will wonder what's going on if my car isn't here when they turn up."

"When are they due home?"

"They left a note on the fridge this morning. I'm pretty sure it said about nine tonight."

Brett nodded. "I'll be back before then." He leaned forward and cupped her face with his empty hand. His lips met hers and Kayla reached for him, her hands linking behind his head.

When Brett pulled away, Kayla couldn't stop a smile from forming. "I'll see you later." She headed inside, still smiling as she grabbed an apple, from the basket on the kitchen bench, on the way to her bedroom.

Chapter Eighteen

Sitting at her desk, Kayla finished off the apple as she started studying. She had no idea how long she'd been at her desk when she was startled by a shadow moving closer to her. She bit back a scream, her heart continuing to pound even when Brett stepped forward into the pool of light cast from her desk lamp. He held out a glass of juice, which Kayla took, glad to have something to do other than talk. Taking a sip, she tried to calm her racing pulse. The last few days she'd kept thinking she could see shadows moving closer, but as soon as she turned to look, they were gone. She really needed more sleep.

Brett gestured towards the apple core on the desk. "Have you had anything else to eat?"

Kayla glanced at the time. "No. I didn't realise it was so late." She rose from her chair and stretched. "I think I'll grab a sandwich. What about you?"

Brett reached out to pull her close to him when she started to walk past. "I've eaten. I ended up at Brian's for a bit. Are you okay? You seem a bit jumpy."

Kayla ignored the flicker of yet another shadow in her peripheral vision. "Yeah. Probably too much studying. I should get some sleep after I've eaten." She started to move away, then stopped. "Has Jeff arrived home yet?"

"Yeah. He's locked himself in his room."

Kayla was instantly worried. "He… ahh… did you ask… is…"

"He needs some time alone. I told him to unlock the door when he was sick of his own company. Preferably some time before I'm ready to head to bed."

"Okay." Kayla smiled in relief and started to move away again.

Brett pulled her closer, instead of letting her go, and kissed her. "Miss me?"

Kayla grinned. "Would it bother you if I said no?"

Brett chuckled. "Go have something to eat before you dint my self esteem."

Still grinning, Kayla headed for the kitchen. Her grin faded as she passed her brother's closed door. She paused, the muffled sounds of music the only sign of life. Should she see if he wanted food? She took a step closer to his door and raised her hand. At the last second she changed her mind. He'd promised not to kill himself until next year. Surely he'd keep his promise. He always had before. Lowering her hand, she forced herself to move away from the door and head to the kitchen to make a sandwich. She ate it while she cleaned the mess from the kitchen bench and then walked to her bedroom, a couple of bites left.

She paused at her door, which was closed, and shoved the rest of her sandwich in her mouth. Had Brett closed the door for a reason? She'd left it open. Too bad. It was her room. Turning the doorknob, she swung it open. She nearly choked on her mouthful of food when she saw Brett lying on the carpet, struggling with a tall, anorexic looking man with grey skin, bare chest, black pants, and a black hooded cloak that was pushed to one shoulder from their struggles.

Kayla swallowed her food as she ran forward ready to pull the man off Brett. She reached out and froze. Brett's skin was turning the same grey as the man's.

"Get away, Kayla. Run." Brett's struggles weakened. "Please. Run."

His words jolted her into action. She couldn't run. Not when Brett was in danger. She took the last couple of steps forward and grasped one of the man's arms. Her fingers instantly felt like they had pins and needles. She tugged on his arm, the sensation increasing. Her mouth rounded in surprise as she saw her fingers turn grey. Ignoring the pain and colour fading from her hands, Kayla tightened her grip and pulled as hard as she could.

The man drew away from her, shaking her off his arm like she was little more than a minor irritation.

Freed, Brett stumbled to his feet and staggered to her side. "Get out of here." He pushed her towards the door.

"I'm not leaving you behind." Kayla watched the grey man as he turned to walk towards them, her feet refusing to obey her instinct to run when she caught the lifeless look in the dark eyes.

Brett stepped in front of her. "Get out of here. Now." He again pushed her towards the door.

Kayla stumbled and grabbed Brett by the arm. "What is that thing?"

"I don't know. But it's after me, not you. Go before it changes its mind."

Brett had barely finished speaking when the grey man went from a shuffling walk to a blur as he crossed the room and launched himself at Brett again. Kayla was knocked backwards, colliding with the door. Clinging to the door frame, she struggled to regain her balance. She took a hesitant step forward, her mind whirling as she tried to understand what was happening. There was no time for thinking. She had to get the grey man off Brett. Before he was as grey as the man who had his hands wrapped around his neck, forcing him to the floor.

Kayla spun, rushing to the laundry that was to the left of her bedroom. A frantic glance around showed nothing she could use. Her heart pounded, as the sounds of the struggle in her room grew quieter. With shaking hands, she flung open the door of the broom cupboard and grabbed the only item that looked like it might make some kind of weapon. A wooden handled broom. Kayla raced back to her room, refusing to think about what would happen if the broom didn't help. Brett was pressed against the floor, the grey man choking the life out of him.

"Get off him." She swung the broom as hard as possible and nearly shouted as the timber cracked when it connected with the grey man's head. He stumbled back soundlessly and landed on his back, struggling to untangle himself from his cloak. "Brett." Fear made her voice wobble. She was unable to take her gaze from the grey man to check how Brett was.

"We have to get out of here." Brett struggled to his feet, his voice raspy.

Kayla nodded. She tightened her grip on the broom handle in the hope it would stop her hands from shaking and backed towards the door, Brett beside her. She grabbed her handbag off the floor as she passed it and pulled her door closed once they were out of the room. Kayla started to slow at Jeff's door.

Brett grabbed her arm. "Keep going. We don't have time. It only seems to want me."

When they reached the kitchen, Kayla stopped abruptly, the broom dropping from her hands. Brett opened his mouth to speak and Kayla pressed her hand against his lips and tugged him towards the dining room and out the glass doors that led onto a deck. She closed the door behind them.

"What's wrong?" Brett whispered.

"I heard my parents' car pull up. Come on. We'll head along the side of the house and out to the front. I'll ring Jeff to ask him to cover for me once we're on the road." She was amazed at how calm she sounded considering how her heart raced and her mind struggled to grasp exactly what was happening.

"Won't they recognise the sound of your car?"

Kayla shook her head then smiled ruefully when

she realised Brett wouldn't be able to see the movement properly in the shadows of the deck. She almost laughed, then realised it was probably hysteria and forced herself to focus. "Nah. Besides, they're probably on the phone or checking emails or something. They live and breathe work." She swung her legs over the low rails of the deck to stand on dew dampened grass.

Brett swore as he joined her. "Looks like the grey man stepped through the wall of your room."

Kayla grabbed his hand. "Then let's go." She forced back the panic that wanted to swamp her. Later. She could scream and go completely insane later.

They ran towards the grey man, dodging to the side as they approached him. Kayla felt his fingers brush against her arm as they passed. Pins and needles instantly formed and she felt her arm weaken slightly. Then they were at the front of the house and Brett took the car keys from his pocket and hit the central locking button.

"I'll drive." He let go of her hand as he headed for the driver's side.

Kayla glanced behind her and, when she saw how close the grey man was, didn't argue. Brett started the car before the doors were closed and drove down the road as Kayla struggled to pull on her seat belt. Once buckled, she stared out the back window, watching as the grey man broke into a run.

"He's following us. But he can't keep up." She turned to Brett. "Are you okay?"

"I feel like I could sleep a week. Have you got Irene's card?"

"Yeah." She rummaged in her handbag until she found it. Irene answered the phone almost immediately. Kayla put it on speaker so Brett could hear too. "Irene, we have a problem."

"I was wondering when you would ring. Do I take it you haven't been in one place for long tonight?"

"You knew? Why didn't you warn us?" Brett demanded.

"It's against the rules. Surely you didn't think this was going to be easy. Regaining a life isn't meant to be easy. Ever. Now what questions are you going to ask? I can't volunteer the information, you have to ask the right questions."

Kayla's fingers tightened around the phone. "Who's the grey man?"

"A soul stalker."

"What does he want?" Brett asked.

"Why, your soul of course."

Brett swore and hit the steering wheel with the base of his palm. "How long will he be after me?"

"Sixty days. Counting from tomorrow. If you make it to late August you'll be safe. I'm sure you can figure out the exact date."

"What about me?" Kayla asked. "Is there any chance he'll go after me?"

"Only if you lay hands on one of them."

Brett swore again. "How do we protect ourselves against him. Hang on. Them?"

"You didn't think it'd be easy to stay alive, did you? Of course there's more than one. But they are scattered. I'd be surprised if you have more than a handful after you for now."

"You said something about not being in the one place for long. How does that help?" Kayla asked.

"They can run at a speed of thirty kilometres an hour, non-stop, but have no other way of going faster."

"That'll cost a fortune in petrol if we have to keep driving all the time. When are we meant to sleep?" Kayla demanded.

"During the day when they don't hunt."

"Isn't there anything else we can do to protect ourselves from them?" Brett demanded.

"Were you buried or cremated?"

"Cremated."

Irene was silent a moment. "Not as good."

"Why?"

"If you were buried you could stay on your grave and you'd be safe. You need to use your ashes to make a circle around you. They won't be able to cross it. At daybreak, try and pick up all your remains. Two months is a long time to make them last. Especially since each day there'll be less and less of them until there are none left at all. They might last the full sixty days, but I doubt it."

Brett swore. "Why didn't you tell us?"

"Why didn't you ask me?" There was silence as neither Kayla or Brett answered her. "If that is all your questions, I'll leave you to it."

"Great," Brett said dryly.

"Call if you need to know anything else," Irene said cheerfully before she hung up.

Chapter Nineteen

Kayla stared at her phone, anger and panic flooding her. "I can't believe her. Stupid rules. She could have at least hinted we should ask questions when she said she'd help."

Brett was silent for a minute, his face lit by the dash lights. "We need to see Brian. I have to find out what happened to my ashes."

Kayla looked at the time. "It's ten o'clock. By the time we get there it'll be eleven. What if he's asleep?"

"Then he gets woken up."

Kayla started to protest, then closed her mouth. What was a sleepless night when a friend was in danger? Feeling almost lost, she dialled her brother's number.

"Are you checking up on me?"

Kayla laughed, desperately trying to keep hysteria

from creeping into the sound. "No, but obviously you haven't been checking up on me."

"What's that supposed to mean? What happened?"

"We're in a bit of trouble." She explained everything to Jeff.

"I could meet you somewhere. Catch a taxi or something."

"No. I don't want them after you too."

Jeff hesitated. "Is there anything I can do to help?"

"Yeah. Cover for me. We left just after Mum and Dad got home. And I left a broom in the kitchen."

"Okay. Check in regularly and let me know how you're doing."

"I will."

"Just because I think death is the solution for me, doesn't mean I see it as your solution."

"I don't think it should be anyone's solution," Kayla said softly.

"I'm not in the mood for any more arguments today."

"Jeff–"

"Ring me later and let me know what's happening."

"Okay." Kayla put her phone away and sat quietly. She rested her hand on Brett's thigh.

Brett placed his hand over hers. "I'm not going

to let them beat me. I've got this far. We'll make it through the next sixty days."

Kayla leaned forward and turned the stereo up with her free hand. The beat of the music filled the car and she closed her eyes, letting the sound push the worries from her mind. She focused on the music for the rest of the drive, to Brian's place, as she tried unsuccessfully to ignore the feeling of danger lurking in the shadows. Panic threatened to swamp her and she forced it away. Not now. Focus. Time to focus. Panic later.

They pulled up in front of Brian's house to find it in darkness. The sound of the car doors shutting echoed along the quiet street. Kayla slipped her hand into Brett's as they strode towards the front door. She glanced around and hoped there were no soul stalkers in the neighbourhood. Every shadow seemed to move and shift, forming eerie figures waiting to reach out and grab them. Kayla forced herself to keep her gaze on the door ahead of them. They were shadows. Only shadows. There was nothing hiding in the dark. Kayla wished she could truly believe that.

Brett's knock on the door brought Douglas stepping through it. "What do ye want? It's late to come calling."

Kayla spoke before Brett could, in case he

antagonised Douglas. "We're in a bit of trouble. Can you wake Brian for us, please?"

"A bit of trouble? What an understatement," Brett muttered.

Grumbling, Douglas slid back through the door. Moments later a light flickered on in Brian's room. He answered the door with unbuttoned jeans sitting low on his hips and rubbed his eyes, yawning.

"Better be good." He held the door open until they were through and then swung it shut. "I have to get up early tomorrow." He glanced at his watch. "It's barely still today."

"I need to know what happened to my ashes," Brett said.

"What?" Brian looked wide awake.

Kayla shook her head. "You're hopeless, Brett." She explained the basics of the situation to Brian.

Shaking his head, Brian swore. "You're both up the creek without a paddle."

"Why?" Brett demanded.

"Chelsea has your ashes. Although it could have been worse. Jake tried to get them off her, but she wasn't letting go. He wanted to scatter them."

Brett sighed heavily. "How the hell are we meant to get hold of them?"

Kayla looked from Brian to Brett and back again. "Why is it such a problem that Chelsea has them?"

"Ah…" Brian looked uncomfortable. "That's his old girlfriend. And well, she…" he glanced nervously at Brett.

"Spit it out," Brett muttered.

"You dying made her popular. Everyone wanted to help cheer her up. Your ashes are…" Brian looked uncomfortable again.

"A prop?" Brett suggested.

"Yeah," Brian mumbled. "That's as good a word as any."

"What's with the girls you pair hang out with?" Kayla demanded.

Brian shook his head. "Chelsea isn't normally like that. But I guess going from being average to almost celebrity went to her head a bit. And she is grieving for Brett."

"Then I guess we break in and get them," Brett said.

"Be sensible. It'd be easier to break into the Reserve Bank," Brian said.

"I could get in there," Douglas suggested.

"Jake might be able to help." Brian looked uncomfortable again.

Brett sighed. "We can't sit around here all night. Spit it out why don't you?"

"You know how she was chasing after Jake until she met you, well she's sort of gone back to it. You could try asking him to get them for you."

"We can't turn up on his doorstep and ask for help. That's no way to let him find out Brett is alive," Kayla protested.

Brian laughed sharply. "Why not? Isn't that what you did to me?"

"That was an accident." Kayla gave both Brett and Douglas a pointed look.

"You two head on over there. I'll give him a call and warn him you're coming," Brian said.

Brett stared at his friend for a moment before he nodded. "Okay."

Ten minutes later they pulled up in front of Jake's home. Kayla reached out to take Brett's hand when he continued to sit in the driver's seat. Sitting there with shadows pressing in around them was making her nervous.

"Do you think we could see Jake so we can get hold of your ashes? I do need some sleep tonight. I have exams tomorrow." She glanced at her watch. "Okay, I have exams today." She groaned. "They're probably going to find me snoring at my desk instead of answering questions."

"I'm sorry. I didn't mean to put you in danger like this."

"Then let's sort it out so we can stop the soul stalkers from getting us."

Brett nodded and got out of the car. He took Kayla's hand again as they walked towards Jake's house. Instead of heading for the front door, Brett led her around the side of the house to a glass sliding door and knocked on it.

"Why this door?" Kayla whispered.

"Jake lives at his uncle's place, in a granny flat."

A light went on behind the drawn curtain a minute before the door slid open. Jake was taller than Brett by nearly ten centimetres. He was solidly built and wouldn't have looked out of place on a football team. His black hair was barely a centimetre long and his dark eyes stared at Brett while his jaw dropped.

"Brian didn't warn you, did he?" Brett asked.

Jake continued to stare at Brett for almost a minute before he closed his mouth and grinned. "You owe me ten bucks."

Brett laughed. "Not likely. I would have lasted until daybreak if it hadn't been for that kid."

"Brian told me I would be amazed. And to forget

all my current beliefs regarding life and death. What the hell is going on?"

"Think we can come in?" Brett asked.

Jake stepped back, his gaze falling on Kayla. "Sorry. I didn't notice you."

Kayla smiled. "I can understand that."

"This is Kayla." Brett led her to a faded brown lounge and sat down beside her.

"So what happened? I mean, I saw you. No pulse, all dressed up and heading for the incinerator." He swore and shook his head slowly. "I even saw the urn." Jake opened a door in the television cabinet and pulled out a bottle of scotch. He gestured towards Brett with it. Brett shook his head. Jake grabbed a glass, poured a nip, glanced at Brett and then with a shake of his head, doubled the amount.

Brett grinned. "Isn't it meant to be sweet tea for shock?"

Jake took a mouthful. "Bugger that. It'd ruin the flavour of the scotch."

Brett laughed then became serious. "I need your help."

Jake sat in one of the armchairs. "Name it."

Brett explained what had happened and why he needed his ashes.

Jake put his empty glass on the floor beside his seat. "How long till the soul stalker catches up with you?"

Kayla glanced at her watch. "At a guess, maybe ten minutes."

Jake nodded. "Okay, let's put more distance between you and the soul stalker. Head to the lookout. Have you got a number I can reach you on?"

Kayla nodded and rattled off her number when Jake took out his phone. "Where's the lookout?"

Brett rested his hand on hers. "Don't worry. I know where it is." He looked over to Jake. "How is that going to help?"

"Trust me. Make sure your car is hidden. Mine will be in the parking area. When I call, don't bother answering, head straight for my car and your ashes should be on the back seat."

"How are you going to manage that?" Brett asked.

"I did once think I could manage miracles, but I'm beginning to think I'm an amateur compared to you." Jake grinned.

Brett laughed. "All right. We'll head to the lookout."

"And whatever you do, don't let Chelsea see you and don't stick around once you have your ashes. Chelsea would ring every newspaper, she could think of, with the story of your resurrection. What trick will you do for Easter since you've already pulled this one off?"

"Good thing that's not until next year. I think I'm going to need a lot of time to figure out something to top this one." Brett rose to his feet and stepped forward as Jake also stood.

Kayla watched as they hugged, hearty slaps on each other's backs. She slipped her hand into Brett's as he returned to her side. "Thanks for helping." She met Jake's gaze.

"Thanks for bringing my mate back."

Kayla nodded. Her throat tightened and she blinked her eyes. "I'm glad I could." She walked quietly beside Brett as they headed to her car, peering into the darkness as she watched for soul stalkers. She was relieved to be in the car again and on the move. At least the speed limit was a lot faster than a soul stalker was capable of going.

When they reached the lookout, Kayla sat wordlessly beside Brett. The windows of the car fogged up and she took the picnic blanket out of the boot and returned to the front seat, wrapping it around her. It didn't help much and she thought of her jacket at home. She glanced towards Brett who wore a light, long sleeved shirt. Reaching out, she rested her fingers on his wrist, which was cool to her touch.

"Why don't we hop in the back seat so we can share the blanket," Kayla suggested. Before he could reply, her phone rang. Her heart leapt as she checked the number. Not recognising it, she handed the phone over to Brett.

"That's Jake. Let's go." He handed the phone back as it stopped ringing.

Getting out of the car, Kayla kept the blanket wrapped around her as she walked at Brett's side. They couldn't move too quickly. There wasn't enough light. When they reached Jake's car, Brett paused and glanced around. The night was quiet and still, their breath misty on the air.

Brett opened up the back door and the interior light came on. An ice cream container sat on the back seat. Written in permanent marker on the lid was, 'Sorry about the container. It was all I could find on short notice.' He reached out to pick up the container, but at the last minute he drew back. Kayla gently pushed him out of the way and picked it up. He stepped back when she turned towards him, the container in her hands.

Seeing his expression, Kayla tucked it under her

blanket and closed the car door. "Come on. We don't want to be sprung by Chelsea."

Brett nodded and led the way back to the car. He kept several paces away from her the entire distance. When Kayla put the container on the back seat, he kept his gaze forward, tilting the rear view mirror up a little more.

Kayla reached for him once she was buckled up. "Brett-"

"Get some sleep. Maybe wind the seat back a bit. I'll keep heading out this way and turn around in time to get us home around daybreak. That way we won't have to worry about the soul stalker for tonight."

Kayla started to argue with him, but thought better of it when she saw the slight tremor in his hands as he put the car in reverse. "Okay," she said softly. "I'll give Jeff a call first."

Chapter Twenty

Kayla looked blankly at the exam paper and wished she didn't feel so sluggish. She yawned. Although she'd managed six hours sleep, most of them had been in the car and had been more along the lines of drifting in and out of wakefulness. She wished she could have stayed home, like Brett, and slept the entire day. She yawned again and frowned as she tried to make sense of the question at the top of the page. She guessed she had at least a twenty-five percent chance of getting each question correct in the first half of the exam. The multiple-choice section was probably the only part she'd be able to answer.

"Seems like most people answered 'B' for the first question, lass."

Kayla's head came up quickly at the words spoken just behind her. She glanced over her shoulder to see Douglas grin at her. She almost forgot where she was and went to speak. At the last second she faced forward and was relieved the supervising teacher hadn't noticed her strange behaviour.

"Give me a minute and I'll check the answer for the second question."

Kayla watched as Douglas strode around the room. She was tempted to ignore him, but she knew there was no chance she could pass the exam without help. Not while her brain was barely functioning. She didn't know how she was going to answer the second part of the question. An essay wasn't going to be as simple as multiple choice.

By the time the exam was ended and Douglas had helped her with both sections, Kayla felt ready to collapse. She stumbled to the door and lost herself in the students making their way along the corridor outside the room. She had one more exam today and then none the next day. She wished today had been her exam free day. Kayla jumped as a hand grabbed her by the shoulder. She spun to see Red.

"Give me a heart attack why don't you?" Kayla shrugged Red's hand off.

"You were the one ignoring me. I must have called your name a dozen times."

"Sorry. I don't think I'm awake yet. Don't be surprised if I start snoring."

Red laughed. "You look like crap."

"Gee, thanks. With compliments like that I really look forward to hearing what you have to say next."

Red shrugged. "No point lying. You probably already know. You must have looked in a mirror at least once today."

"I've been trying to avoid them. I have enough nightmares these days without finding more inspiration for them."

Red dropped her arm around Kayla's shoulders. "Come on. I'll get you a caffeine and sugar hit. That should help get you through the rest of the morning."

"And what will help me through the afternoon?"

"Don't get pushy. Be grateful for what I've offered."

Kayla stumbled. "I feel like a zombie. I need my bed. Desperately."

"And you look it too."

"Need me this afternoon, lass?" Douglas fell into step beside Kayla.

She wondered how she could say yes without making it obvious and be certain Douglas would know she was talking to him. "I wish someone else could take this arve's exam for me."

"I'll be there, lass." Douglas strode away.

Red snorted. "If you had an identical twin sister

instead of a useless twin brother you might have been able to manage that."

Kayla was too tired to come to her brother's defence. All she could manage was a grunt in reply. They stopped in front of a vending machine and Red put money in so she could buy drinks and chocolate.

Red handed one of each to Kayla. "Caffeine and sugar as promised."

Another yawn interrupted Kayla's smile. "I feel like I'm about to break my jaw with how much I've been yawning."

"You didn't say why you're tired. And why did you leave your car with Brett? He hasn't got a license. What if he gets pulled over?"

Kayla glanced around. "I'll tell you all about it when he picks us up after school."

"Torture. You must hate me since you're making me wait so long to find out."

"Nah. Too tired to think straight."

Red grabbed Kayla's wrist and turned it so she could check the time. "You have a bit over an hour before your next exam. Let's head to the library and you can find a comfy spot to take a nap. I'll wake you with plenty of time to get to your next exam."

Kayla hesitated. But she didn't have much choice. The world wouldn't come into focus and it felt like she was looking through a camera lens and some lunatic kept messing with the zoom function. "Thanks. You can't imagine how desperate I am for sleep."

* * *

That afternoon, Kayla was relieved to see Brett waiting for her when she crossed the school grounds heading for the parking lot. The last few metres to reach the car seemed to stretch out like they were kilometres. As soon as he saw her, Brett strode towards her. When he reached her side and put his arm around her waist, she sagged against him.

"You look terrible."

"The compliments are flowing today," Kayla muttered.

"Are you okay? You're not going to pass out at my feet are you?"

"Depends on if you're likely to catch me."

Brett laughed. "You can have a bit under two hours sleep before the soul stalker arrives."

Kayla groaned. "I need more than that."

"I'm sorry. I–"

"Forget it," Kayla muttered.

"Hey." Red interrupted. "Do I get to hear everything yet?"

"Give us a chance to get in the car." Kayla squinted and blinked as she tried to bring her car into focus. She blinked again and realised Jeff was already there, waiting for them. She stumbled the rest of the way to her car, grateful she was able to lean against Brett. It was probably all that kept her from tripping over her own feet and landing face first on the ground.

Red slid into the back seat of the car. "Now do I get to hear what's happening?"

Kayla sighed. "Yeah, but if nothing makes sense, that's not my problem. I didn't ask to be up all night." She explained everything and nearly dozed off to sleep as she waited for Red to comment.

Red sat there quietly for nearly the whole trip. Kayla was relieved she didn't have to answer any questions. She was even more relieved when they pulled up in front of her home. With a mumbled goodbye to her friend, she staggered to her room, used the bathroom and collapsed onto her bed. When she heard her bedroom door open, she didn't have the energy to open her eyes to see who it was. She felt a hand brush against her hair.

"I'll wake you before they arrive," Brett said.

Those were the last words Kayla heard before Brett

shook her awake. She groggily sat up and wondered why he hadn't let her sleep longer. It came back to her in a flash. She groaned and dragged herself out of bed. As soon as she'd used the bathroom, Kayla looked warily at Brett who was on the opposite side of the bedroom to where the ice cream container sat on her desk.

She strode over and peeked at the contents. Reaching in, she scooped up a handful of the ashes. They didn't remind her of any ashes she'd seen before. More like whitish grains of sand. She let them drop back into the container when she saw the sickly look on Brett's face. "What's the plan?"

"We need to make a circle to protect ourselves through the night. It's half past four. Sunset is a few minutes after five. We'll want it large enough for comfort. Especially since sunrise isn't until twenty to seven."

Kayla glanced at the contents of the container again. "You know, if we pulled my bed into the middle of the room, I bet we could make a circle around it."

"Sounds like a good idea to me. The night is going to feel extremely long. A bit of comfort might help."

Once the bed was in the middle of the room, Brett glanced towards the container several times. Kayla picked it up and held it against her chest. "Sit down. You're the one who looks terrible now. I'll make a circle around the bed. But I do have one question. What if I need to go to the toilet? How do I go about leaving the bed if the circle is meant to keep them from harming us?"

"Guess you'll have to hold on until morning."

"Great." Kayla glanced around her room for something to use to scoop up the ashes. She took an empty glass off her desk and carefully made a barrier around the bed, making sure there were no gaps in it. Before she was a quarter of the way through, Brett had left the room. She didn't blame him. She doubted she'd feel very comfortable if it were her ashes being spread around the room. Straightening, she put the empty container on her desk, leaving the glass in it. There was no way she was ever going to drink out of it again.

Her mobile phone rang and she checked the display. It was Jake. She'd saved his number on the way to school that morning. "Yeah?"

"It's Jake. Is Brett about?"

"I'll find him." She strode towards her bedroom door.

"Before you do, can I ask you something?"

Kayla hesitated. "What?"

"Will he be okay? I mean, honestly, will he make it through all this? I don't think I can watch him die twice."

"Honestly… I don't know. I hope so. I'll be doing everything possible to make sure he survives."

"Do you mind if I come over and see him?"

"Ahh…"

"Please? I… last night… this morning… it seems like a dream."

Kayla could understand that, although she leaned more towards the word nightmare. "Yeah. Come over. But I don't know what's going to happen. It'll be dark soon. We'll be stuck in a circle of his ashes."

"Yeah, I realise that. But the soul stalker won't be interested in me, will he? I mean, he's only after you and Brett. Didn't you say as long as no one touches him, they should be right?"

Kayla stepped back as her bedroom door swung open. "That's the theory. But I'd be surprised if you could see him."

"I'll be there in about an hour. I'll talk to Brett then."

"Okay." Kayla gave him her address and tossed her phone onto the bed once Jake had hung up. She met Brett's gaze. "Jake will be here in an hour."

"What! The soul stalker will be here soon."

Kayla pressed a hand to his chest. "Calm down. He should be safe. He probably won't be able to see the soul stalker."

"I hope not."

Kayla glanced behind him. "What's going on?"

"I conned Brian into handing over some of his cash. I pointed out that he wouldn't have had any of it without you."

Kayla stared at the television and DVD player Jeff wheeled into the room on a low cabinet. "But–"

"You and I will be stuck in the circle for nearly fourteen hours." Brett gestured towards her bed. "We're not likely to be able to sleep the entire time. Unless you had another entertainment in mind..." He grinned. "I thought movies might be a good idea."

Red entered the room and handed a bottle of water to Kayla. "Don't drink it all at once. The next toilet break is a long time away."

Kayla nodded and faced Brett. "Movies?" When he nodded, she said, "I do have to study." Her eyes rounded and her jaw dropped open. "Oh no."

"What?" Three concerned voices asked together.

"I cheated. I cheated on today's exams. Douglas helped me."

Jeff laughed. "Why didn't I think of that?" He clapped Kayla on the shoulder. "Brilliant idea, sis."

Kayla shook her head. "It wasn't my idea." Her eyes narrowed as she looked at Brett.

"You looked like you were about to pass out. I didn't tell him to help you cheat. Just to watch out for you. That you hadn't had much sleep."

Kayla dropped onto her bed with a groan, careful not to step on the ashes. "I can't believe I cheated."

"There's hope for you yet." Jeff sat beside her.

"Hope."

"Leave her alone, Jeffery."

"Stay out of it, Mildred."

"The pair of you get out of my room. I'm not in the mood to listen to you argue over nothing." Kayla glared at them, both open mouthed at her outburst. She was tempted to apologise, but was too tired. She watched as they left the room, with frequent glances over their shoulders.

Brett closed the door before he sat beside her on the bed, drawing his feet up off the floor. He checked the time. "Five minutes. Anything you need to do before we're imprisoned for the night?"

Kayla shook her head and then nodded. "I don't know." Her words were almost a wail.

"You have your phone. You can ring your brother if you need anything."

"If he answers after I yelled at him."

Brett smiled. "He will." He got off the bed and plugged in the television. After putting in a DVD, he brought the remotes back with him. Minutes after he returned to the bed, the grey man walked through the wall and into the room.

They watched warily as he paced around the bed. He stared at them for several minutes before retreating to a corner of the room. Brett and Kayla shared a look and, with a shrug, Brett turned on the movie. They were halfway through it when Jake arrived, shown to Kayla's room by Jeff. Brett paused the movie.

Jeff stopped in the doorway and pointed to the man in the corner. "Is he what I think he is?"

"What are you looking at?" Jake asked.

"Well, that answers that question," Brett said.

Kayla nodded. "I didn't think he'd be able to see him. But I did wonder."

"Do you think someone could tell me what's going on?" Jake came further into the room, a nervous glance towards the ashes around the bed.

Kayla pointed towards the desk. "Grab a seat. Just make sure you don't break the circle."

"I'll leave you to it. I better get back to my room before Red trashes my computer." Jeff shut the door before Kayla could ask him what was going on.

"I hate being stuck in here," Kayla grumbled.

"You hate not being able to find out what's going on."

"She's not the only one." Jake pulled the chair close to the bed.

Kayla pointed to the corner. "The soul stalker is waiting for one of us to step out of the circle."

"That's it? He's waiting?"

Kayla nodded. "For now. Hopefully that's all he does."

Jake glanced at the corner again. He shook his head. "You do know I can't see anything. Not even a haze, a difference in colour, nothing."

"That's okay. I didn't think you would. I guess he's sort of like a ghost," Kayla said.

"And you can see ghosts."

Kayla nodded.

Jake looked from one to the other. "This is too bizarre."

"Tell me about it." Brett linked his fingers with Kayla's. "What happened last night after we left?"

"Well…" Jake looked from Brett to Kayla. "How much do you want to know?"

"Every little bit," Brett said.

Jake nodded. "Okay. But remember, you asked for it ...

Chapter Twenty-One

The moment Jake closed the door on Brett and Kayla, he grabbed his phone and rang Brian. He grinned when Brian answered the phone. "Arsehole."

"I take it they've been?"

"You could have warned me."

"Seeing is believing."

"You're full of it."

Brian laughed. "You had more warning than I had. So, do you have a plan?"

"Yeah, I think so. But Chelsea's probably going to hate me." He paused a moment. "I keep thinking all this is impossible."

"I know exactly what you mean. Good luck getting the ashes."

"I'll probably need it. I'll call you tomorrow. Sounds like we have a bit of catching up to do."

"Yeah. Night, Jake."

As soon as he hung up, Jake rang Chelsea. He paced back and forth in his living room as he waited for her to pick up.

"Jake? What time is it?"

"I'll be over to pick you up in five minutes. Bring the urn. We're going to the lookout to scatter the ashes. We have to let him go, Chelsea."

"No!"

"You and me. Together. Come on, Chels. We need to move on. I need to do this. I haven't had a decent night's sleep since… well, for weeks. I think this will help. Please."

There was silence before Chelsea answered, her voice a whisper. "I miss him, Jake. This is all I have left of him."

"No it's not. That's part of his death. Let it go and focus on the good stuff. Then tonight you and I can go out to dinner and celebrate Brett's life."

"We could go out and do that without getting rid of his ashes."

"No, we couldn't. I'll be there in five minutes. Be out the front waiting or I'm knocking on the door."

"You'll wake my parents."

"Then be out there waiting for me."

"Jake–"

He disconnected the call, ignoring it when it

instantly started to ring. Leaving his ringing phone behind, he let himself into his uncle's house and grabbed two empty ice cream containers from the kitchen cupboard. His next stop was the lounge room where he opened up the glass door of the fireplace and shovelled cold ashes into one of the containers. They were different, but hopefully Chelsea wouldn't notice in the dark.

Back in his part of the house, he pulled out a permanent marker pen and wrote on the lid of the empty container. Then he grabbed his jacket, phone and car keys and headed outside to his car. The containers went in the boot and within a couple of minutes he pulled up in front of Chelsea's home. He grinned when he saw her hurry towards him, the urn clasped to her chest. His grin vanished as she drew near the car.

"I'm not happy about this," Chelsea said.

Jake got out of the car and took the urn from her, putting it on the back seat. He turned and hugged Chelsea, holding her close. "It's what we need to do."

She relaxed against him. "I guess."

Jake walked her around to the passenger side and opened the door for her. Leaning against the top of the door, he stared down at her once she was seated.

"You'll feel better letting him go." He closed the door and returned to the driver's side.

The drive to the lookout was mostly silent and Jake was tempted to turn up the stereo. He glanced at Chelsea and saw she'd gone back to sleep so he left the volume alone. He didn't want to wake her. Conversation would be an effort. His mind was full of questions after seeing Brett. Brian, who was the most practical, non-imaginative person he'd ever met, believed the story. If Brian hadn't, he would have thought it a hoax.

He finally pulled up in the parking area of the lookout and reached out to gently shake Chelsea awake. She yawned and stretched. Jake got out of the car and grabbed the torch he kept under his seat. He switched it on as he opened the passenger door.

Chelsea stumbled out. After regaining her footing, she turned to reach in for the urn. Jake drew her back. She looked up at him with a puzzled expression. "Weren't we going to-"

"Let's see which way the wind is blowing first. Come on. No point if they're going to blow straight back on us."

Chelsea nodded and let Jake lead her up the winding path that led to the top of the lookout. Half way up, Jake stopped and handed her the torch.

Frowning, she automatically took it. "What's wrong?"

"I need to grab my jacket. No point in both of us going back to the car. I won't be long." Jake started to move away from her as he pulled out his keys that had a small LED light on them.

"Jake!"

"You'll barely notice me gone." He kept going and reached the car in a few minutes with several glances over his shoulder to make sure she didn't follow. He shuffled the ashes, both the wood ones and human ones, pulled on his jacket and left the ice cream container of human ashes on the back seat. Taking the urn with him, he dialled Kayla's number as he walked back along the path. He listened to it ring and hung up before he reached Chelsea.

"You were ages." Chelsea shone the torch in his face.

"Hey."

"Sorry." She pointed the light at the ground. "I thought you said we'd wait and see about the ashes."

"I thought we'd probably end up finding a reason to put it off. It has to be done." He strode along the path and Chelsea fell in beside him, shining the torch on the path.

"I don't know, Jake. It doesn't seem right."

Jake draped an arm around her shoulders. "Of course it's right. Come on. It's freezing out here. Let's get up to the lookout."

An uncomfortable silence fell between them as they continued to walk. As soon as they reached the lookout, Jake opened the urn and tossed the contents out into the breeze. It tore the wood ash away from him before Chelsea could see what the urn had actually contained.

"Jake!"

"What?"

Chelsea grabbed the urn off him. "You didn't say goodbye or anything. You dumped him over the side like you were throwing out the trash."

"I didn't want to give us time to rethink. It was the right thing to do."

"But–"

"Come on, Chels. You know we would have stood here all night arguing. Aww now, don't cry." He pushed his hands into his pockets and pulled them out empty. "I don't have any tissues."

"How could you?"

"Chels–" but he was talking to her back. Sighing, he took out his keys, so he could see the path, since Chelsea marched ahead with the torch. He hoped Brett and Kayla had already taken the ashes. If

Chelsea ran into Brett all his plans would have been for nothing.

* * *

"What are you doing here if you're meant to be taking her out to dinner tonight?" Kayla asked.

"I wanted to check and see how everything was. I'm meeting her in the city centre in…" Jake glanced at his watch. "About an hour." He hesitated. "I also wanted to ask you about Nick and Trevor."

Brett shook his head. "Not yet. Let's wait in case-" he glanced towards the grey man.

Kayla's fingers tightened on his. "Brett-"

"Not yet." His words were firm.

Jake rose to his feet. "I better get moving." He returned the chair and glanced at the corner. "Call if you need me. No matter the hour."

Brett nodded. "Thanks."

Jake grinned. "I'll see myself out. No need to stir yourself."

Brett laughed. "Thanks," he said dryly.

Kayla waited until she could no longer hear Jake's footsteps in the hall. "Have you known him long?"

"Yeah. We grew up together. Nick and Trevor too. I didn't meet Brian until I was sixteen. But the other three, even when I lived hours away, I kept in touch with them. They're what brought me back to the area. I guess you could say they've been my family over the years. Ever since I lost mine." When Kayla opened her mouth, Brett pressed a finger against her lips. "Shh. No more questions. Not tonight." He glanced at the grey man. "Let's watch the rest of the movie."

Kayla nodded and snuggled down beside him. She didn't see the end of the movie, drifting off to sleep and not waking until nearly four in the morning. When she struggled to sit up, Brett instantly woke, looking around blearily.

Kayla glanced towards the grey man and saw by the light from the desk lamp he was in the same place. "It's okay."

Brett rubbed at his eyes. "This bed isn't big enough for two. Especially since you keep hogging all the space."

Kayla grinned. "I did not. I bet it was you."

"How are you feeling? Better?"

"Yeah." She nodded towards her desk lamp. "Who put the light on?" Earlier, only the television had lit the room.

"Jeff. He also turned the TV off and told your

parents not to disturb you because you were studying."

Kayla sighed. "Sixty days is going to go very slow."

"Another few hours and it'll be fifty-eight days."

Kayla groaned. "Don't remind me." Her gaze was drawn to the grey man. "What are we meant to do between now and daybreak?"

"Do you want me to ring your brother and ask him to put a movie on?"

Kayla shook her head. "Let him sleep."

Brett's lips slowly curved into a grin. "There aren't many things you can do in a bed in the early hours of the morning."

Kayla lightly hit him on the chest. "Tell me something."

"What?"

"I don't know. How about your earliest memory?" When he nodded, Kayla laid her head against his chest, smiling as she listened to his childhood stories.

Chapter Twenty-Two

Kayla tipped the last bit of the ashes out around her bed. There was a gap of a few centimetres and she used her fingers to spread them out.

"Eww. How can you touch them?" Red sat on the edge of Kayla's desk, watching.

Kayla shrugged as she stood up. "Guess I'm used to them."

"This sucks. I wish you could go to the party tonight. School's ended for a fortnight, we should be out celebrating."

"I'll celebrate when all this is over." Kayla put the empty container on her desk and laughed when Red jumped off. The only thing she was happy about was that exam week was over.

"Hello? Keep that stuff away from me."

"That'll be what you look like one day."

"Nope." Red shook her head. "I'm gonna be buried."

"I'm sure the worms will appreciate that." Jeff stood in the doorway.

"Eww. I'm never gonna die. How revolting."

Kayla laughed. "You won't have a choice in the matter. Besides, I'd rather be crushed bone fragments than worm food."

Red winced, covering her ears. "Stop. I'm not listening."

"We found a good website that describes the whole process," Jeff said.

Red kept her hands over her ears. "Still not listening."

"Did you ask her?" Jeff asked.

"Didn't have time." Red lowered her hands.

Jeff grinned. "I thought you weren't listening."

"Ask me what?" Kayla demanded.

"We want to borrow your car," Jeff said.

Kayla shook her head. "No way. You're mad even thinking I'd let you have it."

"That's so unfair. Neither of us have a car. Come on, Kayla. We really want to go to the party. Well, I do anyway," Red said.

"You're going too?" Kayla stared at her brother in surprise.

Jeff shrugged. "I guess."

Brett stepped into the room. "Take a taxi." He walked over to Kayla. "Five minutes."

Kayla nodded. She turned to Jeff and Red. "Have a good night. I have to finish getting ready." She headed for the bathroom ignoring Red's pleading. When she came out only Brett was in the room and the door was closed.

Brett held up three DVDs. "Which one do you want to watch?"

Kayla tapped the case of one as she walked past him and flopped onto her bed. "This is so lame. I can't believe I'm spending the first night of the school holidays locked in my room."

Brett joined her on the bed as soon as he'd put the movie on. He threaded his fingers through hers, a wry smile on his lips. "Should I apologise again?"

She momentarily tightened her fingers on his. "Nah. It sucks, that's all."

He plumped up the pillows and lay beside her. "Yeah."

They fell silent as they watched the movie. This time Kayla lasted until the credits before she drifted off to sleep. It seemed like she'd barely closed her eyes when Brett was jerked away from her.

She sat up, blinking as she tried to focus. The grey

man held Brett's outstretched arm, trying to pull him off the bed. Brett gripped the bed head as he fought to stay in the circle. The arm held by the soul stalker slowly turned grey. Kayla felt a slight tingle and a weakening in her body where it pressed against Brett.

She jumped off the bed, warily watching the soul stalker. He loosened his grip on Brett and when Brett managed to pull away, started around the circle for Kayla.

"Get on the bed." Brett reached for her.

Kayla climbed on the bed, avoiding the ashes. Her heart felt like it raced a hundred kilometres an hour. She wrapped her arms around Brett. "Are you okay? You're not..." She drew back so she could look him over. His arm was grey, the colour, or lack of colour, crept up his neck. Tugging at his shirt, she checked his chest. The grey travelled over part of it. "Brett." Fear washed over her, his name barely a whisper.

"Shh." He pulled her close. "Don't think about it. We're safe for now."

"What happened?"

"I guess I must have let my arm go outside the circle in my sleep."

Kayla recalled how he'd slept on the mattress in Jeff's room, one arm flung out. "I'm tying your arms to your body."

Brett laughed.

Kayla pulled away from him. "I'm serious."

Brett continued to smile. "I know." He rubbed at his shoulder.

"Does it hurt?"

"Pins and needles. And it sort of feels like it's not part of me. Like there's no energy in it, or something."

Kayla stared at him. "No life?"

He was silent a moment. "Yeah."

Kayla glanced at the grey man who watched them from the corner he'd retreated to. "I thought… when I saw he had you…"

Brett brushed her hair back from her face. "I know."

She leaned forward and pressed her lips to his, pouring all her fear and relief into the kiss. One hand clutched at his shirt and the other splayed against his back. Brett's hands went to her waist and tightened for a moment before he pushed her away slightly.

"This isn't a good idea while we're stuck on a bed."

Kayla stared at him. "You nearly died. I nearly," she looked away, her voice dropping, "lost you."

Brett's fingers rested against her jaw, turning her head so she faced him again. "You didn't. I'm not going to die." He pulled her close and lay down, taking her with him. "Go back to sleep."

"How can I? What if one of your arms goes outside the circle again?"

"I'll hold onto you instead." He tightened his arms around her.

"Make sure you do." She held onto his arm that was across her, afraid to let go.

He pressed his lips against her forehead. "Sleep."

"Impossible," she muttered, but fell asleep the moment she closed her eyes.

* * *

Kayla stared at the thin line of the ashes that didn't quite meet. She sat back on her bedroom floor with a sigh. There was no way she could get the circle to join. If she made the rest of the line any thinner it wouldn't be solid. Every day it had become harder to make the circle.

"What's wrong?"

Kayla turned to face Brett, who stood in her doorway. "We don't have enough."

He stared at the circle thoughtfully before he nodded. "I'll get Jeff. We'll move the bed and bring in the mattress. It takes up less room than your bed."

Kayla sighed as he left the room. Thirty-two days. Another twenty-eight to get through. What were they going to do when there were no ashes left? She stood up when Jeff and Brett came into the room. While they moved the bed, she went to Jeff's room and rolled up the mattress, letting the bedding and pillow bunch up in the middle.

"We'll get that." Brett grabbed one side of the mattress while Jeff took the other.

Kayla trailed them to her room and waited until they'd rolled the mattress out and remade it. She fixed the circle the moment they were finished. The three of them stared down at the mattress.

Kayla turned to Brett. "We're not going to have much longer, are we?"

"I thought a recliner might be a good choice," Brett said.

"What?" Kayla wasn't sure she'd heard correctly.

Brett shrugged. "At least they're comfortable. We won't be able to lay it back, but we might be able to get some sleep. Do you feel like going shopping with me tomorrow to buy one?"

Kayla closed her eyes for a second. When she opened them again, Brett smiled slightly. "You're serious, aren't you?"

Brett grinned. "Yep." He glanced at the alarm clock. "Four minutes till curfew."

Kayla didn't bother answering. She used the bathroom and joined Brett on the mattress. He had the remote controls in his hand and the television was on, showing the movie menu.

"Well?" Brett asked.

Kayla frowned. "What?"

"Shopping tomorrow?"

"Why not? It's Saturday. Not like there's anything better to do," she said dryly.

Brett ignored her tone and turned to Jeff. "What about you?"

Jeff shook his head. "Nah. Red and I are going to the beach tomorrow." Jeff had used some of the money he'd put in Kayla's bank to buy a cheap car.

"Really?" Kayla immediately forgot her annoyance over wasting her Saturday. "What's going on with you two?"

"Nothing. She needs a chauffeur." Jeff shrugged and his shirt tightened across his shoulders.

Kayla eyed her brother. "Looks like you're the one who needs to go shopping. That shirt barely fits you." She grinned. He'd tried out for the swim team at school and been accepted. He wasn't one of the best swimmers on the team, but he also wasn't one of the worst. And she'd seen a few girls talking to him at school since he'd joined the team and started going to the afternoon practices at the heated indoor pool.

Jeff shrugged again. "Whatever." His eyes widened.

Kayla turned to see what he looked at. "Not two of them."

Brett swore as each grey man took a different corner. "What do they think this is? Soul stalker central?"

"Do you think we'll end up with more of them?" Kayla looked from one soul stalker to the other.

"I hope not." Brett pulled her close. "We're safe in here. No matter how many of them turn up."

Jeff shifted awkwardly in the doorway. "Do you want me to stay home?"

"You're going out?" Kayla asked.

Jeff nodded.

"Where?"

"Party."

Kayla was speechless for a moment. "You've been to a party every Friday night since the school holidays. What's going on? And who are you going with?"

"A couple of people from school."

"Is Red going with you too?"

Jeff shrugged. "Yeah, but she hassled me to pick her up. I hadn't planned to take her or anything."

Kayla grinned. "Are you sure? The pair of you seem to be hanging out together a lot lately."

"Maybe because you've been neglecting her and she's had to make do with me to drive her places. I wish she'd hurry up and buy her own car," Jeff grumbled.

Brett laughed, turning to Kayla. "Isn't there a saying about protesting too much?"

Kayla looked thoughtful. "Hmm, you know, I think you're right."

"Oh, forget it." Jeff slammed the door behind him.

"Jeff. Don't run off. I'm sorry." Kayla ruined her apology by bursting into laughter.

"At least he remembered to lock the door before he shut it."

Still grinning, Kayla picked up her phone. She sent a text to her brother. *Jeff and Red sitting in a tree…*

Brett laughed when he saw what she wrote. "You do remember we rely on him if we need anything during the dark hours."

Kayla nodded. "Yep. But he won't let me down. No matter how much we hassle each other."

"That must be nice to have. Someone who's always there for you." Brett looked wistful.

Kayla met Brett's gaze, her expression serious. "You do have that." She linked her fingers through his.

Brett stared back at her. He smiled slightly then brushed his lips across hers. "Thank you."

Chapter Twenty-Three

Jeff came into the room and groaned when he saw Brett and Kayla making out on the recliner they'd bought a couple of weeks ago. "Do you pair have to?"

Kayla broke off their kiss and turned in Brett's arms to look at her brother, laughing. "Yep. Besides, it's my room."

"Did you want something?" Brett asked.

Jeff looked at the five soul stalkers ranged around the room. "Ah… yeah." He frowned. "Wasn't there four last night?"

Brett nodded. "We seem to be collecting them fairly quickly. But we've only got another twelve nights to get through."

"Thirteen. We aren't halfway through this night so you still have to count it," Kayla said.

Jeff eyed the circle. "It's looking a little thin."

Brett sighed. "It's the last night we'll be able to use the recliner."

"Then what?" Jeff glanced down the hall then stepped into the bedroom, closing the door behind him. Before anyone could answer, they heard Robyn call Kayla's name.

Kayla checked her watch. "How come Mum's home? It's only eight."

"Put a DVD on." Brett pulled out the remotes that were tucked between the cushion and the side of the recliner.

"Kayla. Where are you?"

"Bedroom, Mum."

Brett skipped through the movie until they were about halfway through it. He shifted onto the armrest of the chair. "Squish over, Kayla. Jeff, you sit on the other armrest."

"She better not expect me to get off the chair." Kayla moved to the centre of the recliner as her brother joined them.

The bedroom door swung open. Robyn glanced at each of them, her gaze resting on Brett as he paused the movie. "Don't you have a home to go to?"

"Mum. We're trying to watch a movie here," Jeff complained.

Robyn looked at Jeff for a moment before she

turned her gaze to Kayla. "I received a letter from your school today."

"Yeah?" Kayla tried to rack her brain, but could come up with no reason why they'd send a letter to her parents.

"They've asked me to see them. Do you know why?"

Kayla shook her head. "I wouldn't have a clue. Didn't they give you an idea in the letter?"

"No." Her gaze returned to Brett. "I want you to go home after this movie. Understand?"

Brett nodded.

Kayla yawned. "That was the plan. I'm heading to bed then."

Robyn looked at each of them in turn. She nodded sharply then closed the door behind her. They could hear the tap of her high heels as she strode down the hallway.

Kayla stared at the door. "Good thing she didn't notice the ashes. I have no idea how we could have explained them to her."

Brett pressed play and the movie started again. "Now what are we going to do?"

"I'll wait until she's in her office and pretend to see you out. In case she ever asks, you don't live far from here, okay? You walk home." Jeff got off the arm of the recliner, taking a large step to avoid standing on the ashes.

Brett moved Kayla over on the chair and joined her on the seat. "Why would she get a letter on a Sunday?"

Kayla laughed. "They don't pick up Friday's mail until today. Easier to get a park at the post office and it gives them plenty of time to deal with it before Monday morning."

Jeff frowned. "Maybe you should stay somewhere else for the last few days. Especially if you're in trouble at school." He grinned. "I can organise you a doctor's certificate saying you're in hospital with pneumonia."

"You're kidding, right?" Kayla eyed her brother, but he didn't look like it was a joke.

Jeff shook his head. "Nope. What do you say?"

Kayla hesitated. It seemed wrong, like cheating on a test. "I don't know."

"I'll need at least a day's notice, so keep that in mind."

Kayla nodded. "How do you know these… ahh… useful people?"

Jeff grinned. "If I told you, I'd have to kill you."

"Yeah, right. Come on, Jeff. Don't leave me in suspense."

"People I've helped online."

"Doing what?"

Jeff shook his head. "I'm going back to my room." He glanced at the television. "I'll be back in about forty minutes to let you know if my plan worked. If Mum's safely in her office that is."

"Thanks."

"Yeah, I owe you one," Brett said.

Jeff looked at Brett for several seconds then shook his head. "No, I probably owe you." He closed the door behind him before they could ask what he meant.

"What did you do for him?" Kayla asked.

"Nothing I know of."

"There must be something."

"Then I wouldn't have a clue. I've forced him to go swimming every morning with me. And jogging. Oh, and made him use your home gym. Not to mention dragging him shopping for new clothes and hassling him when he needed his hair cut."

"You don't think-" Kayla could barely voice her thoughts. When Brett opened his mouth to speak, she covered it with her hand. "Don't say it. I don't want to jinx it if it's true."

Brett pressed a kiss against her palm and grinned when she dropped her hand. "You'll have to talk to him about it eventually. There's four and a half months left of the year."

"I know. But for now, let's not risk jinxing it."

Brett nodded. "Where were we when your brother interrupted us?"

Kayla grinned. "Hmm, let me see. I think my hand was here." She slipped her right hand under his shirt and slid it upwards until it rested against his heartbeat.

"That seems about right. But what about your other hand? I know it wasn't resting in your lap."

Kayla laughed. "And neither were yours." She moved closer, her lips meeting his.

* * *

Brett stood in the doorway of his old room at Brian's house. Kayla hovered in the hallway behind him, Brian a few steps behind her.

Brian cleared his throat. "No one's been in it since you. I cleaned it thinking I'd rent it out to someone, but… you know, Douglas and everything. Not like I can have a flatmate with him about."

Douglas stepped through a wall and into the hallway to rest his hand on Kayla's shoulder. "What's wrong with having me about, lad?"

"Nothing. I don't think we should let too many

people know you exist. We wouldn't want reporters camped on our doorstep," Brian said. "Anyway, I'll leave the two of you to it. The spare key is on the chest of drawers. And, uhm… we'll have to be out of here at the end of the week. I've bought a place closer to the city centre. It makes more sense than wasting money on rent. It's an area that's going ahead."

Brett nodded, his gaze fixed on his old room. He didn't turn his head even when Brian and Douglas left them alone. Kayla moved closer to him and slipped her arm around his waist. He automatically draped an arm around her shoulders.

Kayla tried to step forward with him. He didn't budge. "Come on. It's only an hour till dark. We need to move the bed to one side so we can make a circle with your ashes." Kayla ran her hands through her hair, glad to find a couple of loose strands. "Douglas." She stepped into the bedroom, leaving Brett in the doorway.

Douglas stepped through a wall. "What's wrong, lass?"

Kayla moved to the foot of the bed, holding out the strands of hair to Douglas. "I need help moving this against the wall."

Douglas took the strands and stepped up to the head of the bed. Before Kayla could lift her end of the bed, Brett moved to stand beside her and, with a look, took hold of it. Kayla stepped away and managed to hold back a grin. She watched as the queen-sized bed was pushed up against the wall near the window.

Douglas dusted his hands on his trousers. "Anything else, lass?"

Kayla shook her head. "No, that's all." As soon as he'd left the bedroom, she gasped. "Oh no, we should have asked first."

"What about?" Brett sat on the bed, leaning back on his hands.

"Irene. We should have asked her about the soul stalkers and if they'd go after Douglas." She took out her phone and dialled the number, tapping her foot as she waited. When it rang out, she tried again. No luck. "Now what?"

Brett shrugged. "I don't know. We might have to share our circle with him."

"I hope not. It's going to be crowded enough as it is." Kayla picked up the ice cream container she'd put on the hallway floor earlier. "There's not much left."

"Wait until there's none."

"Don't remind me." Kayla used the glass in the container to pour a thin line of the ashes. She frowned when she saw the size of the circle. "How are we meant to fit in there?" Fear raced through her. She couldn't lose him. There had to be enough space for two of them, but she didn't see how.

Brett rose to his feet and came to stand next to her. He sat in the middle of the circle. "Guess you'll be on my lap."

"We're not going to have a circle for much longer, are we?" She eyed the small gap between Brett and the ashes.

Brett met her gaze, not replying straight away. "No."

Kayla's phone rang, making her jump. Staring at the name displayed, she didn't know if she was relieved or more worried. Taking a deep breath, she answered her phone. "Irene."

"You have more questions?"

"Yes. The soul stalkers. They won't go after Douglas, will they? The ghost who lives here."

"As long as he's only a ghost. Give him no weight in the real world."

"Huh?" Kayla frowned, trying to figure out the cryptic comment.

Irene sighed. "Don't make him visible to those who can't see the deceased. Then he'll be safe."

"Oh. Thanks."

"Any other questions?"

"No."

"Call if you have any. It's not long now." Irene hung up before Kayla could reply.

She slipped her phone in her pocket. "I have to tell Douglas not to use my hair while it's dark and we're here."

"I'll do it. I need to talk to Brian for a minute anyway."

Kayla nodded and went to sit on the bed. Staring at the circle, she wondered how many more nights they'd get through before there was only standing room. And after that? There wouldn't be too much longer before there were no ashes left.

Chapter Twenty-Four

Kayla checked her watch. Time rapidly raced towards sunset. And a sleepless night. She couldn't imagine how it would be possible to get any sleep at all tonight. Luckily she'd taken Jeff up on his offer and he'd be taking a doctor's certificate to school for her tomorrow. As uncomfortable as it had made her feel to cut school for a while, she knew she couldn't cope. She needed more than a few hours sleep each day. Her phone rang again and she checked the display. Her heart missed a beat. "Hi, Mum."

"I had an appointment with your school today."

"Really? What did they want?" She held her breath. Surely it couldn't be too bad.

"They said you don't seem to be paying as much attention in class and your grades have been slipping."

Kayla wondered if that would help convince them the doctor's certificate, Jeff was taking in, was real.

"You know how much trouble I have with school work. I'm trying my best, it's getting harder."

"Do we need to organise a tutor for you?"

"Nah. I have it under control. Jeff is helping me now."

There was a moment of silence before Robyn spoke again. "Where are you?"

Kayla thought of and discarded several comments. "You remember the article Dad read in the paper a while back and left on the kitchen bench for us to read? The one about Brian Macrae who found the money behind his ancestor's portrait and had the sense to get it valued."

"Yes. Of course I do. What a wonderful find. Many young people wouldn't have thought them worth much at all."

"Brett knows him. We're at his place. I'm not sure what time I'll be home. It'll probably be late."

"Really?"

"Yes." Kayla held her finger to her lips when Brett stepped into the room.

"Do you have any of your father's business cards with you? Maybe he'd like to look at some different investment opportunities."

"I've been invited back for dinner tomorrow night.

I'll give him one then. If you leave some in the kitchen I'll grab them in the morning."

"I'll do that now. And Kayla…"

"Yeah?"

"You should be cultivating a friendship with Brian more than Brett."

"Ahh, yeah, sure Mum."

"Take care."

"Yeah. Bye." Kayla slipped her phone back in her pocket and turned towards Brett after a glance at her watch. "Seven minutes."

"I've used the bathroom. It's all yours."

"Back in a minute."

When Kayla returned to the bedroom, Brett sat in the circle. He smiled wryly and patted his lap. "Come tell Santa what you want for Christmas."

Kayla laughed as she tried to find a comfortable position. She froze when she heard Brian laugh from the doorway, turning her head so she could see him. "What?"

Brian shook his head, a grin on his face. "My warped sense of humour." He wandered into the room and walked around the circle. "You won't be able to move much at all. Not without going past the boundaries."

"I don't think I can do this." Kayla started to rise, but stopped when Brett's arms tightened around her.

"You have to. It's too late now to figure out something else. The sun has set."

"They have to get over here from my home. Maybe." She frowned. Unless there had been some nearby when the sun had risen that morning.

"Kayla, I'm not going to risk your life. We'll see how we manage tonight. Maybe tomorrow night we'll have to spend it driving around in the car."

"Do you want me to set the TV up in here?" Brian asked.

Kayla shook her head. "I don't think I want to see another movie this year."

"I'll grab some sheets and make up the bed so you can crash the moment the sun rises." Brian headed for the door.

"Can you bring me my book from my overnight bag? It's on top of everything." Kayla squirmed, trying to get comfortable. "Not as good as the recliner and nowhere near as good as the bed."

"Stay still. You're going to make the night even longer if you keep moving around."

"Eleven nights left. We're not going to make it."

Brett pulled her tight against his chest, his breath

grazing her cheek. "We will. We've managed forty-nine days, eleven isn't many at all."

Brian came back into the bedroom holding a pile of sheets and a book. He handed the book to Kayla. "Anything else I can get you?"

"We'll yell if we need anything," Brett said.

Brian nodded before he moved to the bed and started to make it.

Kayla's phone rang and she wriggled so she could pull it out of her pocket. "Hey, Jeff."

"I saw the grey men wander through the house and then pause outside like they were dogs scenting the air. They ran off in your direction."

"How many were there?"

"Six." When Kayla remained silent, Jeff asked, "Are you still there?"

"Yeah."

"Everything okay?"

Kayla laughed, a sharp, bitter sound. "What do you think?"

It was Jeff's turn to be silent for ages. "Mum wanted to know why I wasn't with you tonight."

"What?"

"She thought I should be meeting Midas." Jeff referred to the name one of the magazine's had called Brian.

Jeff's words brought the hint of a smile to her lips. "I should have expected that."

"So I'm thinking I could come with you tomorrow night and we could text her and say it got so late we were invited to stay the night."

"No."

"You didn't even think about it."

"Jeff, please. We barely have a circle. There are so many soul stalkers you wouldn't be able to move in the room without running into one. I don't want them after you too."

"But it's okay for them to be after you?"

"Since when has something like that bothered you?"

"You're not facing a schoolyard bully, Kayla. And it's always bothered me when you've faced them. Especially when it was for me. But, you know what I'm like when it comes to pain. Even the thought of it makes me freeze."

"Bullies don't scare me. Well, not at the time. I'm usually too angry with them to think about being scared."

"I know. That's why this is getting to you. You have plenty of time every day to worry about what will happen in the night."

"Yeah," Kayla said softly.

"I'd better go. I have homework to do."

"Okay. Oh, and can you collect Dad's business cards from the kitchen tomorrow morning after they've left? And mail one to Brian. That way I can honestly say I made sure he got one."

Jeff chuckled. "Sure. And you call me if you want my help."

"Okay. Bye."

"See you later."

As soon as Kayla put her phone on the floor, outside the circle, Brian came to stand near them. "Why do I need one of your father's business cards?"

"He wants to hassle you about investing money." Kayla shrugged. "I guess he does okay, he's had many of his clients for a lot of years. I don't expect you to see him."

"Will it help you to stay away from home longer if I do?" Brian asked.

"Yeah, probably."

"I'll give him a call. I don't promise anything. Maybe I can have him send out some info or something."

Kayla smiled. "Thanks. That'd be good."

Brian looked from one to the other. "Anything else?"

Kayla and Brett answered at the same time. Kayla said, "Nah," while Brett said, "We're right."

As soon as Brian left the room, Kayla picked up her book. She had placed it outside the circle since there had been no space for it inside. She turned to the first page and tried to focus. Many of the lines she had to reread so the story would make sense. By the time she'd read two chapters, Kayla thought it was time to give up. It was the longest she'd ever taken to read so little. She felt Brett tense and glanced around. Two grey men had arrived. They each picked a corner to stand in. Kayla put her book down outside the circle and the grey men moved in the moment her hand crossed the ashes. They continued to wander around for several minutes after she'd hastily withdrawn her hand.

"It's too soon for them to be here from my house, isn't it?" Kayla stared up at the soul stalkers as they passed in front of her again.

"Yeah."

"When the others arrive, that'll make eight."

"Yeah."

"What are we going to do?"

"Stay in the circle."

"Brett."

"What can we do? Nothing. We can't fight them, I

doubt they can be killed, so what do you suggest we do?"

Kayla picked up her phone and dialled Irene, glaring at the soul stalkers who moved in to hover around them for a moment. The phone was answered on the third ring. Kayla didn't bother returning Irene's hello. "Can soul stalkers be killed?"

There was a slight pause before Irene answered. "When they absorb a soul they go."

"Does that mean they can't be killed?"

"Not in the usual sense."

Kayla clenched her teeth and took a deep breath. "Is there any way to fight, damage or kill the soul stalkers?"

"Why didn't you ask such a clear question to start with?"

Kayla opened her mouth to yell at Irene, but Brett took the phone from her. He put it on speaker mode.

"You can weaken them," Irene said.

"How?" Brett and Kayla asked together.

"With Brett's ashes."

"What?" Kayla glared at the phone. "Why didn't you tell us?"

"You didn't ask."

Kayla let out a sound of annoyance. "Irene–"

Brett interrupted her. "Can you tell us how to

damage them with my ashes. And how much does it damage them?"

"Throw a pinch of the ashes at one of them. It affects them immediately. They weaken and are unable to move. It lasts for three to five hours, depending on the strength of the soul stalker. And I'm not talking physical strength."

"What sort of strength?" Brett asked.

"Some steal the soul quicker than others. Those are the stronger ones."

"Thanks, Irene," Brett said.

"Yeah. Thanks." Kayla's tone was sarcastic. "Not telling us information because we haven't asked is a stupid idea."

"Those who don't question things always feel that way. It's sensible to seek as much information about something before you jump into it. As I've said before, regaining a life isn't meant to be easy. Nor are those who can help meant to make it easy. It's something that must be earned."

"That doesn't help us much now," Kayla muttered.

"Is there any other information we might find useful to know about the soul stalkers?" Brett asked.

"What I might think useful is more than likely to differ from what you would find useful."

Kayla clenched her teeth again and forced herself to

bite back the words she wanted to speak. She guessed alienating Irene wouldn't be a good plan.

"Okay, thanks Irene. We'll call if we think of anything else to ask," Brett said.

"Good luck."

Brett put Kayla's phone on the floor, his hand outside the protection of the circle for mere seconds. It was enough to bring the soul stalkers close. He stared at them. "What do you think? Should we give it a go?"

"Yes. We can't sit in the circle all night. My legs are already going to sleep."

"Yeah, mine too. I've lost nearly all feeling in my feet." Brett carefully picked up two pinches of the ashes, making sure he didn't break the circle. As the soul stalkers passed in front of them again, he flung the ashes at them.

They staggered back, black spots like burn marks flecking them. First one and then the other collapsed to the floor within seconds of the ashes touching them. They lay still, no movement of their chests to show breathing. No movement at all.

Chapter Twenty-Five

Kayla staggered to her feet and stepped cautiously forward. She started to reach out and touch one.

Brett grabbed her arm, pulling her back. "Are you mad?"

"Absolutely." Kayla grinned. "I talk to ghosts, so I'd have to be."

"Don't touch them. Who knows what might happen."

"Okay." She glanced around the room. "It's so good to stand up after being stuck in the one position for ages."

"A couple of minutes out of the circle and then we wait for the other soul stalkers inside it. We can't take them all out at once."

"We can manage four of them easily. I bet we could get the last two before they reached us."

"We're not going to risk it."

"Sure thing, Grandpa."

"You can't make me change my mind. No matter what you say. I'm not going to let you risk your life."

"Fine." Kayla stalked over to the bed and dropped onto it, gazing at the ceiling.

Brett came to stand over her. "Ten minutes and we're back in the circle."

Kayla sat up, swinging her legs over the side of the bed. "They're an hour away." She rose to her feet so she could face him. "I'm not getting back in the circle for at least another three quarters of an hour."

"What if others turn up?"

Kayla stared at him for a moment then strode to the circle and carefully took a pinch of the ashes. "Then we'll see how well all the years of playing sport have payed off." She smiled.

"Kayla–" Brett crossed the floor to place his hands on her shoulders.

"No. I'm sick of hiding in the circle night after night. Sick of not fighting back. I always fight. You want someone to cower behind you and let you take care of everything then you'd better find someone else." She glared at him.

Brett glared back at her for a moment. His expression softened. "I'm worried you might get hurt. If anything happened to you…"

"I could say the same thing about you. We'll fight them together. And beat them. Let's see what small containers Brian has so we can have some of the ashes ready to use." Kayla pulled away from Brett and headed out of the room.

"What are ye doing out here, lass?" Douglas sat in the lounge room watching a documentary on the sharemarket.

"Do you know where Brian is?"

"In the kitchen."

"Thanks." Kayla headed for the kitchen, Brett on her heels.

Brian jumped to his feet, a coffee mug on the table in front of him. "What are you doing out of the circle?"

"We've found out some more information." Kayla grinned.

"If we throw my ashes at the soul stalkers they pass out for several hours," Brett said.

"How'd you figure that out?"

Kayla's smile disappeared. "The witch told us. After she made us ask the right question first."

"Witch?"

"It was the nicer of the names I considered calling her."

"Irene," Brett said.

Brian laughed. "Now I'm following. I think."

"Anyway." Kayla waved her hand as if to brush away the conversation. "We need some small containers. Something quick to open and that can be kept in our pockets."

Douglas joined them in the kitchen, invisible to Brian. "Ye don't ask for much, do ye lass."

Brian momentarily frowned. "You know, I think I have exactly what you need." He opened the third kitchen drawer and rummaged around in it before closing it. He rummaged in the next drawer down. "Found them." He turned and held up four half filled glitter vials.

"What are you doing with glitter?" Brett asked.

"An old girlfriend dragged me to a fancy dress party. She went as a fairy and used the glitter to decorate her wings. You'd think that would have been enough of a warning to make me run."

"I remember her. Should'a been smothered at birth. Would have done the world a favour. Hope ye don't turn out like her, lass. One minute sane, the next ye'd think she was the devil's daughter."

Kayla giggled at Douglas' words and Brian sent her a funny look. He glanced around the kitchen. "He's in here, isn't he? Talking."

Kayla nodded.

"What did he say?" Brian tipped the glitter into a neat pile on the table and held the plastic vials out.

Kayla took one of the vials and sat at the table. "Pretty much the same as you said about your ex-girlfriend." She carefully put the ashes in the narrow vial and stared at them in the bottom. She eyed the glitter on the table and with a grin picked up a pinch and added it to the vial. She pressed the white lid on and shook it.

"What do you think you're doing?" Brett took the other three vials.

Kayla laughed and shrugged. "I don't know. It seemed like a fun thing to do."

Brett shook his head as he put a pinch of the ashes he carried into one of the vials. He capped it and slid it into his pocket.

"Boring." Kayla looked from Brett to the glitter and back at Brett, her lips still curved in a smile. Now they had a way of fighting back it felt like they had a chance.

Brett handed over one of the empty vials. "Get that filled." He turned to Brian. "Do you think you could try and track down some more tonight? You sometimes see them in supermarkets."

Brian nodded. "Will you be okay here on your own?"

"Yeah." Brett frowned when he saw Kayla add a pinch of glitter to her empty vial. "Do you have to?"

"Yep. Don't hassle me. I'm happy. I feel like celebrating. So I'm making my own little party popper. A soul stalker party popper."

Brett chuckled. "Fair enough. Let's finish making your second party popper." He wrapped his arm around her waist and walked with her to his bedroom. Within minutes they had their vials ready.

Kayla glanced over at the two soul stalkers. She frowned, moving closer. "Only one of them is wearing a hooded cloak."

Brett joined her. "I noticed. Not many of them seem to wear them. I wonder why."

"Hmm." Kayla reached out to touch the cloak.

Brett grabbed her hand. "What do you think you're doing?"

"I want to see if we can take it off him."

"Don't even think about it."

"Then help me find something we can use to manoeuvre it off him."

Brett sighed, slowly shaking his head. "Okay."

It took several minutes to settle on a wooden handled mop and a pair of thick plastic industrial gloves. Brett used the gloves while Kayla levered the grey man with the handle of the mop.

"Maybe we should get a couple of pairs of these gloves. I can't feel any numbness at all." Brett tugged at the cloak.

"Why don't you try touching him without a glove on and see if the numbness still comes when they're unconscious."

Brett hesitated. He drew off one of the gloves. His bare hand hovered over the grey man. He closed his eyes for a second and the moment he opened them he fleetingly touched the arm of the soul stalker. The tips of his fingers lost colour. He drew his fingers away, staring at them.

Kayla leaned closer to check. "Guess they suck the life from you even when they're unconscious."

Brett slid his hand back in the glove and tried to remove the cloak. Kayla pushed the handle under the body and levered it up so he could pull the cloak a little higher. Eventually, with a last tug, the cloak came over the grey man's head. The second every last thread of the cloak left his body, he seemed to dissolve into nothingness.

Kayla's jaw dropped and Brett reached out to touch the floor where the grey man had been. He grasped the cloak in his other hand, looking up at Kayla, questions in his eyes. She slowly shook her head, guessing her own eyes were filled with similar queries.

Brett checked the cloak in his hands. "It feels light and thin even though it looks like a heavy woollen cloak. I wouldn't have a clue what it's made of."

"Think we should ring Irene?"

"The witch?" Brett teased.

Kayla shrugged. "She might be, but we don't have anyone else we can question."

Brett nodded. He dropped the cloak on the floor and rose to his feet. Pulling off the gloves, he dropped them near the cloak. Kayla picked up the phone she'd left on the floor near the circle and redialled Irene's number.

"Hello?"

"Irene. We took a cloak off an unconscious soul stalker and he dissolved."

"What?"

"A soul stalker's cl–"

"You're still alive? How did you manage that? Or was it Brett? Did he become a soul stalker?"

Kayla turned back to Brett as he reached out with a bare hand to pick up the cloak. She dropped the phone, reaching for him. "No!" Brett faced her, as she threw her arms around him and tugged at him to draw him away from the cloak.

"What's going on?" Brett let her pull him in her direction.

"I don't know." Kayla swore as she spotted her phone on the floor. "Hope she's still there." She picked it up and put it on speaker mode.

"Hello? Kayla? Brett?"

"Irene. What did you mean?"

"About what, Kayla?"

"The cloak. Can it kill? Harm? What?"

"You will become a soul stalker if you wear their cloak. Or touch it. You must burn it. Be very careful not to let it touch your flesh. It's different when a soul stalker wears it. That neutralises it."

Kayla felt her knees weaken. She grabbed hold of Brett to steady herself. So many days and they'd nearly been for nothing. She could barely whisper. "Why did it vanish when we removed the cloak?"

"I don't know, dear. No one takes off the cloaks. It's too dangerous. We know what would happen if someone was to touch one that wasn't worn by a soul stalker. You really should learn to ask more questions."

Kayla forced her legs to take her to the bed so she could sit down. "So we burn it."

"Yes. As quickly as you can. How did you manage

to remove the cloak without becoming a soul stalker?"

"Brett used thick plastic gloves. You know the ones with the roughened fingers so you can grip things. The industrial ones."

"What a marvellous idea. Did you have any other questions?"

"No." Kayla dropped the phone onto the bed beside her as soon as Irene had hung up. She covered her face with her hands. "I can't believe…"

"You didn't know."

Kayla raised her head. "It doesn't matter. It's not a game. I guess I forgot for a moment. I was so happy to get out of that circle during the night. I wanted to have some fun."

Brett smiled slightly. "Like when you were making soul stalker party poppers."

Kayla smiled weakly. "I guess."

"Kayla. Get in the circle." Brett raced back to the circle, grabbing two pinches of the ashes.

Chapter Twenty-Six

Kayla spun to look behind her as she stumbled off the bed. Six soul stalkers walked through the wall, one barely an arm's length from her. She fumbled in her pocket for a vial as she hurried backwards. She pushed the lid off with her thumb and her fingers tightened around the vial as she threw the contents at the soul stalker. He collapsed to the floor seconds after two on his left also dropped. A grey man on his right managed to wrap his hands around Kayla's throat.

Brett threw another pinch of the ashes at him and he collapsed onto the floor. Kayla fell at her sudden release. She tried to scramble away, but another one grabbed her by the ankle and pulled her towards him. His other hand grabbed her calf, then his fingers slackened and he sprawled across her leg. Kayla scurried away from him in time to see the last one crash to the floor.

She didn't have time to shift away from the downed bodies, or stand up, before Brett was there. He crushed her to his chest, his heartbeat racing loudly in her ear. She guessed hers raced equally as fast.

Kayla pressed against Brett's chest with her hand. "Need to breathe."

Brett loosened his arms slightly. "They didn't hurt you?"

"Some pins and needles."

"I had to stay in the circle. I couldn't come to you."

"I know. It would have been stupid to do so. I guess we lost track of time with Irene's little bombshell."

"Never again." His arms tightened again.

"Need oxygen."

"Sorry."

She stared up at him. "It worked though."

"What did?"

"One of us for bait while the other attacked."

"No! No way. You aren't going to use yourself as bait while I attack them."

"The circle is getting smaller and you have better aim than me. Only one of us will be able to stand in it soon."

"Then it'll be you."

Kayla shook her head. "Don't be stupid-"

"Kayla, I'm not going to stand safely in the circle while you're mobbed by them. It's not going to happen."

Kayla pulled away from him. "We'll see." She moved over to have a look at the one she'd thrown the contents of her vial at. She grinned. "I think some of the glitter's stuck to him."

"Don't change the topic. You will be the one in the circle."

She glanced around at the bodies. "There's two more cloaks. How about we get them off and burn all of them at once."

"Are you listening to anything I'm saying?"

Kayla faced him. "Yes. But that doesn't mean I agree with it. It doesn't matter tonight, anyway. We'll figure it out tomorrow. We have things to do right now."

"There's nothing to figure out tomorrow. It's already settled. You will be in the circle if there's only room for one. Now let's deal with these cloaks."

Brian returned while they were burning the cloaks in the backyard. Douglas stood by, watching them, having already been told the dangers of touching soul stalker cloaks.

"What's going on here?" Brian looked first at the small fire and then at Brett and Kayla.

Kayla explained. Brian looked at the burning cloaks thoughtfully.

"What are you thinking?" Brett asked.

Brian turned away from the fire. "It's a pity you didn't keep one of the cloaks."

"Why?" Kayla frowned as she tried to figure out the benefit.

"The other soul stalkers might have disappeared too if you had put the cloak on them and then removed it," Brian said.

"Hey, that's not a bad idea." Kayla grinned. "Tomorrow night we'll have to try it. That's if any of the cloaked ones come after us. A pity you took so long to get home."

"I have twelve vials of glitter. They're on the kitchen table." Brian looked towards Kayla and grinned. "Still full of glitter."

Kayla laughed, half apologetic, partly defiant. "And the ashes worked perfectly having that bit extra with them."

Brett checked the burning cloaks with a stick. The thin curls of ash broke apart like paper had been burned, not material. "We should go inside to set up the vials and see if the soul stalkers are still unconscious."

Kayla looked reluctantly towards the house. "I

guess." She glanced up at the stars. "It's been ages since I've been outside at night. I miss it."

Brett put his arm around her. "Not much longer and you'll be able to stay outside, all night if you want."

"Considering how cold it is, I don't think I'll want to for long. I just like having the option." She leaned against him, feeling his warmth through her jacket.

They walked silently inside. Once in the kitchen, they emptied the glitter from the vials and headed to the bedroom. Kayla's six vials had a little bit of glitter in the bottom of each of them. When he noticed, Brett slowly shook his head, a hint of a smile on his lips.

Kayla grinned when she saw Brett looking at the vials. "At least you'll know which ones are mine."

"We'll have to empty them into the container each night. We don't want to risk not having enough of the ashes in them if some of it… disappears." He shrugged. "Evaporates. Or whatever it does."

Kayla opened her mouth to answer when one of the soul stalkers behind Brett rose to his feet. Without thinking, she flung a pinch of the ashes at him. Brett spun to face the soul stalker who crashed to the floor.

She glanced at her watch. "Looks like that one only managed three and a quarter hours."

"We're going to run out of the ashes quickly using them like this."

Kayla shrugged. "We're losing more of them each day. We should put them to good use while we still have them." She yawned.

"Do you want to sleep while I stand guard?"

"If you promise to wake me in a couple of hours and let me stand guard so you can sleep. Oh, and have Douglas watch with you. In case you get into trouble you can't handle. He can yell at me to wake up."

"I'll find Douglas. You get comfortable. But don't go to sleep until I get back."

Kayla didn't mean to fall asleep. But once her head hit the pillow, her eyes wouldn't stay open. The next thing she knew, light fell across her face, making her eyes blink open. A shaft of daylight snuck in at the side of the curtain and landed on her face. She turned her head to see Brett fast asleep beside her. She yawned as she sat up. The ice cream container sat in the middle of the circle of ashes, the vials capped and waiting in the container. She pressed her hand against her pockets and found one vial left in them. She guessed Brett must have taken the rest of the vials once the sun rose.

She slid carefully over the foot of the bed so she didn't wake Brett and made her way to the bathroom.

As soon as she finished in there, she headed for the kitchen, starving. It was a long time to go without food, but since they couldn't leave the circle after sunset to use the bathroom, it was the only option. Well, it had been up until now. Kayla jumped as she heard a sound behind her.

Brian stepped into the kitchen. "Hungry?"

"Starving."

"You want cereal or would you rather I cooked up eggs or something?"

"Cereal. Cooking would take too long."

Brian grinned. "Not liking the enforced fasting?"

"Not at all." She took the bowl and spoon he handed her and then looked at the cereal choices in the cupboard he opened. She grabbed a box and carried it to the table.

Brian took milk from the fridge and sugar off the kitchen bench and put them in front of her. "What are your plans for today?"

Kayla made her breakfast. "I wouldn't have a clue." She filled her spoon and leaned forward to eat.

Brian sat across from her. "Do you mind if I ask you something?"

Kayla shrugged and swallowed her mouthful. "I don't know. Guess you'll have to ask and find out."

Brian smiled fleetingly. "What's it like to see ghosts?"

"I don't know."

"What?"

It was Kayla's turn to smile. "I didn't realise I could until I met Brett. And then well," she shrugged. "I don't know. He didn't seem like a ghost."

"Do you think there are other people who can see them? As clearly as you can."

Kayla nodded. "There'd have to be. Jeff and I aren't all that special. The odds are we're not the only ones in the world who can see them. I bet the other people who can, don't realise either."

"I guess that'd make sense."

Kayla scraped her bowl clean and leaned back in the chair. "So, still interested in cooking me breakfast?"

Brian laughed as he rose from the table and headed for the fridge.

Chapter Twenty-Seven

Kayla helped Brett fill the glitter vials, seated at the kitchen table in Brian's new house. She tried not to think about how low the contents of the ice cream container were. She hoped it got them through to almost the end. Besides, they hadn't had a single cloaked soul stalker in the last handful of nights. She wanted to see if Brian's theory about the cloak worked. And it wasn't something they could do unless the soul stalkers were unconscious. Well, she couldn't imagine it'd be an easy task if they were conscious.

Brett put the cap on the last vial. "Good thing there's only six days left. We've used up nearly all the ashes between the sixteen vials."

Kayla looked at the scattering of the ashes in the bottom of the ice cream container. She ignored the sensation in her stomach. The sickly, twisting feeling made her think disaster awaited them. "We're going to have to hit the road tomorrow, aren't we?"

Brett stared at her for a moment before he nodded. "I doubt there'll be much, if any, left by then." He gestured towards the container.

Kayla reached out to hold his hand. "Less than a week. We can do this."

"I hope so."

Her gaze travelled over each of the vials. "If one of the cloaked ones doesn't come tonight we probably won't get to try out Brian's theory." She slipped half the vials into her pockets.

"Did I hear my name mentioned?" Brian entered the kitchen. "Do you have to do that at the table? I eat there."

Kayla grinned when she saw his expression. "With the temperatures they use to cremate people nothing harmful or contagious is left behind. Actually, soft tissue and organs are vaporised so this is bone."

"Please." Brett looked pained. "Can we skip talking about the process?"

"Baby."

"Baby! See how comfortable you'll feel talking about dying once you've died," Brett said.

Kayla shook her head. "I'm not coming back as a

ghost. I'm going to do the sensible thing and go to wherever you're meant to go."

"What if you die young?" Brett slipped the rest of the vials into his pockets.

Kayla stared at him for a moment. "I'm glad you came back."

"If you pair are going to get mushy, I'm outta here," Brian warned.

Kayla laughed. "Can't please some people. No getting mushy. No playing with human remains at the table. Is there anything we're allowed to do?"

They all turned at the rap on the front door.

Brian groaned. "I hope it's not the neighbours welcoming me to the neighbourhood. That happened at my old house and I couldn't get rid of them for hours."

Kayla checked her watch. "We don't have hours."

"You've just moved in. Surely they wouldn't hassle you so soon," Brett said.

Brian shrugged. "They did last time." He headed for the front door, Kayla and Brett close on his heels.

"Jeff. What are you doing here?" Kayla looked at the basket in her brother's hands. "And what on earth is that? If you're going to grandma's house remember to keep an eye out for the big bad wolf."

"Ha, ha. Very funny. Some old lady who lives

next door. She wanted to welcome you to the neighbourhood. I told her I live here too. I didn't think you'd want visitors. Said we'd see her once we're settled in."

Brian took the basket and peeked inside. "Thermos and cake?"

"Coffee apparently." Jeff stepped inside with a glance over his shoulder. "Not sure we should touch any of it. She reminded me of the wicked witch from Snow White."

"Have you been watching kid's cartoons again, baby brother?" Kayla walked beside Jeff as they returned to the kitchen.

"You're such a comedian, Kayla." Jeff's tone contradicted his words. "But evil like that makes an impression when you're three-years-old. I had nightmares about that witch for months. And so did you." Jeff pointed at Kayla when she opened her mouth to speak.

"Did not. Your screaming woke me and made me scream. I thought you were being murdered." Kayla took the thermos from the basket and opened it. She sniffed. "It smells okay."

"So did the apple Snow White ate." Jeff took the thermos from Kayla and tipped it down the sink. He glanced around the kitchen. "It didn't take you lot long to get this room unpacked."

"Priorities." Brian grinned. "Beds are set up too. The rest of the house is complete chaos though."

Kayla eyed the basket Brian had put on the table. "What about the cake? It looks good."

"Have you got a pet rat you can use as a test subject?" Jeff opened the container and looked suspiciously at the cake.

Kayla shook her head. "Talk about paranoia."

Jeff offered the cake to Douglas who had appeared in the kitchen moments after them. "You could eat it. It's not like you can die when you're already dead."

"Thanks, lad. I'll have it with me morning coffee once all the soul stalkers are gone. Leave it on top of the fridge, will ye?"

Jeff put the container on the fridge and turned to face Kayla. "Don't touch it."

"Yes, Dad."

"Be serious, Kayla."

"Then maybe you should test it." Kayla barely noticed the kitchen empty.

"Is that what you want?" Jeff crossed his arms over his chest.

"Isn't that what you want?"

Jeff shrugged one shoulder. "I don't know. Sometimes."

"What about when this year ends?"

"How do I know?"

"Then how am I meant to know either?" Kayla glared at her brother. She had too much to worry about. Getting rid of one worry would have been nice.

"Will you stop turning my words back on me?"

Kayla's hands went to her hips. "I want to know if I'll have a brother next year. Is that such a tough question to answer?"

"Yeah. It is."

Kayla's anger left her and she stepped forward to rest her hand on his crossed arms. "I don't want to lose you."

"I know."

"I want to know what you're thinking. Are you still considering killing yourself?"

Jeff pulled away from her, his back to her. "It's complicated. Some days I think it'd be the easiest option. Before, I thought that every day. Now…"

Kayla stepped forward so she could look at him. Hope struggled to life. "Now, what?"

Jeff shrugged. "Some days seem like they might be worth living through."

"Are you going to the shrink Mum and Dad want you to see?"

Jeff shook his head. "Nah. I'd rather figure it out on my own."

"But if–"

"Drop it, Kayla."

"Promise me you won't try and kill yourself without telling me first?"

"That'd defeat the purpose."

Kayla grinned. "That was the idea."

"How about I don't kill myself unless I've said goodbye first?"

"A letter doesn't count."

"Fine."

"Or a text, email or anything else other than face to face."

Jeff glared at her. "Don't push it."

"Let me know if you work things out. So I'm not left wondering."

"Okay. That I can promise."

"Ah, Kayla?"

She turned to see Brett in the kitchen doorway.

"Time to get ready."

She nodded and turned back to Jeff. "What are you doing over here? And at this time of the day."

"I thought you might need some help. Besides, I'm

sick of Mum and Dad asking why I'm not spending more time with Midas."

"You're not going to put yourself at risk too." Kayla's hands went back to her hips and she glared at her brother.

"I won't touch them. I'll wear those industrial gloves you bought and use a wooden broom handle." Jeff gestured towards the two sitting against the wall in the kitchen. They had them in each room. They, like every other object, only became solid against the soul stalkers when Kayla or Brett held them, which meant they should work for Jeff too.

"Fine. But you touch one and I'll make your life miserable." Kayla pointed a warning finger at him.

Brett stepped forward with three vials in his hand. "You'll need these."

Jeff took them and slipped them into the pockets of his jeans. "Thanks."

Brett faced Kayla. "Meet you in the bedroom?"

Kayla nodded. "I'll use the bathroom first."

When Kayla entered the bedroom, which only contained Brett's bed pushed up against the wall, both Brett and Jeff waited for her.

She grabbed the broom handle from where it leaned against the wall beside the door. "I guess we'll be able to watch all the directions easier with another pair of eyes."

Brett placed the ice cream container, he'd brought with him from the kitchen, on the bed. "Any minute now."

They stood back to back, a vial in one hand, a wooden broom handle in the other. Silence filled the room as they scanned the area, waiting.

They came from Kayla's direction. "Thirteen. We can't take them all. We'll be left with three vials and a handful of the ashes. We're going to have to run."

"They're faster than us." Brett held his vial ready.

Kayla swore. "None of them have cloaks."

"I can hold them off." Jeff said. "What are they waiting for? Why don't they attack?"

"They're getting wary. These ones have spent the last few nights unconscious," Kayla said.

"I think they're communicating. Silently." Brett warily eyed the soul stalkers.

"We're not staying." Kayla glanced at Jeff. "You be careful."

"The moment I hear the car start, I'm letting them follow." Jeff backed up towards the hallway.

Brett grabbed Kayla's hand and dropped the broom handle. "Get moving if this is what you want to do."

Kayla dropped her broom handle and followed

Brett into the hall. She glanced back to see Jeff plant one end of his broom handle against the hall wall while the other end protruded into the bedroom. He rammed it forward and seconds later it was driven back into the wall.

"Move!" Brett dragged her towards the front door.

"What are you doing to my new house?" Brian stepped into the hallway.

"Too many of them. We have to run." Brett pulled the front door open.

"Here." Brian threw his keys at Brett when he turned. "Take mine."

"Thanks." Brett ran towards the new four-wheel-drive in the driveway, Kayla on his heels. He hit the central locking button and they jumped in.

"Hurry up. They're coming through the walls." Kayla pulled her seat belt on.

Brett started the vehicle, threw it into reverse and floored it. As soon as he hit the bitumen he braked and put the vehicle in drive. Kayla twisted in her seat to watch as the soul stalkers were left behind, running after them.

"Slow down, Brett. If we're pulled over for speeding they'll catch up to us. Not to mention you'd have to explain not having a licence." And how he happened to be alive.

Brett eased off the accelerator. "I should see if Jeff can get something done about that."

"Why don't we get through the next six nights first?"

Brett reached over and took hold of Kayla's hand. "Anywhere you wanted to go?"

She looked out the window. "I wouldn't have a clue. You do realise we ran out of there without my handbag and our jackets."

"Have you got your phone?"

"Yeah." Kayla took it from her pocket.

"Get your brother to meet us somewhere with what we need. Tell him to bring my wallet too."

"I wanted to ring and check on him anyway."

"Tell Brian if the wall was damaged by the broom handle I'll fix it tomorrow."

Chapter Twenty-Eight

Kayla rang her brother, relieved when he answered. She'd been worried he might have been caught. She arranged to meet him at the beach.

Brett waited until Kayla had hung up. "Don't you think it'll be too cold to go to the beach?"

Kayla shrugged. "I don't care. I've always loved the moon on the water. I don't know why. It looks cool. A bit like being on another planet. One with two moons."

Brett grinned. "And you reckon your brother's weird."

Kayla lightly punched him in the arm. "Hey."

"Don't distract the driver. I might have an accident."

"Yeah, like that was such a big distraction." Kayla couldn't help occasionally looking behind.

"You might try and get some sleep. That way you can drive later."

"It's barely dark and my heart's going faster than a race horse. What do you think the chances are I'll manage to sleep?"

"Slim?"

"I wouldn't even rate them that high." They fell silent. Kayla went back to glancing behind, checking for soul stalkers. Only cars followed.

When they reached the beach, she gratefully climbed out of the vehicle and stretched her legs. Brett joined her and pulled her close, an arm around her waist. She couldn't help shivering at the chilly breeze coming from the sea.

"Don't even think about saying I told you so," Kayla said between chattering teeth.

Brett pointed up the beach to where flames flickered. "What about seeing if we can share the warmth?"

"I thought fires weren't allowed on the beach."

Brett shrugged. "I guess there's no one around to complain. Not many people hang out at the beach this time of year. Too cold."

"I guess. But what about Jeff?"

Brett took the half dozen steps towards the sand and scooped up a handful. He used it to draw an arrow on the bonnet of the vehicle, pointing in the direction they planned to walk. The breeze swirled some of the sand around the edges, but left the shape intact. "If he doesn't notice that I'm sure he'll ring."

Kayla nodded and walked quietly beside Brett, holding his hand. She glanced towards the vehicle and wished there was more light to see where they were going. The houses and high-rises lining the beach were mostly in darkness. She supposed they had better things to do on a Sunday night than sit at home waiting for the workweek to start. She sighed.

Brett's fingers tightened on hers. "What's wrong?"

"Just thinking that there's better things to do on a Sunday night."

"Better things than walking along a deserted beach holding hands? And I thought girls were meant to be more romantic than boys."

Kayla reluctantly smiled. "You know I was talking about running from the grey men."

"That's a relief. And here I thought you had a problem with the company."

Kayla moved closer so their arms bumped. "Idiot." She smiled up at him.

Brett grinned. He turned to face the fire as they reached it. "Hey."

A slim girl with her dark hair drawn back in a

ponytail rose from the sand. "Hey." Her voice sounded cautious.

"Mind if we share your fire?"

She shrugged. "Suit yourself." She waited until Brett and Kayla sat before she dropped onto the sand, the fire between them.

"Do you live around here?" Kayla asked.

"Nah. I thought it'd be cool to visit." The girl shrugged.

"I'm Kayla and this is Brett."

"Gem."

Kayla grinned. "Nice to meet someone else with an unusual name."

Gem smiled. "It's not really. It's short for Gemma." She wrinkled her nose. "But you can see why I don't tell many people."

"I'm the opposite. I hate it when people shorten my name."

"Where are you from?" Brett asked.

Gem shrugged. "Nowhere near here. I wanted a complete change of scenery. You know how it is."

"So you decided to ditch school for a bit and go to the beach instead," Brett said.

Gem glared at him. "Who said I'm still at school? I look young for my age."

"How old are you?" Kayla asked.

"Eighteen," Gem said defensively.

"I would have put you at sixteen," Brett said.

"I told you I look young for my age. What do you want? To see a driver's licence?"

Brett shrugged. "Sure. Why not?"

"I don't have it on me. It's back at the hotel." Gem tensed like she was ready to run.

"Don't tease her, Brett. It's not like I can talk. How many days has it been since I turned up for classes?"

"I don't like being lied to. She could have said it wasn't our business. No reason to lie about it." He turned to see what had caught Gem's attention. "Looks like your brother's here with our jackets."

Gem jumped to her feet. "This place is getting too crowded."

"We aren't staying long. We'll leave you to your peace as soon as we've talked to my brother." Kayla rose to her feet.

Gem hovered near the fire. She glanced between it and Jeff. "Good."

Jeff dropped Brett's jacket and wallet in his lap and handed Kayla her jacket. He looked over to Gem. "Where'd you come from?" He turned to Kayla with a frown. "She doesn't look like a-"

"No." Kayla interrupted him, worried he'd say

ghost. "We were enjoying her fire while we waited for you. We didn't want to turn into ice blocks."

"You could have sat in the car with the heater on." Jeff slid a backpack off his shoulders and sat down in the sand in front of it.

"I thought you lot weren't staying." Gem continued to stand.

Kayla gestured towards Gem. "Gem." She waved towards her brother. "Jeff."

Jeff nodded in greeting as he took a thermos from the backpack. "Anyone for coffee?"

"I could just about kill for a cup," Brett said.

Kayla shrugged. "At least it'll warm me up."

Jeff turned to Gem. "I didn't bring a fourth cup, but you can use the lid of the thermos."

"Ah… I guess." Gem sat down again, a little further away from the fire. She buttoned up her denim jacket.

Jeff handed cups around. "And I have pizza. I can't promise it looks pretty. I folded it in two so I could get the box to fit." He grinned. "We could call it a pizza sandwich. Might be a new craze or something."

Gem's gaze followed the box as Jeff took it out of the backpack and unfolded the cardboard so he could open it. The pizza was on one side of the box only.

Jeff handed a doubled over slice to Gem. "Here."

"Thanks." Gem had hers eaten and was looking

wistfully at the empty box before the others were even halfway through theirs.

Jeff threw a packet of chips at Gem who caught them with a startled look. She handed them back. "I'm fine."

Jeff shrugged. "We're not going to miss them. Save you going home to get something to eat if you want to stay at the fire longer."

"I'm here on holiday," Gem said.

"Well, save you going back to wherever you're staying." Jeff held out the packet of chips again.

Gem slowly reached for them. "Thanks."

"How long are you sticking around here?" Brett asked.

Gem shrugged. "I haven't decided yet."

"Good plan. If you get bored with the place you just take off," Jeff said. "I've been thinking of doing some travelling after school finishes."

Kayla looked at her brother in surprise. "You have?"

"Yeah."

"When did you think of that?"

Jeff grinned. "Are you still fishing for info?"

Kayla smiled. "Do you blame me?"

Jeff shook his head. "Nah. But you've already

grilled me today. I'm not about to figure things out that quick."

Gem looked puzzled. "What's going on?"

"My sister's worried I'm going to try and kill myself again."

"Oh!" Gem eased back some more.

Jeff laughed. "You don't have to worry. I don't hurt other people. Just myself. Actually, hurt wouldn't be the correct word. I can't stand pain. But then dying doesn't have to be a painful process."

"Ahh... right." Gem didn't look reassured.

Kayla hit her brother's arm with the back of her hand. "Stop scaring the girl."

"I'm only telling the truth." Jeff popped the last piece of pizza into his mouth.

Kayla checked the time. "We should get back on the road." She turned to Jeff. "You'll understand if we don't want to stick around anywhere for long."

"Yeah. Give me a call to let me know you've made it through the night." Jeff handed over the backpack. "Your handbag is in it and a few other things I thought you might need."

"Thanks." Kayla got to her feet. She glanced towards Gem then back at her brother. "You didn't... the grey... ahh..."

Jeff grinned. "All safe and unharmed. They didn't

get close enough before they realised it'd be easier to go around rather than through me to get to you."

"You're on the run?" Gem demanded.

Brett rose to his feet and automatically put an arm around Kayla. "Something like that. Nice meeting you, Gem. We won't stick around and bring our troubles here. Thanks for sharing your fire."

Gem looked dazed. "Thanks for the pizza."

Kayla looked at her brother. "Are you coming?"

"I might enjoy this fire a little longer. If Gem doesn't mind." He turned towards her.

Gem shrugged. "Suit yourself."

Jeff handed over the three vials of the ashes Brett had given him earlier. "Take care."

Kayla nodded. "See you later." She wrapped her arm around Brett's waist as they turned in the direction of Brian's vehicle. Brett carried the backpack. As soon as they were in the vehicle, Kayla went back to searching for soul stalkers.

"Maybe we should have stayed on the beach longer. At least you didn't seem to be constantly looking over your shoulder then."

"There's something about a campfire I find relaxing."

"Do you want to go camping during the next school holidays?"

"Ahh…" Kayla looked uncertain.

Brett grinned. "A group of us. Not just you and me."

"Okay."

Brett reached out to take Kayla's hand. "You know I wouldn't pressure you into anything, don't you?"

Kayla smiled slightly. "You mightn't."

"What's that supposed to mean?"

Kayla rolled her eyes. "Figure it out because I'm not explaining it."

Brett laughed softly. "Are you trying to give me a compliment?"

"You would take it that way."

"It sounded like one to me."

Kayla turned to stare out the window so she could hide her grin from Brett. It was kind of a compliment, but she wasn't about to tell him so. She turned towards him when he swore.

Chapter Twenty-Nine

Kayla's jaw dropped when she saw the four soul stalkers on the road in front of them. Brett pressed harder on the accelerator, heading straight for them.

Kayla grabbed the handle attached to the roof and clung to it. "What are you doing? The car won't hurt them. They'll be in our laps."

"Shh." The vehicle sped towards them, Brett's knuckles white on the steering wheel.

"Brett! There's a car in the other lane." Kayla resisted the urge to close her eyes as Brett swerved around the soul stalkers at the last second. Then he was back in his lane, the car coming towards them honking repeatedly. A fist came out the window of the other car as it passed, a single finger raised. She twisted in her seat to see the soul stalkers running towards them again. "Why are you slowing down?"

"Because we're getting off the motorway. We don't know where the rest of them are."

Kayla did close her eyes as they took the next exit ramp too fast. She opened them when the vehicle slowed, continuing to grip the handle. One by one, she forced her fingers to relax so she could let go. She pressed her hand against her heart. "I wonder if that's how people feel right before they have a heart attack."

"You're too young for one."

"I don't know. It's possible." Kayla looked at Brett. Her eyes widened. "You enjoyed that."

"I wouldn't exactly say enjoyed."

"Then what would you say?"

"I wonder if your brother is still at the beach."

"Don't change the topic."

"Kayla–"

"My life flashed before my eyes and you're sitting over there grinning."

"I'm not grinning."

"Not now. But you were before."

Brett sighed. "I was relieved we beat their trap. So sue me."

"And that's all?" Kayla stared at him suspiciously.

"I guess it was a bit of a rush."

"See. You enjoyed it."

Brett laughed. "Fine. I enjoyed it. Can we drop the conversation?"

"Hmph." Kayla turned her head to gaze out the window.

"You're not going to sulk all night are you?"

"I don't sulk."

"Fine. Then how about you tell me what you're doing."

She continued to stare out the window, letting the silence drag out between them. "What happens when all this is over?"

"What do you mean?"

"The danger, the excitement," she emphasised the last word. "When you have your life back."

"I guess I'll see if I can get Jeff to speak to his friends about ID, get a job and look at going to uni next year. Have you got any idea which ones you're applying to?"

"And that's it?"

"What exactly are you trying to ask me, Kayla?"

"Us?"

Brett pulled over onto the side of the road.

Kayla glanced behind them. "What are you doing? The soul stalkers will catch up to us."

Brett faced her. "We have at least ten minutes before they do."

"Brett-"

He stopped her words with a kiss. When he pulled back from her, he smiled. "We are going camping during the September holidays. And since that's less than a month away, you better start thinking about where you'd like to go."

"I..." words failed her.

"You were the one who told me not to start anything with you because you were convenient. After all you've done to help me, do you think I'd do that to you?"

"No. But..." she shrugged.

"It's not gratitude either." He paused a moment. "You're the last person I'd expect to be insecure."

"I'm not normally." She glanced behind them. "I guess things have happened quick and we've been so focused on trying to stay alive."

Brett's hand went behind her head to cup it. "What I feel for you has nothing to do with the soul stalkers, dying, or anything else."

Kayla slowly smiled. "Good." She leaned forward to kiss him. Minutes later she pulled away from him. "Can we get out of here now? Before the soul stalkers catch up with us and how we feel about each other is no longer a concern."

Brett laughed. "Absolutely." He pulled back out onto the road. "So… camping?"

"What about it?"

"Did you have any other plans for the school holidays?"

Kayla turned towards the window again. She grinned. She considered making him wait for her answer, but decided that wasn't exactly fair. "Camping might be okay. Can Jeff and Red come along?"

"Yeah. I was thinking of inviting Brian and Jake."

"What about your other friends?"

"Nick and Trevor?"

"Yeah."

Brett shrugged. "I don't know. Maybe it'd be better if I didn't tell them."

"Would they tell everyone the truth?"

"No."

"Then what's the problem with telling them?" Kayla smiled when Brett didn't answer. "And I thought you wouldn't be insecure either."

Brett glanced towards her. "That's not the reason."

Kayla's smile became a grin. "Sure?"

Brett shook his head slowly. "Fine. I'll tell them."

"Good."

"Why?"

Kayla looked puzzled. "Huh?"

"Why is it good?"

"Because then you'll pretty much have your old life back. Weren't you worried you'd lose it?"

Brett smiled. "Yeah. Thanks."

They fell silent. After a while, Kayla began to feel sleepy, the hum of the engine making her yawn. She closed her eyes to rest them for a couple of minutes. Next thing she knew, she opened her eyes to find the four-wheel-drive stopped and the driver's seat empty. Fear struck her.

Straightening, she blinked, trying to focus on the view outside her window. Relief rushed through her when she saw Brett at the petrol bowser. Stumbling out she stretched, covering her mouth as she yawned again. She checked the time. Another couple of hours until daylight.

"Where are we?"

"A couple of hours from home."

Kayla smiled. "Good plan."

Brett tried to answer her smile with one of his own. The pump clicked and stopped. Brett hung the nozzle up and seemed to take a long time putting the fuel cap back on.

"What's wrong?"

"Nothing." Brett shut the fuel cap door.

Kayla grabbed Brett's arm when he turned away from her. "Don't give me that crap. You're just about growling at me."

"Let me pay for the fuel so we can get back on the road."

Kayla stared at him. She glanced over to the petrol station then back at Brett. "I'll pay for it." She let go of him and grabbed her handbag out of the vehicle.

"Wait here." Brett started to walk towards the door of the petrol station.

Kayla fell in beside him. "I'll put it on my credit card. My parents won't notice it amongst all the other purchases."

Brett stopped and turned to glare at her. "I told you to wait at the vehicle."

"Not unless you give me a good reason." She watched as his jaw clenched then he turned away and stalked off. She hurried after him, reaching the counter at the same time as he did. Her credit card was in her hand before Brett had a chance to take out his wallet.

"Quiet night out there?" The young man behind the counter took the card.

"Yeah." Kayla glanced at Brett who kept looking behind him.

"Credit?"

Kayla nodded in answer and keyed in her pin number, taking the receipt the man handed her when the transaction went through. "Thanks."

"Bye."

Brett walked silently beside her, his gaze darting around. He relaxed slightly the moment they were in the vehicle.

Kayla continued to watch him as he started the engine and drove off. Comprehension dawned on her in a rush. "Is that the same kind of service station where you were shot?"

Brett glanced towards her, but said nothing.

"Brett–"

"Drop it. Okay?"

"Yes or no?"

"Then you'll drop it?"

Kayla hesitated. She guessed some information was better than none. "Yeah."

"Yes."

She reached out and rested her hand on his thigh. "Do you want me to drive yet?"

"No."

"Okay."

They fell silent again. Half an hour later, Brett pulled off the road and turned the engine off. He faced Kayla.

When he continued to look at her, she spoke. "What?"

"Sorry."

"For?"

"Snapping at you earlier."

Kayla shrugged. "I understand."

Brett took her hand. "Thanks."

"Is that why you pulled over?"

Brett smiled. "Nah. Starting to find it difficult to stay awake. Do you want to drive?"

Kayla grinned. "How hard was it for you to admit that?"

Brett opened the door instead of answering. Kayla laughed as she climbed over to the driver's seat. She started the engine and pulled out onto the road the moment Brett had buckled up.

"We'll be more organised tonight. Music for the stereo for starters," Brett said.

"And more food. I was going to grab something to eat when I paid for the fuel, but you made me forget all about it."

"Good."

"Oh, yeah. Sorry."

"There wasn't another one open. And I couldn't go much further without running out of fuel. I know it wasn't the servo. It could have been anywhere. I…" he shrugged. "Those servos bring it back."

"It's okay. We'll make sure we use one of the other franchises in future. Now, weren't you going to have a sleep?"

"Probably not. I doubt I could sleep even though my eyes feel like they have a beach load of sand in them."

"Have you been camping before?"

"What?"

Kayla grinned. "I'm trying to get your mind on more pleasant subjects."

Brett laughed. "Okay. Thanks."

"Well?"

"Well what?"

Kayla rolled her eyes. "Camping. Have you been before?"

"Yeah."

"And?"

"What?"

She let a sound of frustration escape. "Details. You don't expect me to drag every comment out of you, do you?"

"Details. Okay. But don't complain if I bore you senseless."

"Don't bore me to sleep and you'll be all right.

You wouldn't want me to have an accident." She grinned when he slowly shook his head. Her grin settled into a smile as she listened to him talk, asking the occasional question, her gaze on the road ahead.

Chapter Thirty

Kayla was woken by Brett jerking awake, gasping. She reached over to him, his face and chest streaked with sweat. "It was only a dream." She tightened her arms around him when he pulled her close.

"No it wasn't."

"I know it happened, but this time it was a dream. You're here. Beside me. Alive."

Brett exhaled heavily. "For now."

"We're never going to those service stations again. You've had nightmares ever since."

"What, no suggestions I talk to a shrink like you keep telling Jeff?"

Kayla laughed and pulled back so she could look into his eyes. "And what would you tell them? I keep dreaming about my death and I don't want to go through it again. And by the way, I'm meant to be dead and was a ghost for a while, but I figured out a way to deal with it. Yeah, right. I wonder how many pills they'd be filling you with for that story."

Brett smiled slightly. "So I take it no shrink?"

"Definitely no shrink. You'll have to make do with talking to me or your friends."

"So you can tell me I'm being an idiot."

"I wouldn't say that."

"Yeah, but I feel like one when I have a nightmare that wakes me, like a little kid afraid of the dark."

Kayla pressed herself close. "Then how about I take your mind off your worries instead?"

Brett grinned. "I like that idea much better." His lips met hers.

When they finally broke apart, Kayla stared at him. "What were we talking about earlier?"

"I wouldn't have a clue. Want to help me forget some more things?"

Kayla glanced at the time and groaned. "I had planned to get in at least another two hours sleep."

"You expect me to sleep now?"

Kayla grinned. "Well-" she giggled when he pounced on her and she ended up beneath him. When they surfaced from the kiss she tried to pull him back to her.

Brett shook his head. "Cold shower time or I won't be getting out of this bed any time soon."

Kayla reluctantly let him get off the bed. She sighed. "How am I meant to go back to sleep?"

Brett smiled. "Glad I'm not the only one suffering."

Kayla threw a pillow at his retreating back and smiled when he laughed. She plumped up her pillow and lay back down, her arms behind her head. Two more nights to get through and then they'd be safe. And they'd have the weekend without being hunted. She wondered if there was a party planned for Saturday night. She guessed Red would know. She made a mental note to ring her later.

Red had been extremely understanding over how preoccupied she'd been. She couldn't ask for a better friend. Brett's pillow landed on her face and she pushed it away, turning to see Jeff striding towards her.

"What are you doing here? School's not out yet."

Jeff shrugged. "I had permission to leave early since you came home from hospital today."

"Huh?"

Jeff laughed. "Hope you don't do that Monday when everyone asks how you are."

"Oh. Right. Pneumonia."

Jeff clapped his hands lightly together a couple of times. "Yay. We have brain action."

Kayla threw the pillow at her brother. "Go away. I didn't get enough sleep."

He caught the pillow and grinned as he slowly stalked forward the last few paces.

"You wouldn't."

Jeff laughed evilly.

"You'll regret it." She sat up and swung her legs over the side of the bed.

He answered her with another laugh and swung the pillow. Kayla grabbed the other pillow as she dodged and swung back at him. She managed to get in an equal amount of blows.

"Well, lass, I thought ye more mature than that."

Kayla turned to face Douglas, still grinning. The pillow hung limply at her side. "Morning."

Douglas grinned back at her. "Afternoon."

Kayla glanced at her watch again. "Oh, yes, of course. Those soul stalkers are playing havoc with my sleeping pattern. And sense of time."

"Two more nights left." Jeff threw the pillow on the bed.

"And the nights are getting shorter." Kayla hit her brother with her pillow before she threw it on the bed. She grinned at the daggered look he sent her.

"It wouldn't be that much of a difference, would it?" Jeff asked.

"Since we started I think the nights are about an hour shorter."

"That can't be right." Jeff frowned.

"Check it online if you want. That's where we get the rising and setting times for each day."

"Marvellous thing the internet," Douglas said. "The things ye have these days. I spent nearly twenty-four hours on it without a break and there were more sites to look at from the search I did."

"That's easily done," Jeff said. "What were you searching?"

Kayla smiled as Jeff and Douglas talked about different sites they'd been on. She slipped from the room and headed for the kitchen, pausing in the doorway. The room was empty. Out of habit she glanced around for a glimmer of grey, then forced herself to stop mid-glance. With a sigh of annoyance she entered the kitchen and helped herself to cereal. It might be the afternoon, but it was her breakfast time.

"Any left?" Brett pointed to the box of cereal on the table.

Her mouth full, she nodded, glad to have company. Running from the grey men was making her jumpy. She watched as he grabbed a bowl and spoon and joined her at the table. Her gaze took in his damp hair and jeans sitting low on his hips. Her gaze travelled up his chest when his jeans were hidden below the table. When he stopped moving, she looked at his face to find he watched her.

She grinned. "What?"

"I think I should be saying that."

"Just admiring the view. I'll have to thank Brian for getting a house with central heating." Her gaze dropped to his bare chest again. Laughter from the doorway had her turning towards it. "Hey, Brian." She grinned.

"Should I keep that in mind when the electricity bill arrives and charge you for a share of it?"

"Nice try. I bet you'd have it on anyway."

Brian turned the kettle on and leaned against the kitchen bench. "Yeah. Douglas has a tendency to chill a room if I don't. I always thought it was the house I lived in. Old timber house, drafts, you know."

Kayla nodded. "I've noticed the chill in the air is worse when they're annoyed."

"Which Douglas regularly is." Brian grabbed out a coffee mug and held it up. "Anyone?"

"Definitely," Brett said.

Brian put a coffee in front of Brett as soon as he had made them and slipped into a chair at the end of the table. "How was it last night?"

"I think there were eighteen of them. A bit hard

to be certain since we try not to stick around in one place for long and at sunset they appear where they were at sunrise," Kayla said.

"Any cloaked ones?" Brian took a sip from his mug.

"Nah. We've been keeping an eye out for them. Maybe they know we get rid of them or something." Kayla put her dish and spoon in the sink. She grabbed the ice cream container off the top of the fridge.

Brian winced when she sat back at the table. "Do you have to do that right now?"

"I want to know how much is left." Kayla put the last of the ashes in the vials. She stared at the four small containers. "Let's hope we don't need to use them." She handed two over to Brett.

He looked at the contents before he slipped them in his pockets. "Nearly over."

Brian's gaze was drawn to the ice cream container. "You know I could almost hate Jake."

"Why?" Kayla frowned.

"Because I haven't been able to eat ice cream ever since I've seen what that container holds. I'll probably never be able to think about glitter the same way again either."

Kayla grinned. "Aw, does that mean there's none in the freezer?"

"There is, but I can't bring myself to eat it."

"I don't have a problem with ice cream containers." Kayla rose from the table and took the ice cream out. She opened it and peered inside. "Mmm, double choc-chip." She turned to Brett with a grin. "Want to share it with me?" At his shrug she grabbed out two spoons.

"You pair are sick." Brian rose from the table with a shake of his head.

"Let's go laze in bed and eat it." At Brett's nod, she headed for the bedroom, pausing in the doorway. "Are you going to be in here all afternoon?"

Douglas and Jeff turned to look at her. Jeff looked at where she'd stood earlier and then back at the doorway. He grinned sheepishly as he stepped forward. "I didn't know you'd left the room." He snagged one of the spoons and helped himself to some of the ice cream.

Brett grabbed the other spoon and looked at Kayla. "You can have the spoon your brother slobbered over."

"Thanks," Kayla said dryly as she took the spoon off her brother. She headed for the bed and flopped down on it, frowning as she looked at Jeff. "You didn't say why you're here. Just gave me some crap about me getting home from hospital."

Brett frowned. "Hospital."

"My excuse for ditching school. Remember?"

Brett scooped up some ice cream. "Vaguely."

"I'm glad I'm not the only one who forgot." She turned back to Jeff. "Well?"

"I'm coming with you tonight. If they corner you, there's no way you can fight off… ahh, how many is it now?"

"At least eighteen." Kayla dipped her spoon into the ice cream that was rapidly melting around the edges.

"Eighteen!" Jeff stared at her.

Kayla shrugged. "Maybe more." She licked the stray ice cream off her spoon then dipped it back in the container.

"The pair of you can't face them on your own. Red said she'd help too."

"How does she think she can help? You have to be able to see them to do anything about them." Kayla frowned. "Can we discuss this later? I'm trying to enjoy my ice cream and you're ruining the moment."

"Hair."

"Huh?" Kayla stared at her brother, her spoon halfway to her mouth.

Brett shoved the container under the spoon. "Watch it. You'll drip it on the bed."

Kayla popped the ice cream in her mouth. "You

want to explain a little better? Lack of sleep is my excuse for my brain not working well today. What's yours?" She raised an eyebrow as she stared at her brother.

"Our hair. I bet it works the same as it does for ghosts. It's worth a go anyway. And one more person to help fight them off, if we're cornered, would be good."

"I don't know." Kayla spoke her words slowly. "I don't want to risk anyone else."

"I'm coming tonight. Even if I have to follow you."

Kayla recognised the determined look on her brother's face. Probably because she regularly wore the same look. It wasn't often that she saw it on her brother. "Okay. But no one else. We have two more nights to get through. Let's try not to involve too many people."

Jeff nodded and checked the time on his phone. "I'll be back in about an hour. I have a few things to get together."

"Like what?"

"Food."

Kayla rolled her eyes. "Don't tell me. Let me guess. Tim Tams and a can of whipped cream." She shook her head when Jeff grinned. "I don't know how you can eat them together. Talk about too much of a good thing."

Jeff shrugged. "Don't leave without me or I'll go out looking for you."

"We'll wait." Kayla glanced down at the ice cream container the moment her brother left the room. "Brett! You're a pig." She pulled the container away from him. "The rest is mine."

Chapter Thirty-One

Kayla changed the music on the stereo and put the USB stick into the coin purse she stored them in. "Even with a million songs you need to change them when you're on the road this many hours."

Jeff yawned. "I thought it'd be more interesting than this."

"Ah… I hate to tell you, but I think it's about to get interesting." Brett slowed the vehicle.

Kayla looked ahead to see a line of soul stalkers stretched across the two lanes of the bridge they were on. "Reverse back." She twisted in her seat and swore. At the start of the bridge soul stalkers fell into place. "Now what?"

"We could launch it over the side and hope we land on the river bank," Jeff suggested.

Kayla shot her brother a look. "This isn't an action movie."

"For some reason I think Brian mightn't like that plan either." Brett stopped the vehicle.

"They're standing there. Why aren't they coming for us?" Kayla looked first at the ones ahead of them then the ones behind.

"What about jumping into the water and letting the current take us downstream." Jeff wound down the window, peering outside. "A pity it isn't a full moon. We need more light."

Kayla took out two vials of the ashes, turning them in her hands. They had to do something.

"They won't help. The wind will blow it back in our face," Brett said softly.

"I'm not giving up. There has to be a way out of this." She shook the vials, listening to the sound of the contents moving up and down. "I don't suppose you have glue in your backpack." She twisted in her seat to look at her brother.

Jeff shook his head. "Not much left other than whipped cream."

Kayla stared at him for a moment then slowly smiled. "Give it here." She held out her hand.

Jeff rummaged in his backpack. "You know drowning your sorrows in comfort food isn't exactly going to help you figure out what to do next."

Kayla squirted whipped cream into her palm and

let the can fall onto her lap. "I'm not going to eat it." She tipped the contents of one of the vials into the whipped cream and smeared it across her palm. She held her hand up and grinned when it stayed in place.

"Nice." Jeff grinned back at her.

"They're starting to close in. Guess they got sick of waiting." Brett gestured to the soul stalkers in front of them.

Kayla handed the can of whipped cream and the other vial to Jeff. She held out her other hand. "Load it up."

Jeff looked at his fingers once he'd finished. "I'm certainly not going to lick them clean."

Kayla giggled. "Tell me about it."

"Are you ready?" Brett demanded.

"Yep." She looked at her brother. "Sit behind Brett." She faced forward, her hands held out, aimed at the two soul stalkers who would end up in the front of the vehicle. "Floor it. We don't want to give them time to figure out what we're doing."

"Don't miss." Jeff shifted over on the back seat.

"Not likely," Kayla muttered. She looked straight ahead, barely daring to blink. She gritted her teeth when her hands impacted with two soul stalkers, half in the dash. Their eyes seemed to grow large, their mouths silently gaped and their bodies seemed to shudder. Kayla pulled her hands back and they slipped downward and through the floor of the vehicle like it didn't exist. She turned to look out the back, staring at the two shapes lying on the highway.

"I think they were trying to scream." Jeff grabbed tissues from the box sitting on the floor in the back and handed them to Kayla.

"They became solid when I touched them." Kayla shuddered. "While they were stuck inside the car."

"That couldn't have been comfortable." Brett glanced in the rear view mirror. "You do know we have to cross that bridge again later to get back to the city."

"No way." Kayla cleaned the mess off her hands and grabbed more tissues to get off the last smears of whipped cream.

"One of them wore a cloak," Jeff said quietly.

Kayla blinked, thinking back to what she'd done. "I didn't register that. I was too busy trying to keep my hands in the correct place. And then when they became solid..." She shuddered. "Let's not go there. And let's completely forget about turning around and seeing if Brian was right."

"What if we give it a couple of hours and then head back. They should still be unconscious and we can do it then," Jeff suggested.

"I vote no." Kayla turned to Brett. "What do you think?"

"I'm guessing we're not the only ones who've been through this. We should find out for the ones who go through this after us. Someone found out all this info for us. And I bet it wasn't through reading a book. They would have dealt with it while they hadn't a clue about what they were doing."

"Irene only gave us the information when we asked the right questions."

"She did give it to us. As she said, this isn't meant to be easy. I'm cheating death."

"Brett." She placed her hand on his arm. "It's dangerous and we're so close to it being over."

"We have to do this." Brett glanced at her.

She looked away, dropping her hand. "I feel like saying, screw everyone else. But, I guess you're right. I just don't like it."

"None of us like it." Brett took her hand and rested it on his thigh, his hand on hers.

"Remember we only have two vials left." Kayla looked at his hand, almost completely covering hers.

Brett lightly squeezed her hand before he let it go. He wriggled in his seat, pulled the vials from his pocket and handed them to Kayla. "You're the first priority."

"No." She tried to give them back to him.

Brett closed her hand around them. "Stop distracting the driver."

Kayla felt like her heart missed a beat as she stared at the vials. She faced Brett. "I…" She closed her eyes for a second. "Brett, I-"

"Shh. One and a half nights left to get through. We'll make it." Brett brushed his knuckles across her cheek. "I promise."

"You can't pr-"

He interrupted her. "I promise."

Kayla fell silent. She wanted to believe him. She desperately wanted to know he spoke the truth. Even Jeff was quiet. She looked over her shoulder, meeting her brother's gaze. He reached out and rested his hand on her shoulder for a moment. She smiled weakly before she faced forward. Her brother had it right. There wasn't much to be said in a situation like this. She stared at the dotted line of the highway, listening to the music. What else could she do? Think about removing the cloak from the soul stalker? No way. She wasn't going to think about it until she absolutely had to. She closed her eyes and tried to focus on the music playing on the stereo. It didn't help.

Time to think about removing the cloak came far too quickly. Kayla stood on the deserted highway next to Brett. Jeff stayed near the vehicle and scanned their surroundings.

Brett tugged on his industrial gloves. "Standing around isn't going to make this job any easier."

Kayla sighed and pulled her gloves on. "How are we going to do this?"

"I'll lift him enough for you to get the cloak over his head." Brett knelt beside the soul stalker.

Kayla pulled the cloak up and over the soul stalker's head the moment Brett sat him up. The grey man dissolved. Brett didn't have time to let him go.

Brett rubbed at his hands. "That wasn't a pleasant feeling."

"Don't tell me. I don't think I could handle knowing what it felt like." She eyed the other soul stalker.

Brett moved over to him and lifted him enough to get his head off the ground. "Quickly. Before any others turn up."

Kayla stepped behind the body and slipped the cloak over the head. It took Kayla a few seconds to register the grey man was awake and had his hands wrapped around Brett's throat. "Let go." Grabbing hold of his wrists she tried to drag him away from Brett. She couldn't budge him and he wasn't interested in her. Letting go of him, she tried to pull the cloak over his head. He flung out an arm, knocking her to the ground.

Jeff ran towards them. Before he reached the soul stalker Brett struggled with, another came out of the scrub at the side of the road and barrelled into him. He landed on the bitumen, trying to get to his feet.

"Jeff. Get away from here." Kayla struggled to her feet, torn between helping her brother and Brett. She made another grab at the cloak. The grey man turned towards her, releasing Brett who swayed on his feet.

Brett made a grab for the cloak too. The grey man didn't know which direction to turn in. The moment the cloak was removed, he dissolved.

"Get in the vehicle."

Kayla ignored Brett's raspy command and ran to her brother. "Keep the cloak away from him. He has nothing to protect himself from it."

Brett swore. "Use a vial." He ran towards the vehicle with the cloak.

Kayla punched the soul stalker in the side. "No. We only have two left." She punched him again and this time he turned on her, letting Jeff go. "Run!"

"Get in the vehicle. The pair of you." Brett raced towards them, a wooden broom handle aimed at the soul stalker. He knocked him backwards. The three of them ran to the four-wheel-drive and jumped in.

Brett threw it into gear and pressed hard on the accelerator. He swerved as the soul stalker threw himself at the vehicle.

"Where's the cloak?" Kayla glanced around.

"In the boot. Brian put a solid plastic toolbox in there in case we came across one." Brett stared at the end of the bridge, speeding up as it came closer.

Chapter Thirty-Two

Kayla exhaled as they reached the end of the bridge, feeling slightly light headed from holding her breath as they crossed it. "Do you think it's too late to ring Irene?"

"What for?" Brett rubbed his throat, his voice a little raspy.

Kayla frowned at him, staring at the grey colour of his skin. "Are you okay?"

Brett nodded. "I will be. Just a sore throat."

"Tell me about it." Jeff rubbed his own throat. "They certainly know where to grab you so you can't easily escape them."

Kayla took out her phone. "I'm going to ring her."

"Why?" Brett glanced at her.

"To tell her about the cloak and ask about Jeff." Kayla dialled the number.

"Why do you need to ask her anything about me?" Jeff demanded.

Kayla glared at him. "You were meant to stay back." She put the phone on speaker mode.

"Hello." Irene sounded half asleep.

"The cloak works. The problem is they wake up when you put it on them."

"Kayla?"

"Yeah."

"Hmm. That isn't very good. Maybe someone should stand by with remains to sprinkle on them again."

Kayla hesitated. "I've also got a question."

"Lovely. Questioning is good."

"One of them touched Jeff."

"Was it the one you took the cloak off?"

Kayla was silent a moment before she said softly, "No. What does that mean for him?"

"Not very good. Although not terribly bad either. If you all get through tomorrow night, and the rest of tonight of course, then he'll have one soul stalker following him. Maybe you could use the cloak to get rid of it."

"How are we meant to tell which one it is?" Kayla glared at the phone.

"Hmm, yes. That is a dilemma. I'm sure you'll

figure it out. Or he'll have sixty days of one soul stalker after him. The sixty days start from the first moment the soul stalker touched him. That goes the same for any other soul stalker he might come in contact with."

"Is there anything he can use for protection? Like we've used the ashes," Kayla asked.

"Nails or hair can be burned and flung at the soul stalker. It does the same as the remains."

"Great," Jeff muttered. "Do you know what burning hair smells like?"

"Of course, dear. Now was there anything else?"

"Would that work for Brett?" Kayla asked.

"It is different for the recently deceased. Only their remains will work." Irene paused. "Was that all?"

Kayla glanced at Brett and Jeff who both shook their heads. "Yes."

"Goodnight then."

Kayla sighed. "I always think of something when she's gone."

"What did you want to ask her?"

"Would the ashes of anyone do? Or the burnt hair or nails of anyone."

Brett glanced at her. "How would you get hold of the ashes of someone else?"

"I could manage," Jeff said.

Kayla shook her head, a smile twisting her lips. "Not another one of your odd friends."

Jeff shrugged. "They obviously come in handy at times."

Kayla didn't know how to answer his comment so she remained silent and looked out the window. The trees and shrubs were little more than a flicker of dark shadows as they drove along the quiet stretch of highway. Brett reached out and took hold of her hand. She faced him when he lightly squeezed it. When his gaze momentarily met hers, she smiled slightly. They had to get through this.

She slid her left hand down the side of her seat and lowered it slightly so she could get more comfortable. Continuing to face Brett, she let her eyes close, drifting off to sleep. It seemed like only minutes before she felt something brush her cheek, waking her up.

She reluctantly opened her eyes to find Brett's face close to hers, early morning light creeping into the vehicle and chasing most of the shadows away. Brett pressed his lips against her forehead before he leaned back in his seat. Kayla glanced in the back seat and noticed her brother wasn't in the vehicle. She frowned.

"He went inside to get something to eat."

Kayla checked out the window and realised they were at Brian's home. She guessed it was Brett's home too since he had a room there. She yawned, unable to keep her eyes open while she did. When she opened them, she saw Brett get out of the vehicle. She watched him walk around to her door and open it.

He grinned at her. "It looks like I should get you into bed."

Kayla laughed softly. "That sounds like a lame pick up line to me."

Brett reached out and took hold of her hand, his other going to her waist to help pull her towards him. "It seems to be working."

"Not quite the way it sounds."

"I can live in hope." He winked at her as her feet hit the ground.

Kayla smothered another yawn. "I take it there were no more problems?"

Brett shook his head. "One more night left to get through."

She groaned. "It's going to be the worst. Everything hinges on surviving it. And look what happened tonight."

"No more bridges. And no directions where there's only one way back."

"There's other ways they can stop us. What about heavy traffic?"

"We'll make sure we head out of the city before sunset. Jeff and I were talking about different roads to take while you were snoring."

Kayla hit Brett's shoulder with her open palm. "I don't snore."

Brett grinned. "Are you sure? It's not like you know what you do in your sleep."

"Yep. I do." She grinned back at him. "Red and I recorded ourselves for several nights a few years ago. Grade nine I think it was." She frowned as she tried to recall. "Anyway, neither of us snore, but I do mumble in my sleep sometimes." Kayla couldn't stop yet another yawn.

"Come on. Let's get you inside. You look half asleep."

Kayla leaned against Brett as they went inside. "I feel it. I'm going to sleep for a week once this is over."

Brett stopped at his bedroom door. "Do you want something to eat before you crash?"

Kayla shook her head. "Nah. I'd probably fall asleep in it. I can see the headlines. Girl drowns in cereal."

"I'm going to grab something quick to eat. I'll be back soon."

Kayla nodded. Brett smiled at her before he pulled

her close and kissed her. She stared after him, leaning against the door frame as he disappeared down the hallway. She sighed. Moving seemed like such an effort. She finally managed to stagger to the bathroom before returning to the bedroom and collapsing on the bed. Seconds later she was asleep.

Kayla sat up suddenly and looked around. The room was dim, the heavy curtain drawn at the window. She breathed a sigh of relief when she saw Brett beside her, his arm flung out so it hung over the edge of the bed. She smiled as she looked at him. His other hand was behind his head. She resisted the urge to reach out and check he was real. Even as a ghost, he'd felt real to her. Shifting her pillow to a better position she lay down, her gaze remaining on Brett. She was tired, but dreaded falling asleep to relive the moments when the soul stalkers had been stretched across the road in front of and behind them.

As if feeling her gaze on him, Brett's eyes blinked open. He smiled when he saw she watched him. "What's the time?" His voice sounded slightly raspy.

Kayla's gaze was drawn to his neck. "You're bruised."

Brett gingerly touched the colourful marks. "Doesn't surprise me." He turned her wrist to look at her watch and groaned. "It would have been nice to sleep until a couple of hours before sunset."

"Tell me about it. I wish this day was over and we were watching tomorrow's sunrise."

"Try and get a bit more sleep. We've barely had six hours."

"I did sleep a little in the car."

"How restful was that?"

Kayla sat up and shrugged. She sat cross-legged on the bed to stare down at him. She smiled slightly. "There's one thing I will miss when the sun rises tomorrow morning."

"And what's that?"

"Being with you nearly twenty-four seven."

Brett slowly smiled. "There's a solution to that problem."

"I'm not moving in with you."

"Why not?"

Kayla shook her head. "Because I'm seventeen."

"So? I'm only a year older than you."

"I haven't finished high school."

"What about staying here weekends?"

"Maybe."

"Is your maybe leaning more to yes or more to no?"

Kayla rolled her eyes. "I'm going to have a

shower." She started to crawl over the top of Brett so she could get off the bed, which was against the wall.

His hands captured her when she was above him. A smile curved his lips. "Do you want to go somewhere Saturday night and celebrate?"

"Ask me at sunrise."

Brett laughed softly. "Deal." He lifted his head off his pillow so his lips could graze hers. "I'll ask you again at twelve past six."

"I'll have an answer for you then." Kayla hopped off the bed, grabbed her overnight bag from the corner of the room and headed for the bathroom.

She felt better after showering. More alert. She dropped her bag in Brett's room. The bed was empty. She tracked him down in the kitchen where he sat at the table with his hands wrapped around a coffee mug. When she placed cereal, milk and sugar on the table, Brett snagged her hand before she could move away.

"Grab me a bowl and spoon too? Please?"

Kayla nodded. She collected the bowls and spoons and sat across the table from him. The meal was silent, her mind full of questions, problems and worries. As soon as her bowl was empty, she took the ice cream container off the fridge and returned to the table with it. She stared at the closed lid, her fingers resting on the edge, silently reading the words Jake had written on it two months ago. 'Sorry about the container. It was all I could find on short notice.'

"Do you want me to open it?"

She met Brett's gaze, holding it for a moment. Shaking her head, she returned her gaze to the container, slowly opening it up and placing the lid beside it on the table. The container was empty. Panic raced through her and she shook out the four vials. A couple of specks of glitter fell out, joining the sprinkle of glitter on the bottom of the container. After placing the vials on the lid, along with the drinking glass she'd used as a scoop, she slightly shook the container. The glitter shifted across the bottom. Nothing had changed. She placed the container on the table and met Brett's gaze.

"It's empty, isn't it?" His voice was low, his gaze steady.

Chapter Thirty-Three

Kayla nodded in answer to Brett's question, fear keeping her silent. Nothing. Absolutely nothing. She didn't know what they'd do if they ran into soul stalkers they couldn't avoid. She took a shuddering breath and dropped her gaze to the container. There was only glitter. Not a single bit of pulverised bone was left.

Brett reached across the table and took Kayla's hand in his, his thumb rubbing back and forth. "We expected that."

"I know." Her words were barely a whisper, but at least she'd finally managed to say something.

"Jeff and I thought the beach would be a good place to see the sun set."

"Why?"

"Because it's the opposite direction to where we were last night."

Kayla nodded. "I guess that makes sense."

Brett grinned. "Here I am asking you to watch a sunset at the beach with me and all you can ask is why. Where's your sense of romance?"

"It's a little grey right now."

Brett laughed. "Do you think sunrise might resuscitate it?"

Kayla closed her eyes and, continuing to hold Brett's hand, rested her other elbow on the table so she could lower her head onto her hand, the heel of her palm pressed against her forehead. How were they going to survive long enough to see the sun rise. When Brett squeezed her hand, she raised her head to meet his gaze. "How can you laugh?"

"By not thinking too hard about it. I know they're coming." He rose from the table and walked around to stand behind her, his hands dropping onto her shoulders. "We have wooden broom handles, industrial gloves and a cloak. I know the odds are a bit on the slim side. But we have less than thirteen hours to get through. I'm sure we could sit down and figure out how many hours we've survived if we wanted to, but I know it's been more than thirteen hours. I have to believe we can do this."

"Why do you?"

Brett pulled out the chair beside her and sat so he

could look her in the eye. "Because the alternative isn't acceptable."

"But–"

Brett pressed a finger to her lips. "We will survive the night. All three of us."

Kayla nodded her head. What else could she do? She desperately wanted him to be correct. She let him pull her against him, her head pressed to his chest, his heartbeat loud. It raced as quickly as hers seemed to, fear keeping it from slowing its pace. "Okay, but I need to ring Irene."

"If it's about those questions you had this morning, I've already talked to her."

Kayla pulled away enough to see his face. Nothing she saw in his expression looked like it had been good news. "There's nothing else we can do, is there?"

Brett shook his head. "But they were good questions."

"Yeah, just no help," Kayla muttered.

"You know there's a bedroom."

Remaining in Brett's arms, Kayla faced Brian, forcing herself to grin and lighten her tone. "And deprive you of something to complain about?"

"I'm sure I'd survive." He headed for the kettle and filled it before he turned it on. He gestured towards Brett's mug. "Another one?"

Brett shrugged and smiled wryly. "It's not like I have to worry about getting to sleep any time soon."

Brian grabbed the mug and frowned at the ice cream container on the table. "Do you need to have that there?"

"It's empty," Kayla said softly.

"Oh." Brian stared at the container for a moment. "Sorry."

"We'll manage," Brett said.

"You better." Brian grabbed a coffee mug from the cupboard. "I'd be extremely annoyed if I had to go to another funeral for you so soon after the first one."

"I have a feeling there won't be anything left if the soul stalkers manage to win."

Kayla looked at the glass that sat on the ice cream container lid. She turned to Brian. "Do you have a hammer?"

With a nod, he opened the second kitchen drawer and rummaged around in it. "What do you need a hammer for?" He handed it over.

Kayla couldn't help grinning. "Interesting place to keep a hammer. We keep knives, spatulas, tongs and egg flips in our second kitchen drawer."

"So do I." Brian leaned back against the kitchen bench. "Why the hammer?"

Kayla laid the glass on its side in the ice cream

container. "Because there's no way I ever want to drink out of this glass." She lightly hit it with the hammer and watched as it broke.

Brian shuddered. "Thank god for that. I wouldn't want to drink out of it either."

Kayla laughed as she put the lid on the container. "Well, neither of us have to worry about it now."

Brian made coffee and brought two mugs over to the table. He handed Brett his mug before he sat down. He looked at Brett and Kayla for a moment. "Do you need any extra bodies? Jeff said it's possible I'd be able to see them. We tested his hair theory out with Douglas. I can see him clearly as long as I hold a strand.

"No," Kayla and Brett said together. They turned their heads and smiled at each other.

"What if-"

Brett shook his head as he spoke. "I'm not risking your life too. And what if you ended up being touched by one of them and had to survive sixty days without losing your soul? I can tell you that sixty days is a bloody long time. I didn't realise how much time."

"Is there anything I can help with?" Brian took a sip of his coffee.

"No. If there was, I know I could ask you."

Brian nodded. "Of course you can."

Brett grinned. "As long as it doesn't involve money."

Brian nodded solemnly. "Wouldn't want to cause me to have an early heart attack from parting with my cash."

Kayla couldn't resist smiling at them. She knew Brian had given Brett money, so he wasn't penniless, while he was trying to get his life back.

Jeff stepped into the kitchen, yawned and rubbed his bare chest. He stopped when he saw them gathered around the table. "Anything important or can I return to my half zombie state for a while?"

"Zombie away," Kayla said.

Jeff grunted in answer and grabbed himself a bowl and spoon. He looked between the box of cereal already on the table and the cupboard door that hid the rest of the boxes. With a shrug he sat at the table and grabbed the one in front of him.

Kayla rose to her feet. "I'm going to give Red a call."

Brett nodded, snagged her around the waist and rose to stand beside her. He kissed her before he let her go. "I'll get organised for tonight. Any food requests?"

"Anything but whipped cream. If Brian finds the

thought of ice cream difficult to stomach, I can't think about whipped cream without shuddering."

"I don't want to know that story. Don't take all of life's pleasures away from me." Brian tipped the last mouthful of coffee into the sink before he put his mug in the dishwasher.

Kayla grinned, tempted to tell him. She laughed when Brett turned her towards the doorway and gave her a light push. "Spoilsport."

"Be nice," Brett said.

Still smiling, she retreated to Brett's bedroom and took out her phone. She reached Red's message bank, having forgotten all about school. "Is there anything interesting happening Saturday night? Text me if there's something worth going to." She disconnected and lay back on the bed, staring at the ceiling, her mind whirling with worries.

After wallowing for a few minutes she forced herself to get off the bed and track Brett down, helping him put everything into Brian's vehicle that they thought they might need. When they were packed and ready to go, they decided to leave early.

The drive to the beach was quiet. Even the music playing on the stereo didn't help break the silence. Kayla kept glancing towards Brett and Jeff. But what could she say? Sunset loomed in all of their minds. No one wanted to talk about it. It'd come soon enough without dwelling on it. She went back to looking out the window.

People seemed to be everywhere. Carloads they passed, other's that passed them. Crowded shopping centres with gaping doors that barely had a chance to close with the steady stream entering and exiting them. People who seemed to be so immersed in their lives that those around them made no impact. Kayla sighed. She guessed it was an unfair assumption. Knowing how many soul stalkers would be tracking them after sunset was unsettling. Three against more than twenty were not good odds. More than twenty. For all she knew there could be a hundred of them. It wasn't like they'd been able to count them with how spread out they were.

Kayla tried to empty her mind. But every time she thought she had, something would cause a stray thought to enter and she'd circle back to the coming night. She was relieved when they reached the beach and she could get out and stroll along the sand, her hand in Brett's. Jeff walked ahead of them by a couple of metres.

The beach had a handful of people on it, mostly mothers with young children building sandcastles and a handful of surfers in wetsuits, willing to face any weather conditions. The further along the beach they walked, the less people seemed to be about. But mostly, people were gathering their gear and leaving the beach before night fell and the temperature with it.

"Jeff." Kayla waited until he faced her, walking backwards. "Why didn't you leave your backpack in the car?"

Jeff patted the item. "It's my security blanket."

"Yeah right. What's in there?"

Jeff turned to walk forward when they reached his side. "Shortened broom handles, industrial gloves and the cloak, which is in a plastic container for its insulating properties."

"Oh." Kayla's eyes were drawn to the backpack. "It's not dark yet."

Jeff shrugged. "Guess we're paranoid." He glanced towards Brett.

Kayla turned to Brett. "It's your idea too?"

"I thought we should get on the road half an hour after sunset. But I wanted to be prepared. The others won't reach here in time, but that doesn't mean there aren't any in the area," Brett said.

"Yeah, I guess." Kayla couldn't stop herself from glancing at the backpack again. It was like a neon sign that screamed 'here I am', at a deafening decibel.

They fell into silence again, the waves and wind a harmonious melody in the background. None of them spoke until Brett checked the time on Kayla's watch.

He let go of her wrist. "I guess we should turn around and head back to the vehicle in a few minutes. I don't want to leave any later than half an hour after sunset."

Chapter Thirty-Four

Kayla glanced over to where the sun was barely visible in the sky. "Why is it when you want time to go slow it speeds up? And I bet it'll drag once sunset arrives."

Jeff grinned. "Kayla's principle of time. The rate at which time passes is in direct proportion to the dread or anticipation of a situation."

Kayla shoved her brother so he stumbled towards the waves. She stuck her tongue out at him and dashed around to the other side of Brett.

"You think that'll stop me?" Jeff feinted in front of Brett to step behind him at the last second.

Kayla laughed as she jumped out of his reach. His fingers grazed her arm. "Too slow." When Jeff stopped and looked behind her, she shook her head. "You'll have to do better than that if you want to distract me."

"Hey, Gem." Jeff waved to a point behind Kayla.

She started to turn, then hesitated. She looked at Brett, who laughed. He nodded and she turned to see Gem walk down the beach towards them, returning Jeff's wave.

Jeff stepped close to Kayla and with a grin, whispered, "I wouldn't sleep tonight if I was you."

"I have a long memory. Keep that in mind when you retaliate." Kayla smiled sweetly. She faced Gem as she reached them. "Hey. Guess you're not sick of the place yet."

Gem shrugged. "I guess not. I didn't expect to see you lot around here again." She glanced towards Jeff's backpack. "What are you carting this time? An unfolded pizza? That's a much larger backpack than the last one."

"I have Tim Tams in there." Jeff's hand reached up to the strap. "Do you want any?"

"Ah… well." Gem's eyes were focused on the backpack.

Jeff swung the backpack to the sand and rummaged around inside it. He held out the unopened packet. "Help yourself."

"Ah… thanks." Gem opened the packet and had nearly finished a biscuit before she offered them around.

Brett took one. "We better keep heading back to the vehicle."

Kayla checked the time. She frowned. They'd be back at Brian's four-wheel-drive later than they'd planned. She glanced towards the sun that had disappeared behind the buildings overlooking the beach, a glow left in the sky to show where it had gone. She shivered. "I didn't realise how late it was."

"It sounds like your principle of time has struck again," Jeff said.

Gem looked puzzled. "What?"

Jeff laughed. "Kayla was complaining about how time drags when you're doing something you hate but flies when you don't want it to."

Gem nodded. "I know. I hate that too. Time evaporates when you're having fun."

"I have a tendency to lose track of time when I get on my computer," Jeff said.

"Me too. What sort of computer have you got?"

Kayla smiled at Brett and tugged him towards the waves, speeding up a little.

He leaned his head towards her ear when they'd put a few metres between them and their companions. "Are you trying to set him up?"

Kayla's smile became a grin. "No harm in giving it a go."

Brett laughed softly. "A runaway who tends to lie. Hmm, remind me to never let you try and set up my mates."

"We don't know for certain," Kayla protested.

"If she's older than sixteen I'd be amazed."

"Okay, so she exaggerated her age a bit. Are you trying to tell me you haven't done that?"

"Not at all. But only in a good cause."

"Like what? Getting into a nightclub while underage?"

Brett grinned. "I refuse to answer the question in case it incriminates me."

Kayla rolled her eyes. "See, told you. She isn't too bad."

"What about the fact she's run away from home?"

"I don't know. But at least he's talking to her. The last couple of months, well mostly the last month, he's been more sociable. It's great to see. He wouldn't have struck up a conversation with a stranger before. And especially not a girl. Unless it was online. And with some of the odd people he knows online, anyone would be an improvement."

Brett grabbed Kayla's arm, stopping. She looked in the direction he stared and her heart stopped for what felt like an entire minute. As one they turned towards Jeff who walked towards them, talking. He stopped when he realised they headed to him instead of away from him.

Looking past them, he swore, swinging his backpack to the ground and squatting in front of it.

Gem glanced around the empty beach. "What's wrong?"

Jeff handed industrial gloves and wooden sticks to Brett and Kayla. He swore again as he looked between Gem and the soul stalker that ran towards them on the beach. He rose to his feet and pulled a strand of hair from his head. "Hold this."

"What?" Gem took a step back.

"Take it. Then look over there and tell me what you see." He gestured towards the soul stalker with the stick.

Gem backed up further. "You're mad. All of you."

"Forget her. We don't have time for this." Kayla strode towards the soul stalker, Brett at her side.

Jeff slung the backpack into place and walked with them. The three of them attacked the soul stalker at the same time. Gem screamed. None of them paid her any attention.

"Restrain him. I'll use the cloak." Kayla dropped back and waited until Jeff had one of the soul stalker's arms and Brett the other. She grabbed the container from the backpack and made sure it didn't touch any of her flesh. She slipped it over the soul stalker's head and he burst from their grip. "Hold him!"

"You try. It's like fighting a bull." Brett threw himself at the grey man.

The soul stalker managed to fling Brett from him and attacked Jeff who went down under the onslaught. Gem screamed again and ran towards them. Jeff managed to get a couple of blows in with his stick and gain his feet. Kayla attacked the soul stalker from behind, but was knocked aside. Brett used his stick to help himself up.

"No!" Jeff rammed the soul stalker with his stick and spun to push Gem away. "Don't touch him." He spun back and attacked the soul stalker at the same time as Brett did.

Kayla staggered to her feet and launched herself at the soul stalker's back. She grabbed the cloak as Brett struggled with the soul stalker who had his hands wrapped around Jeff's throat. Gem lay sprawled on the beach where she'd landed when Jeff had pushed her away from the soul stalker. Her mouth hung open and she stared at them.

Kayla managed to get the cloak over the soul stalker's head and off again, almost in one move, and they all collapsed in a heap as he dissolved into nothingness. She flung the cloak away as they crashed onto the sand, afraid it would touch the flesh of one of them. They lay on the damp, cold sand, panting.

Kayla was the first one able to speak. "Please tell me it's nearly sunrise."

"Nope, but I think it's time to get out of here." Brett staggered to his feet and reached down to give Kayla a hand up.

Jeff stumbled over to Gem, who was picking herself up. "Sorry. Are you okay?"

Gem pointed to where the grey man had been. "There was… he kept… he wasn't… what was…" she took a deep breath. "He kept vanishing."

Jeff nodded as he put the gloves and stick in his backpack. "Yeah. It's because you can't see them."

"Them?" Gem looked around wildly.

Kayla handed her gloves and stick to Jeff to put away. "There's none of them here now. But we have to go so we can stay ahead of them."

"What was he?" Gem's words were little more than a whisper.

"A soul stalker." Brett put the cloak back in the container before he removed his gloves. "They go after those who've cheated death."

"You mean like, clinically dead for a few minutes," Gem said.

Brett shook his head. "Dead. Never meant to live again type of dead."

Gem frowned. "But…" She glanced around at them. "That's impossible."

Brett shrugged. "Impossibilities are obviously my speciality." He looked up the beach. "We have to run."

Jeff swung the backpack on. "Will you be okay?"

"But… I want… you can't… what's going on?" Gem's voice went from lost and wavering to demanding.

"You have my number. Give me a call and I might be able to tell you some of it. But we have to go before any more of them turn up," Jeff said.

Gem put a hand on Jeff's arm when he tried to move away. "Why did you want to give me a strand of your hair?"

"So you could see him." He flinched when Gem reached out and pulled a strand of hair out. "Hey!"

"I'll call you tomorrow." Gem turned and strode away.

The trip back to the vehicle was done in complete silence and quicker than the earlier walk had been. When they reached the four-wheel-drive, they dusted most of the sand off themselves before they got in.

Kayla glanced at the grains of sand that landed on the seat when she turned her head. "I don't think Brian's going to be happy with the sand in his car. My hair feels like half the beach is in it."

Brett headed for the road. "Sorry. I thought we'd be safe here for a bit."

"At least there was only one of them," Kayla said.

Brett reached for her hand. "But still–"

"I'm not sure how romantic it was, but I feel better after getting rid of him." Kayla glanced towards Brett with a grin.

He laughed. "Good." He looked in the rear view mirror at Jeff. "How are you holding up?"

"Actually pretty good."

Kayla turned in her seat to look at her brother. "Not bad for your first fight. And what was the move you did when you pushed Gem out of the way? I think you've been watching too many action movies or something."

"Probably too many Playstation games." Jeff returned her grin. "I surprised myself."

When Brett swore, they both looked out the windscreen. They echoed him. Brett turned down a side street.

"Should we turn off the main road?" Kayla glanced behind them.

"I spent a couple of hours pouring over maps this morning before I headed to bed." Brett turned another corner.

"Surely you didn't memorise all of them." Kayla stared at him.

Brett shook his head. "Nah. Just which ones to avoid." He reached out and turned on the GPS and hit the home option.

"Cheat." Kayla grinned at him.

"It'll get us back on track when I'm ready." Brett ignored the directions the GPS gave when he made his next turn.

Kayla turned towards her brother again. "Have you got any more sweet food? Something with plenty of sugar." She was starting to feel shaky now the adrenaline was wearing off from the fight.

"Chocolate cake, chocolate, more Tim Tams, lollies and sachets of sugar."

Kayla rolled her eyes at the last option. "Cake. Please." She took the thick slice Jeff handed her and felt a little better after she'd eaten. She licked her fingers clean. "No wonder Mum and Dad didn't take us on any road trips when we were younger."

Jeff took a water bottle out of the backpack and opened it. "What do you mean?"

"I keep having the urge to ask if we're there yet.

I want to get out of the car. I'm sick of being in it."
Kayla sighed. "Nearly enough to make me want to
walk everywhere for the rest of the year."

"That I can't believe." Jeff offered her the water
bottle.

"Nearly. I didn't say definitely." Kayla took the
bottle and had a mouthful before she handed it back.

"Considering we don't exactly have a destination
in mind, I hope you don't start asking if we're there
yet," Brett said.

Chapter Thirty-Five

Before Kayla could reply to Brett's comment, her phone rang. She smiled when she saw Red's name on the display. "Hey."

"Karl is having a party Saturday night."

Kayla laughed. "Not quite the destination I was thinking of."

Red joined in the laughter. "Now why would that be?"

"Any others?"

"Yeah. A few of them. You want the list or the best choice?"

"Best choice."

"Remember you asked for best choice."

"Spit it out, Red."

"Samantha."

"You've got to be kidding!"

"Hey. Don't burst my eardrums. It's open invite

and you did want best choice. Come on. At least if you turn up with Brett and everyone knows he's your boyfriend they can't keep spreading the rumours about you."

Kayla sighed. "I guess."

"I told you it was best choice."

"Yeah, right." Kayla rolled her eyes even though Red couldn't see.

"So how's your night been so far?"

"Terrible."

"You want to tell me about it?"

"Nah. I'd rather not think about it at all." Kayla yelped as Brett took a corner fast. She turned to him. "Watch it. Are you trying to kill us?"

"Nope. Trying to avoid that."

Kayla checked out the rear window. She swore when she saw seven soul stalkers round the corner at a run, chasing them. She swore again when she remembered Red was on the phone. As soon as she put the phone to her ear she pulled it away again.

"Kayla! What's happening?"

"Now who's trying to burst eardrums? We had soul stalkers after us."

"You want to pick me up so I can give you a hand?"

"Nah. But I'd better go. I think I'm going to need both hands to hold on with the way Brett's driving."

"Text me regularly and let me know you're alive?"

"Yeah. I'll see you tomorrow, Red."

"You better. And no letting those soul stalkers get you. Hide behind your brother for a change."

Kayla grinned. "I pretty much have already."

"Great. About time."

"Okay. See you later."

Red became serious. "Stay safe."

Kayla stared at the phone when she hung up, resting it on her lap. She looked over at Brett when his hand covered hers that continued to clutch the phone.

"Everything okay?"

Kayla nodded. "Yeah."

Brett put his hand back on the steering wheel. "Then hold on."

Kayla was glad of the warning. She grabbed the handle attached to the roof and clung tightly as they took another corner fast, barely avoiding running into several soul stalkers. "What are they doing around here? Are they the same ones? How many are there?"

Her words were met with silence. No one could answer her questions. Several more turns and they were back on the motorway. Kayla glanced behind and saw two soul stalkers following. The road ahead looked clear. Even the traffic wasn't too heavy.

They were forced off the motorway about an hour later. Brett avoided the worst of the busier streets in the city centre and headed back towards the motorway and north. The traffic leaving the city was reasonably light and by nine o'clock they almost had the road to themselves.

"Are we headed anywhere in particular?" Kayla turned to Brett.

"Not really. Just trying to avoid our persistent stalkers."

"I feel like we're the cattle and they're the Border Collies. You don't think they're trying to herd us anywhere in particular?"

Brett glanced towards Kayla. He was silent a few seconds before he replied. "I hope to hell not. The only thing they're likely to herd us towards is a soul stalker's convention."

"Isn't that a pleasant thought," Jeff said.

Kayla looked up the road, the headlights leaving too much in darkness. "Should we be heading in this direction? What if they're trying to get us to go this way?"

"If we stay in the city I'm likely to be pulled over

for reckless driving. It's not like anyone else can see the soul stalkers," Brett said. "Unless they're in physical contact with us and I'm not about to let them come that close if I can help it."

Kayla sighed. "I guess not." Glancing out the window, she saw two soul stalkers running towards the road. She turned to look out the rear window and saw them lope along the edge of the other side of the road. The trees in the nature strip soon hid them.

"At least we have less than nine hours left to get through." Jeff rummaged in the backpack. "Anyone hungry?"

Kayla shook her head. The thought of food made her feel ill. Or maybe it was the thought of another nine hours. "No, thanks." Earlier she'd been thrilled they'd destroyed one of the soul stalkers, now she felt hunted again. She wasn't meant to be the one hunted. She always fought. Always. Even when the odds didn't look like they were in her favour she didn't run. Until now. She straightened in her seat. Why should she let them force her to run?

"What are you planning?" Jeff broke a piece of chocolate off the block he held and popped it in his mouth.

She faced Jeff. "What makes you think I'm planning anything?"

"I recognise that look."

She grinned at her brother. "I think we should fight back."

Jeff nearly choked on his chocolate. "Are you mad?"

"No. I'm not. If there's one or two of them, I bet we could deal with them. We have the cloak. What do you think, Brett?"

"I don't know. It sounds risky."

"Really? Riskier than running towards who knows what?"

Silence followed Kayla's words. Jeff was the first to break it. "Maybe if there's only one."

"We managed one without a drama earlier. And two last night. We should have put the cloak on the other one instead of running," Kayla said.

"I guess we could," Brett said slowly, a frown forming.

"Good. Then let's go back and deal with those last two we saw," Kayla said firmly.

"Kayla–"

"Come on Brett. Do you want to leave all of them running around the countryside? What if they end up cornering us? The less about, the better for us."

Brett glanced around. The highway was empty. Slowing, he drove through the lightly treed ditch separating both sides of the road. "I can't believe I'm listening to you." He shook his head.

Kayla grinned. "That's because I make sense."

"It's sleep deprivation. Odd things start to make sense when you're suffering from it," Jeff said.

Kayla ignored her brother. "We should come up with a plan."

Brett nodded. "We'll distract and you use the cloak, Kayla. I doubt you'd be able to hold one steady for long enough. They're fairly strong."

"And to think I complained about all the swimming and hours in the gym," Jeff muttered.

Brett pulled over to the side of the road when he spotted the two soul stalkers running towards them. The headlights lit up the road ahead, making the soul stalkers easy to see. "If more than two show up, we're out of here. I'll leave the vehicle running."

They got out of the vehicle and Jeff handed out gloves and sticks and dropped the backpack on the ground. He raced forward with Brett to attack the soul stalkers. Kayla took the container from the backpack and removed the cloak.

She ran towards the battle. It was nothing like a schoolyard fight. Kayla winced as she saw the soul stalker send Jeff flying into a tree on the side of the road. He barely paused for breath before he threw himself at the grey man again. He tackled him to the ground and Kayla ran forward, reaching them as the soul stalker flipped Jeff off him and wrapped his hands around his neck.

Kayla bunched the cloak up so it became a circle of fabric. Pushing the cloak over his head, she ripped it back off before the soul stalker had time to register what she'd done. She grinned as he dissolved and Jeff groaned. Not having time to stand around and check her brother, she turned to see how Brett was doing. He was pinned against a tree, sagging as his body turned grey.

"No!" Kayla ran towards him and slipped the cloak over the second soul stalker. She wasn't as quick this time. The soul stalker turned on her and, with a swipe of his arm, sent her to the ground. Kayla jumped to her feet while Jeff, swinging his stick, got between her and the grey man who'd returned his attention to Brett. He'd slid to the ground when the grey man had released him to deal with Kayla and leaned against the tree.

Kayla's heart was in her throat when she lunged for the soul stalker. Her fingers tangled in the cloak. The soul stalker turned on her as she tried to lift it over his head, his arms reached for her. Jeff dropped his stick and grabbed hold of the soul stalker from behind, locking his arms around the grey man.

She struggled to get the cloak over his head as he bucked and twisted. Jeff crashed into her as soon as the cloak was off and the soul stalker dissolved. The cloak ended up on the ground half a metre from them. She looked towards Brett who stumbled to his feet. He used his stick to support himself. His eyes widened as he looked behind Kayla and Jeff.

"Run!" Brett's shout came out as a hoarse croak.

Kayla glanced behind and yelped. She scooped up the cloak as she ran towards the vehicle, shoved it in the container and grabbed the backpack. They were in the vehicle within seconds.

Brett drove through the middle of the nature strip to the other side of the highway and headed north. "No way we can take on five of them."

Kayla watched as the soul stalkers fell behind, her heart continuing to race. "At least we took out two." She rubbed her shoulder she'd landed on. It was probably bruised.

"I feel like I went a round with a professional wrestler." Jeff shoved his gloves in the backpack. "I hate pain."

Brett placed Kayla's hand on the steering wheel before taking his gloves off and tossing them to Jeff.

He put one hand back on the wheel and took Kayla's hand in his other. "I don't think I can do that again too soon. I feel like I barely have any energy left."

"Should you be driving?" Kayla's fingers tightened on Brett's.

"I wouldn't have a clue." Brett glanced in the rear view mirror. "Got any chocolate left?"

Jeff took the block out and broke off a row. "Sugar helps." He grinned and broke off some chocolate for himself.

"You worried me when you stayed on the ground for so long." Kayla checked Brett over.

Brett nodded. "You weren't the only one worried."

Kayla looked at her watch. "Almost ten." She sighed. "Why does time have to move so slowly? I was sure it would be nearly eleven."

"That bloody principle of yours," Jeff said.

"Yeah, right." Kayla fell silent, looking out the window. Every now and then she caught a glimpse of a shadow with a grey gleam to it. The skin of soul stalkers seemed to almost glow in the moonlight. At least it made it easier to keep track of them. She glanced at her watch again and groaned.

"What?" Jeff asked.

"One past ten. Time is creeping." Kayla shook her arm then checked her watch again. She supposed it worked properly. She closed her eyes in the hope she could fall asleep. She didn't manage to keep them closed for a minute before she was scanning the night for a glimmer of grey. She spotted another one, off to her right, running across an open paddock towards the road. He wouldn't make it before they passed him, but it was yet another one to chase after them. She couldn't imagine how many followed them now. It wasn't like they were easy to tell apart.

Chapter Thirty-Six

Kayla sent a text to Red letting her know they were alive. She glared at the time on the display. She checked her watch. Identical time. Three minutes had passed. She shook her head. Impossible. It had to be later than that. The time changed as she watched it. Five past ten. She closed her eyes and forced them to stay shut. Five past ten. How were they going to get through the rest of the night? This had to be the slowest night yet.

"We'll have to get fuel soon," Brett said.

Kayla opened her eyes. "But they're everywhere. How are we meant to do that?"

"Only put twenty in. I'll run in and pay while you put the fuel in. We can stop again up the road," Jeff said.

Brett nodded. "If we don't get time to put the full

twenty in at least we'll have paid if we have to make a run for it."

The moment they pulled up at the service station, Jeff hurried in to pay for the fuel. Brett removed the fuel cap while Kayla had the nozzle ready to put straight in. She'd already pressed the buttons to put twenty dollars worth of fuel in the vehicle. Jeff was in the four-wheel-drive before they'd finished refuelling.

"You get in the car. I can get in quicker than you since the fuel cap is on the passenger side," Kayla said.

Brett looked around. "Everything's still clear."

"I think you spoke too soon." Jeff gestured to their left.

Brett swore and headed for the driver's seat. Kayla watched the numbers turn on the petrol bowser. She almost yelled in relief when they reached twenty. Shoving the nozzle back on the bowser, she quickly replaced the fuel cap. She slammed the fuel door shut and jumped into the passenger seat as Brett started the four-wheel-drive. They were on the road before she was buckled, her breath held until the soul stalkers were a glimmer in the distance.

Jeff leaned back in his seat. "That was close."

"We need to stop for more fuel. We don't want to run low," Brett said.

Kayla groaned. "Can we at least wait until my heart rate is back to normal?"

"Yeah. We should give it about half an hour before we stop. We don't want to risk them catching up too soon." Brett glanced in the rear view mirror. "Although there'll probably be others about."

"How comforting of you to point that out." Kayla rolled her eyes. "Not."

They fell silent as they kept watch for soul stalkers, the music still on. Kayla couldn't help checking her watch every few minutes and was almost relieved when they pulled up at another service station. At least it meant they'd got through another thirty minutes. They did the same as before, with Jeff going in to pay for the fuel. This time he had to wait for change, but it didn't take him much longer than the first time. He was in the vehicle before they'd refuelled, on the back seat and glancing in every direction. They pulled out onto the road before any grey men arrived.

Kayla pressed her hand against her heart. "I swear I'm going to end up having a heart attack before sunrise."

Brett reached out and took her hand away from her chest. "No you won't. I'd hate to have to go through this again so we could bring you back."

"I don't think I could go through this knowing what has to be done."

Brett's fingers tightened on hers. "Yes you could."

Kayla fell silent. She didn't have as much faith in her ability to face the soul stalkers again. Especially once the circle of the ashes had reduced in size. And they didn't know exactly what it meant if the soul stalkers got hold of them. Would they join them? She didn't know. But she guessed Irene might.

Brett glanced at Kayla as she took out her phone. "Who are you ringing at this hour? It's ten to eleven."

"Finally," Jeff muttered. "I was beginning to think the next hour would never get close."

Kayla ignored them and rang Irene. She put it on speaker mode.

"Hello?"

"Irene, it's Kayla."

"How are you doing, dear? Not much longer now."

"We're hanging in there. But I've thought of another question."

"Lovely. Go ahead and ask, dear."

"What happens if the soul stalkers get one of us? I mean, I know you said they're after souls, but what exactly does that mean?"

"That you spend eternity as a wandering soul.

Unable to communicate with anyone. Unable to move on. Neither here, nor in the next place. Stuck in a limbo, continually searching for another soul to take your place so you can move on."

"Oh." Kayla couldn't think of another word to say. She remembered the soul stalkers who'd been caught in the dash and had looked like they'd been screaming. There'd been no sound.

"Was there anything else, dear?"

"Ah… no."

"Good luck then." Irene disconnected.

Kayla stared at the phone. She wished she hadn't asked. She didn't want to know. Not now. Limbo. She reached for Brett, placing her hand on his thigh. She'd risked him ending up in limbo because she didn't like to run. She felt sick at the thought of how grey he'd been. How close had he been to limbo? What if they hadn't been able to get the cloak off the soul stalker? It had been a stupid plan. She closed her eyes and tried not to think of how colourless Brett had been earlier. It was impossible. The image was engraved in her mind.

Brett's hand closed over hers. "You okay?"

"I'm not sure." Her voice was barely a whisper.

"Do you think she meant all of us?" Jeff asked.

"Yeah. I think she did," Kayla said softly.

"Oh." Jeff fell silent for a moment. "Limbo doesn't sound so great. I thought I'd die. Not end up in that limbo thing."

"Yeah, me too," Kayla said.

"Then I guess we have to make sure we see sunrise," Jeff said.

"I hope so." There was a waver in her voice that she couldn't control.

"We will." Brett forced his lips into a smile. "You and I have a date Saturday night."

Kayla couldn't meet his gaze. She glanced at her watch and nearly screamed when she saw the time. "It's eleven. It's finally eleven."

"About time," Jeff said.

Brett nodded slightly.

Kayla's eyes blurred and she closed them. Crying wouldn't help anything. Only make Brett feel worse about having involved her. She took a deep, shuddering breath and forced her mind to empty. When that didn't work, she began to count to one hundred, focusing all her thoughts on the numbers. Somewhere along the way, she lost track of what she was doing and drifted into a half waking state, her head filled with grey men chasing after her. And as fast as she ran, they ran faster until they surrounded her. Hundreds of them. Then thousands.

Brett swore and Kayla was startled awake. She blinked as she glanced around. "What are you doing?"

Brett turned off the highway. "They were stretched out ahead of us."

"How convenient they were just after an exit." Thinking of their discussion about feeling like the soul stalkers were herding them, Kayla glanced behind to see eight soul stalkers chasing them. When Brett swore again, she faced forward and echoed him. A line of soul stalkers blocked the road ahead of them. "What are we meant to do now?"

"Kayla, if I don't make–"

Kayla faced her brother. "Don't even think it. We will make it."

"There's nearly a dozen of them." Jeff waved forward.

Brett put the vehicle in four-wheel-drive. "And we're about to go bush." He headed for the side of the road.

Kayla squealed and grabbed for the roof handle. She closed her eyes but when a bump jarred her, they opened again. "I don't suppose anyone knows how to pray."

Jeff laughed. "I don't think it counts if you're not religious."

"I think I'm about to suddenly find religion," Kayla muttered as she gripped the handle, her feet planted firmly in the foot well as she tried to hold on. She screamed as Brett managed to avoid another soul stalker.

"I hope to hell that's not a cop car headed this way," Brett muttered.

"Great. That'd be just what we need." Kayla peered anxiously through the windscreen as a ute raced past on the road they were headed towards. She sighed in relief as it ignored them, gritting her teeth as they hit the bitumen again. "Where are we?"

Brett shrugged. "I didn't notice a sign when we turned off. I was too busy trying to avoid soul stalkers."

Kayla checked the time. "It's four thirty-seven." She grinned. "We've nearly made it."

"Glad to know one of us at least managed to sleep," Jeff said.

"I can't believe I did." Kayla glanced around. The town they drove through seemed empty. Streetlights fell on parked cars, the occasional dog barked, but everything else was quiet and still. She caught a glimpse of a soul stalker down an otherwise empty street. Her heart stuttered in her chest. She forced her gaze forward. "Shouldn't we try to get back out to the highway?"

"If I knew where we were I could put something in the navigator," Brett said.

"Why not put home in it?" Kayla asked.

"Because I don't want to go back the way we came." Brett glanced in the rear view mirror.

Jeff laughed. "So put Cooktown in. It doesn't mean we have to go there, but at least it'll mean we're headed north."

Kayla turned the navigator on. "Couldn't you think of anywhere further north?"

"Sure. How about Cape York?" Jeff rummaged in the backpack. "Anyone hungry?"

Kayla finished entering the new destination in the navigator. "No. Not unless you want me to throw up." Her stomach was filled with dread and worry. Nothing else would fit. She looked ahead and groaned. "Oh no." Two soul stalkers stood on the road ahead of them as they left the town behind.

Brett smiled. "There's only two of them. We've been dodging pairs all night. It's when there's half a dozen or more it gets difficult."

Kayla caught a glimpse of something on the road as Brett started to head around them. She got as far as pointing and opening her mouth before it was too late. She grabbed the roof handle again and swallowed the scream that wanted to escape. She didn't want to distract Brett who fought to keep the vehicle in a straight line after the front tyre blew.

Jeff took out the gloves and sticks, handing a set to Kayla. She pulled on the gloves and jumped out of the vehicle as they came to a stop on the side of the road. Her eyes momentarily closed as she saw where they had pulled up.

Jeff joined her. "How appropriate." He stared at the cemetery with a wry grin before he turned back to Brett. "We'll hold them off while you change the tyre."

Brett nodded once as he opened the rear door. He paused and met Kayla's gaze. "Be careful."

Kayla nodded before she faced the two soul stalkers running towards them. She ran forward, Jeff at her side. She briefly pulled the glove down to check her watch. "An hour and a quarter left. We can do this." She rammed her stick into the stomach of the soul stalker in front of her. She was too busy fighting off the soul stalker to check how her brother fared. But she guessed he was doing well since she caught his constant movement out of the corner of her eye.

"Pity we can't use the cloak." Jeff's voice came in broken breaths as he continued to fight.

"Pity we have no ashes left." Kayla swung the stick at the soul stalker's head and grinned as he landed on the ground. She glanced towards the vehicle. "I reckon we might be able to."

"Kayla. No!"

She ignored her brother and sprinted towards Brett. Grabbing the cloak from the container, she turned in time to attack the soul stalker who'd followed her.

"What do you think you're doing?" Brett laid the flat tyre on the ground and stood up. He swung the wheel brace at the soul stalker and swore as his knees buckled.

The soul stalker went down and Kayla dropped the stick to put the bundled up cloak over his head and rip it off again. She turned to Brett who staggered to his feet. "You okay?"

Brett nodded as he glanced at his grey hands and arms. "Metal obviously isn't a good idea."

Kayla grinned. "At least it hurt him more than it did you. I've gotta help Jeff." She grabbed her stick and, with the cloak in her other hand, raced towards her brother. She checked the time again. An hour. One hour till sunrise. Hope bloomed inside her. They were going to make it. She waded into the fight, her stick cracking the soul stalker across the head.

He went down and she instantly had the bundled up cloak over his head and off before he managed to move.

Jeff leaned against his stick. "You're getting quicker with that move."

Kayla grinned wearily. "Pity I couldn't practice it. We'd have got rid of a lot more of them." When Jeff's eyes widen and his stick wobbled, Kayla frowned. "What?" When her brother didn't answer, she turned to face the cemetery. Her jaw dropped.

"Soul stalker convention." Jeff's voice was shaky.

Chapter Thirty-Seven

Kayla swore. She wrapped the thin cloak around her forearm. It seemed safe enough with how high the glove covered. She tucked one end in to hold it in place. "We have to get back to Brett and warn him." Without waiting for her brother, she raced to the four-wheel-drive. She heard Jeff's footsteps pounding the ground behind her. "Brett!" She waved back the way she'd come as soon as she had his attention.

Brett rose to his feet and swore. "Get the flat in the vehicle." He returned to putting wheel nuts back on.

Jeff bent to help him. "We're not going to get out of here in time."

Brett used the wheel brace to tighten the nuts Jeff had put on. "You will. I'll hold them here."

Kayla stared at Brett, his words taking seconds to sink in. When Jeff nodded in agreement she gasped. "No. I'm not leaving you here."

Brett handed the wheel brace to Jeff and rose to face Kayla. He took the stick from her hands. "I'm glad I met you." He smiled faintly before he kissed her.

She pulled away from him. "No." She tried to grab him as he raced past her. Brett was surrounded within seconds.

"Kayla. Get in the vehicle."

She ignored her brother and grabbed a stick from the backpack. She shook her brother off when he grabbed her by the shoulder and spun her to face him. "I'm not leaving." She checked her watch. "Forty minutes left. You can run if you want."

"Don't be stupid."

She met her brother's gaze. "If it was me in there, would you run?"

"It's not. Let's get out of here. We risk limbo."

She ignored her brother, pulling out of his grip to run across the few metres separating her from the spot where she'd last seen Brett. She could hear the sound of wood hitting flesh. Or whatever soul stalkers were made of.

Several soul stalkers turned to face her and she grinned at them, no humour in her expression. "Come on then." She swung at them, slamming one into another two and knocking them over. They came at her too quickly for her to have a chance to use the cloak. But if she got the opportunity, they better look out.

Jeff joined her, his stick whirling as he lashed out at the closest soul stalker. "You're an idiot."

"So what's that make you?"

He laughed. "Certifiably crazy."

The path cleared enough so they could see Brett. Kayla gestured towards him with her stick. "We should be at his side. He can't protect his back."

Jeff nodded and swung about him. They slowly advanced. Kayla ignored the glare Brett gave her when he saw them. Then a soul stalker was between them and he was forced to focus his attention on the fight. Kayla felt her arms tire. She didn't have a chance to check the time. She hoped it was going faster than it had earlier. All she could do was block the soul stalkers. She gasped when she saw Brett go down under a combined attack.

Ignoring the burn in her arms, she laid about her harder than ever with the stick. Then she was standing over Brett. Four soul stalkers gripped him. She swung at one while Jeff tried to hold the rest of them off. She couldn't get them away from him.

Kayla took a deep breath and dropped her stick. She hoped Jeff could keep the rest of them back. She unwrapped the cloak from her forearm in a quick move and bundled it up so it became a circle of fabric again. She slipped it over the head of one of the soul stalkers and back off before he had a chance to move. She dispatched a second one the same way before the other two released Brett and turned on her. A gulp was all she could manage as she stumbled back. One of them went down as Brett tangled his legs through the soul stalker's feet. Kayla wrapped the cloak around her forearm again, tucking one end in to hold it in place. She ducked under the soul stalker's attack, grabbed her stick off the ground and spun to face him. She wasn't in time. His blow knocked her to the ground.

Jeff jumped in front of the soul stalker before he could reach Kayla. She stumbled to her feet and attacked one that was going for her brother's back.

Brett staggered to his feet, leaning on his stick, his skin almost completely grey. He straightened, striking out at a nearby soul stalker. "Go."

"No." Kayla moved closer to him. Then the three of them were back to back, the circle around them closing in.

"Kayla, please." Brett begged as the soul stalkers stopped fighting them to make an unbroken circle. They slowly moved in, a tight wall of grey.

Kayla backed up until she could feel the warmth of Brett against her. "I love both of you. Obviously not the same." She grinned. "I wonder if we'll be in limbo together."

Brett swore. "Don't you ever listen?"

Jeff laughed. "Not if it's something she doesn't want to hear. Are you scared, Kayla?"

She shook her head. "Not now."

"Me neither. It's strange." Jeff lowered his stick. "I can see one with a cloak."

"He's all yours, bro."

Brett shook his head. "You're mad. The two of you."

Kayla nodded. "Yep. But surprisingly calm. Let's see how many we can take with us." She glanced towards Jeff. It was odd, fighting at her brother's side when so often she'd been his shield. It felt right. "The cloaks are easier to use when you bundle them up into a circle of material."

"Bet I can take more than you," Jeff said.

"Why do I feel like I've stepped into an alternate universe?" Brett asked.

Kayla dropped her stick. There was an arm length between her and the soul stalkers as they continued to close the gap. She yelled and leapt forward, whipping the cloak out and over the head of the closest soul stalker. It was off his head before he had time to blink. She could hear Jeff echo her yell and hoped he was successful getting a cloak. Behind her she could hear the sound of Brett's stick as it impacted with soul stalkers. Then she couldn't hear it anymore.

There was no time to check on him. She had more soul stalkers to dispatch. They were packed too tightly to be able to fight her easily. Behind her she felt them grab at her, but ignored their efforts. There was the occasional tingle and slight weakness as they managed to touch flesh instead of clothes, but then they'd be jostled out of the way in the press of bodies. "Two down."

Jeff laughed. "I've done three."

She reached out to slip the cloak over another soul stalker's head. She grinned as he dissolved, the space he'd left instantly filled by the press of soul stalkers.

"Four!"

She swore. Her brother was beating her. Her grin evaporated when she called out four at the same time he called five. As she reached out to slip the cloak over another soul stalker, he disappeared. The press of bodies that had held her upright vanished and she landed on all fours, relieved the cloak only touched her gloved hands.

Jeff looked around in surprise. "What happened?"

Kayla sat back and pushed the glove down enough to check the time, struggling to understand. "Sunrise." They'd survived? She scanned the ground for Brett and a shudder of relief went through her when she spotted him. Leaving the cloak behind, she crawled over to him. She shook too badly to be able to stand.

Jeff staggered over to them. "He okay?"

Kayla reached out to press her hand against Brett's chest. She swore, removed the glove and touched him again. Tears filled her eyes when she felt the beat of his heart beneath her hand. But he was grey and barely breathed. Was it too late? "Brett. Wake up. Please wake up." She pulled the other glove off and leaned over him, her face a breath away from his. "Please, Brett." She swallowed the lump in her throat when his eyes opened.

"Tell me we're not in limbo." His voice was a whispered rasp, new bruises already forming on his throat.

Kayla half sobbed and half cried as she threw her arms around him. "We're alive. We made it." It didn't seem possible after the amount of soul stalkers that had surrounded them.

Jeff dropped down beside them. "I don't know about you two, but I could eat a dozen blocks of chocolate right about now. Think we can call into a servo and buy a carton? I'm all out."

Kayla drew back from Brett so she could help him sit up. She turned to Jeff. "You okay?"

Jeff nodded. "Is this how you feel after you've beaten up schoolyard bullies?"

Kayla frowned. "Like what?"

"Like you've taken on the world and come out on top. Even though you feel like every bone in your body has been broken."

Kayla laughed at her brother's words and nodded. "Pretty much. Does this mean you won't be hiding behind me anymore?"

"I've never hidden behind you. You've always jumped in front of me while I did a frightened little rabbit in the headlights impression."

"And yet you haven't frozen once when it came to the soul stalkers." Kayla reached out and took her brother's hand, her other arm remaining around Brett.

Jeff smiled. "I know. Completely insane. But after facing the convention tonight," he shook his head slowly, "I reckon I could face anything."

"Tell me about it," Kayla muttered.

"I'll get these cloaks put away." Jeff let Kayla's hand go and staggered to his feet. He glanced around. "Not a bad effort for the night. Two cloaks. They should come in handy for someone."

As soon as Jeff had moved away, Brett reached out to rest his palm against Kayla's face and turned her to look at him. "It's after twelve past six."

Kayla couldn't hold back her smile. "And?"

Brett laughed softly. "Do you want to do something tonight?"

"Hmm. Well... maybe."

"What happened to having an answer for me at twelve past six?"

"I did have an answer then, but you didn't ask me. And as you've pointed out, it's past that time."

"Really?" Brett wrapped his arms around her and kissed her. He pulled back enough to meet her gaze. "Have an answer yet?"

"I'm afraid you've made me completely forget the question."

"Kayla-"

She laughed. "Yes."

"Yes, what?"

"Let's go to Samantha's party tonight."

"The bitch who's been spreading rumours about you?" Brett frowned.

Kayla nodded. "Yep."

"Okay, now you're confusing me. Why would you

want to go to her party?" Before Kayla could answer, her phone rang. "Don't answer that." Brett tried to take the phone from her.

Kayla held it out of his reach, checking the display. "It's Red."

Jeff strode over to them and took the phone. "I'll talk to her."

"Jeff-"

Brett turned her head to face him when Jeff walked away with her phone. "Focus."

"What?"

"Why would you want to go to a party held by someone who's been spreading rumours about you?"

"Red thought it might be a good idea." Kayla glanced away, unable to meet his gaze.

"I should have known." Brett staggered to his feet and followed Jeff to take the phone from him.

"Hey!" Jeff spun to face him. "Oh."

Kayla hurried after Brett and tried to take her phone back. He turned and held his hand up to fend her off. She glared at him. "Well?" She demanded when he returned the phone to Jeff.

Brett smiled. "We'll go to Samantha's party."

"Why?"

"Because Red actually makes sense for a change."

Kayla felt her cheeks heat at what Red had probably

told him. She turned her back on him, when he laughed, and stalked towards the four-wheel-drive.

Brett caught hold of her arm before she reached it. "Kayla."

She stared at his feet and waited for him to speak. When he didn't, she looked up at him to see why. He smiled slightly. "What?"

"I didn't want to tell you earlier. I hoped you might run if I didn't. I wanted you to be safe." He wrapped his arms around her and drew her close. "I love you too."

Her mind stopped being able to think when his lips met hers.

Chapter Thirty-Eight

Kayla followed her brother's car as they turned into Brian's street. She didn't understand why her brother couldn't tell her what he was up to. The surprise he had planned wasn't for her. It was for Brett. And why couldn't they have driven over in her car? She also would have preferred to go home first and get out of her uniform. After an entire week of being back at school she was looking forward to the weekend and ditching her uniform for a couple of days. She couldn't wait until the holidays. School seemed false after having dealt with soul stalkers. A contrived environment.

She parked beside Jeff's car and got out, locking her car as she followed him to the front door. Brett opened the door before they reached it, smiling at her in greeting after a quick nod in her brother's direction. She smiled back, reaching for him and holding him close for a kiss.

"Come on you pair. I do have to get out of here before my mates arrive at sunset," Jeff said.

Kayla pulled away from Brett slightly. Jeff had four soul stalkers following him each night. "We did offer to help you use the cloaks on them."

Jeff shook his head. "And have you risk facing more soul stalkers? I'm fine. I have it all worked out. As soon as I have enough hair and nails collected I'll use them to make one of them unconscious and lead the others away before I go back and use the cloak on him. But I'm going to tie him up first with rope that's been threaded with Kayla's hair. That should make the rope solid for him."

"Now why didn't we ever think of that?" Kayla asked.

"I guess we didn't have time. We were too busy running once we knew about the cloaks." Brett turned to Jeff. "What's your news you wanted to see me face to face with?"

Jeff gestured towards the front door. "Inside first."

Brett led the way. Douglas was in the lounge room sitting in an armchair with a dictionary in his lap and a company prospectus in his hands. He looked up as they came inside. He smiled. "Afternoon, lass." He nodded towards Jeff. "Lad."

Kayla smiled in answer, her attention caught by Nick and Jake who sat in the lounge watching a movie. "Hey."

Jake nodded while Nick looked between Kayla and Douglas. "I can't get used to the portrait walking around like he's alive. Couldn't you have left him in the painting?"

Kayla's smile became a grin. "He wasn't actually in the painting. He's always wandered around the house. You just couldn't see him."

Nick shook his head. "I hope that wasn't meant to make me feel better."

Kayla laughed. "Nope. Just telling you how it is."

"Yeah, well, I have my own father on my back about wasting my life." Nick jerked a thumb towards Douglas. "I don't need him at me too."

"Don't waste yer life then." Douglas looked up from the prospectus.

Brian came into the room with four coffee mugs. "I ran out of hands. There's three more in the kitchen."

"I need to talk to Brett for a few minutes so we'll grab them." Jeff held up a large yellow envelope as he looked at Brett. "I've got something for you."

"You better not expect me to wait in the lounge

room. You've been tormenting me with what's in that envelope all day." Kayla glared at her brother.

"Well-" Jeff began then laughed when Kayla stalked past him, headed for the kitchen.

Jeff grabbed a coffee mug off the kitchen bench and sat at the table. Brett and Kayla did the same. Brett took the envelope, which was addressed to Jeff and stared at it.

"Are you going to open it?" Jeff gestured towards the envelope.

Brett tore it open and tipped the documents out. He frowned. "This is my original birth certificate."

Jeff grinned. "Anything else of interest in there?"

Brett looked up from the document he read. "How did you manage this?"

Kayla took the paper from Brett's hands. "What?" She gasped. "Oh." Her grin couldn't be held back. She jumped up and threw her arms around Brett. "You're alive. I know you've been alive for a week, but now it's official." She turned to Jeff. "How did you do it?"

Jeff calmly took a sip of his coffee. He grinned at the exasperated sound his sister made. "Those odd friends of mine."

"Yeah but-" she waved her hand towards the

document on the table. "That's-" she was lost for words.

Jeff shrugged. "Doctors have been known to make mistakes before. The story is that two were shot and their ID's were mixed up. It was the other victim who died. Everything has been altered to support the story. Apparently it was some homeless person who was out the back of the servo."

"So I've got my old life back." Brett picked up his birth certificate again.

Jeff nodded. "Yep. As far as the world is concerned, you didn't die. Only spent some time in the hospital in an induced coma recovering from life threatening bullet wounds."

"It would have been nice if you'd let me know about this before I told Nick and Trevor the truth," Brett said.

Jeff smiled. "That's why I didn't tell you earlier. You can't have half your friends know and not the others. They'd figure out after a while they were being excluded from something."

"What do you think you are? A shrink?" Brett demanded.

"Nope. But maybe all the hours I've spent with one this past week caused something to rub off on me." Jeff rose to his feet. "I need to get to my sunset, sunrise point. I like to know where they are. Keep them close enough to know what they're up to."

Kayla frowned. "That sounds dangerous, Jeff."

Jeff shrugged. "Life is dangerous."

She let go of Brett to hug her brother. "Take care."

"I am."

Kayla smiled at Jeff. "You've changed in the past week."

"Yeah. I guess facing limbo does that to you." He paused. "I'll be back here for dinner. Will you be about then?"

Kayla nodded. "I'll see you later."

Jeff checked the time on his phone. "I'll be back at seven. Pizza'd be nice."

Kayla laughed. "Sure. I'll let Brian know what he's having for dinner tonight." She watched as Jeff left the kitchen, leaning back against Brett when she felt him step up behind her. "He doesn't seem like my little brother anymore."

"I think he killed the frightened rabbit last Friday night." Brett's arms wrapped around her waist.

Kayla turned in his loose embrace so she could face him. "I think he did too. Enough about my brother. What do you plan to do with your life now you have it back?"

"Sneak you into a nightclub after dinner?"

Kayla laughed. "That wasn't exactly what I was trying to ask you. And how do you think you can manage that?"

"I've got a friend who's a bouncer. He'll be too amazed to see me to card you."

Kayla shook her head. "Seriously."

Brett's lips lightly grazed hers. "I'll see my old boss about a reference so I can get a job closer to here. Look at transferring to a different uni and try and convince you to move in."

"I haven't finished high school yet," Kayla protested.

"But you will in November. You better come up with another excuse before then if you're planning to say no."

Kayla smiled. Who knew what her answer would be by then? She certainly didn't. Her hands crept up to rest on his chest. "Where's the nightclub you're going to sneak me into?"

Brett laughed. "You'll have to wait and see."

Kayla tried to glare at him. "That's so unfair. I hate waiting."

"Yep. I know." His lips met hers before she could try and convince him to tell her where they were going.

As her hands slid up to link behind his neck, she

decided she didn't care where they were going. But if he planned to keep trying to distract her from finding out, she wasn't going to let him know. She pulled back slightly to smile up at him. "That was a feeble effort at distraction."

Brett grinned. "Guess I'll have to try harder then."

Now that was a statement she wasn't about to argue with.

Free Ebook

Subscribe to Avril's newsletter to receive a free ebook. This ebook is exclusive to those on her mailing list. To find out more about this offer visit: www.avrilsabine.com/free-ebook

*

We value your privacy and will not sell, rent, exchange or loan your email address to third parties. Your information is confidential and you are under no obligation to remain on the mailing list and can unsubscribe at any time.

Acknowledgements

Thanks to not only the usual crew, but also a special thanks to all those who answered my many questions. Although I noticed there were a few lengthy pauses. Surely the questions weren't that odd.

To The Reader

If you enjoyed this book, why not consider leaving a review to help other readers discover it too? Reader engagement is one of the few ways that lets an author know readers want more books in a particular series or genre. So leave a review and tell friends, not only about this book but also about other ones you've enjoyed, so you can continue to enjoy books by your favourite authors for years to come.

Dreams are meant to be lived,

Avril.

About The Author

Avril is an Australian author who lives with her family on acreage in South East Queensland. She writes mostly young adult speculative fiction, but has been known to dabble in other genres. You can find more information about her at her website www.avrilsabine.com where you can also subscribe for her newsletter to be kept informed about new releases, current projects, blog posts and exclusive news.

Titles By Avril Sabine

Stories about strong characters and characters who discover their strengths.

SERIES

Assassins Of The Dead- Young Adult Fantasy/ Paranormal

Book 1: Dark Blade

Book 2: Dragon Touched

Book 3: Society Against Vampires

Book 4: King's Request

Dragon Blood- Young Adult Urban Fantasy (with elements of romance)

(5 book series)

Book 1: Pliethin

Book 2: Wyvern

Book 3: Surety

Book 4: Knight

Book 5: Mage

Dragon Mage- Young Adult Urban Fantasy (with elements of romance)

(Series two of Dragon Blood series)

Book 1: Promise

Dragon Blood Chronicles- Young Adult Urban Fantasy (with elements of romance)

(Companion stand alone series to Dragon Blood)

Book 1: Oath

Book 2: Betrayed

Guardians Of The Round Table- Young Adult Fantasy LitRPG

(Co-written with Storm and Rhys Petersen)

Book 1: Dexterity Fail

Book 2: Goblin Boots

Book 3: Singed Feathers

Book 4: Frog Mage

Book 5: Crystal Mine

Book 6: Cursed Harp

Rosie's Rangers- Young Adult Western Steampunk

(6 book series)

Book 1: Justice

Book 2: Vengeance

Book 3: Treachery

Book 4: Accused

Book 5: Wanted

Book 6: Corruption

Mark Of Kings- Children's Fantasy

(Upper middle grade/preteen)

(4 book series)

Book 1: The Arena

Book 2: The Island

Book 3: The Assassin

Book 4: The King

STAND ALONE SERIES

Demon Hunters- Young Adult Urban Fantasy/ Horror (with elements of romance)

Book 1: Blood Sacrifice

Book 2: Retribution

Book 3: Tainted

Book 4: Premonition

Book 5: Cursed

Book 6: Feud

Book 7: Extrication

Plea Of The Damned- *Young Adult Urban Fantasy/Paranormal*

(6 book series)

Book 1: Forgive Me Lucy

Book 2: Forgive Me Aiden

Book 3: Forgive Me Jena

Book 4: Forgive Me Kobe

Book 5: Forgive Me Marti

Book 6: Forgive Me Dawson

Realms Of The Fae- *Young Adult Urban Fantasy (with elements of romance)*

The Sword (short story in Like A Girl Anthology)

Heart Of Stone

Book 1: A Debt Owed

Book 2: Marked By The Hunt

Book 3: The Magic Collector

Book 4: An Unexpected Betrayal

Book 5: Imprisoned By Iron

Fairytales Retold (Short Stories)

Snow-White And Rose-Red

The Twelve Brothers

The Light Princess

Beauty And The Beast

Sleeping Beauty

Aschenputtel

The Golden Bird

The Frog Prince

The Death Of Koshchei The Deathless

Myths And Legends Retold (Short Stories)

Ion, Son Of Apollo

Sir Gawain And The Maid With The Narrow Sleeves

Princess Ilse, The Giant's Daughter

YOUNG ADULT NOVELS

Young Adult Fantasy (with elements of romance)

Elf Sight

Earth Bound

Young Adult Urban Fantasy

Stone Warrior (with elements of romance)

The Jungle Inside

Young Adult Contemporary (with elements of romance)

Through Your Eyes

The Ugly Stepsister

Perfect Little Princess

Young Adult Contemporary/Paranormal

Whispers In The Dark (with elements of romance and same sex relationships)

Over Too Soon (with elements of romance)

Young Adult Sci-Fi

Experiment X-One-Six (Urban Sci-Fi/Superheroes)

An Endless Dawn (Post Apocalyptic Sci-Fi)

CHILDREN'S BOOKS

Dragon Lord (Preteen/early teens) (Fantasy)

The Irish Wizard (Upper middle grade) (Urban Fantasy)

SHORT STORIES

Urban Fantasy

Eternally Late

Dealings With Joe

Glimpses (short story in That Moment When Anthology)

Contemporary

The Brat Next Door

Fantasy LitRPG

(Set in the same world as Guardians Of The Round Table Series)

Tales Of Inadon 1: The Disc (Co-written with Storm and Rhys Petersen) (short story in Game On! Anthology)

Post Apocalyptic Sci-Fi

Compulsive Directive

NONFICTION

A Year Of Weekly Writing Exercises (Creative Writing)

Cooking For Families With Allergies (Cooking) (Co-written with Storm Petersen)

Tell Me A Story, Grandma (Memoir)

For the most up to date details on available titles visit:

www.avrilsabine.com/books/bibliography

Disclaimer

This is a work of fiction. Names, characters, businesses, places, events and incidents are either the products of the author's imagination or used in a fictitious manner. Any resemblance to actual persons, living or dead, or actual events is purely coincidental. The opinions expressed or beliefs held are those of the characters and should not be assumed to be the opinions or beliefs of the author.

www.ingramcontent.com/pod-product-compliance
Lightning Source LLC
Chambersburg PA
CBHW030957190726
48285CB00004BB/1340